NHL HOCKEY

AN OFFICIAL FANS' GUIDE

FIFTH EDITION

John MacKinnon &
John McDermott

WHITECAP BOOKS

ABOUT THE AUTHORS

JOHN MacKINNON has reported on hockey for 18 years. A longtime Montreal resident, he covered Les Canadiens during his eight years with the *Canadian Press*. He was a staff writer with the *Ottawa Citizen* from 1988 to 1995, chronicling the city's successful expansion bid. He now lives and works in Alberta.

JOHN McDERMOTT has been editor of several national sports magazines over the past 10-plus years. In 1995, he helped launch *NHL PowerPlay*, the official magazine of the players and teams of the NHL. He was editor of that publication through 1999. He now lives and works in Michigan.

Picture Credits:

Allsport UK Ltd
Brian Bennett
Gary Bettmann
Bruce Bennett Studios/C. Anderson, Rick Berk, M. Desjardins, M. Di Giacomo, J. Di Maggio, H. Dirocco, A. Foxall, D. Giacopelli, J.Giamundo, P. Laberge, J. Leary, Scott Levy, R. Lewis, R. McCormick, Jim McIsaac, Layne Murdoch, L. Redkoles, W. Roberts, Rick Stewart, J. Tremmel, Nick Welsh, B. Winkler
Hockey Hall of Fame
©NHL Images/Russ Beeker/MLP, Andrew D. Bernstein, Lou Capozzola, Defrisco, Gregg Forwerck, Barry Gossage, Jon Hayt, Mitchell Layton, Craig Melvin, Ronald C. Modra, Nevin Reed, Dave Sandford, Kent Smith, Diane Sobolewski, Ron Vesely

Produced by
Carlton Books Limited
20 Mortimer Street
London W1T 3JW

ISBN 1 55285 165 6

Printed in Italy

Contents

INTRODUCTION

The transformation of the National Hockey League from a parochial league into an organization with a global vision began with the 1972 Summit Series between Canadian stars and the great national team of the Soviet Union—the Big, Red Machine.

After years of seeing their understaffed team whipped by the Soviets at the Olympics and World Championships, Canadians were finally given the chance to see their best players, their professionals, the stars of the NHL, supposedly deliver an overdue lesson to the big, bad Russians. It didn't work out quite that way.

The Canadians won, but it took some desperate, last-minute play and a goal by Paul Henderson with 34 seconds remaining in the final game to give Canada a 6-5 victory in the game and a slender series triumph—four games won, three lost, one game tied. The Canadian-invented sport—and the NHL—would never be the same.

NHL teams soon began to copy the superior Russian training methods, to blend their intricate, purposeful drills into often unimaginative North American practices, to pay more attention to the game's technical aspects.

The Russians, and other European teams, grafted the North Americans' never-say-die competitiveness and physical courage onto their highly skilled brand of hockey.

As the NHL expanded, first from six to 12 teams, then to 14, then 18, then 21 after absorbing teams from the World Hockey Association, and now to 30 this season, teams have to cast their nets wider and wider in search of major-league talent.

The NHL, dominated for its first half-century by Canadian stars like Frank McGee, Howie Morenz, Aurel Joliat, George Hainsworth, Maurice (Rocket) Richard, Gordie Howe, Glenn Hall, Bobby Hull, Bobby Orr and Frank Mahovlich, was adjusting to an influx of European talent.

NHL fans grew to admire players like Borje Salming, Anders Hedberg, Ulf Nilsson, Peter, Anton and Marian Stastny and, in the 1990s, Sergei Fedorov, Pavel Bure, Jaromir Jagr and Teemu Selanne.

Now the NHL has entered the 21st Century and it boasts five times as many teams as it had just three and a half decades ago. There are 17 US states represented, as well as the District of Columbia and four Canadian provinces.

The cliché that the NHL appeals merely to regional interests in the US simply does not apply any longer.

In the fall of 1996, the inaugural World Cup of Hockey was held, a joint venture involving the NHL and the NHL Players' Association. Team USA beat Canada in a best-of-three final series, stunning the favored Canadians in the process.

The 1998 Olympic hockey finals was a triumph for the sport and enabled millions worldwide to watch some of the NHL's greatest stars in action. They reveled in the exploits of Wayne Gretzky, Joe Sakic and Patrick Roy of Canada; Finland's Teemu Selanne and Saku Koivu; Pavel Bure and Alexei Yashin of Russia; Brian Leetch, Keith Tkachuk of Team USA and, of course, the incomparable Dominik Hasek and Robert Reichel of the Czech Republic. The finals also showed that the once dominant North America stranglehold had weakened to such an extent that neither the USA or Canada took a medal home with them. The Czech Republic's stunning victory against Russia in the Final was proof that hockey was truly a global game.

The NHL has come a long way indeed since Henderson's legendary goal on a cold September night in Moscow in 1972. The ongoing progress should be great fun.

That winning feeling: New Jersey captain Scott Stevens—the Conn Smythe Trophy winner—shows off the Stanley Cup after the Devils had defeated defending champion Dallas Stars 2-1 in double overtime at Reunion Arena.

STANLEY CUP

Birth of a Hockey League

The whole world was not watching when a small cluster of men met in a downtown Montreal hotel on November 22, 1917 and formed the National Hockey League. The National Hockey Association, a forerunner of the NHL, had suspended operations, so the heads of the Montreal Canadiens, Montreal Wanderers, Ottawa Senators and Quebec Bulldogs attended a founding meeting and formed a new league.

A single reporter—Elmer Ferguson, of the *Montreal Herald*—reported on the somewhat shaky launch. For starters, the Bulldogs, a poor draw in Quebec City, decided not to operate in the NHL's first season, so the Toronto Arenas were admitted to the league as a replacement.

The league was down to three teams early into the first season, though, after the Westmount Arena, home to the Montreal Wanderers, burned down. With nowhere to play, the Wanderers, too, dropped out. The NHL, then, featured the Original Three for most of its initial season, not the Original Six, a term that would gain common usage years later.

The first president of the NHL was Frank Calder, a soccer-playing British émigrée to Canada who had grown to love the Canadian game of hockey. His name would eventually be etched onto a trophy given annually to the best first-year, or rookie, player in the NHL.

In that first season, the league held the first of many dispersal drafts to distribute the players from the Bulldogs, including their scoring star, Joe Malone, who was chosen by the Canadiens.

In one of two opening-night games for the new league on December 19, 1917, Malone scored five goals as the Canadiens defeated Ottawa 7-4. Malone went on to score 44 goals during the 22-game regular season, easily winning the scoring title and setting a scoring pace never equalled in NHL history. The new league had its first superstar.

The league suffered its first major setback the following season, 1918-19. An influenza epidemic enfeebled many of the players on both finalists in the Stanley Cup playoffs—the Montreal Canadiens and Seattle Metropolitans of the Pacific Coast Hockey Association. Joe Hall, one of Montreal's star players died of the disease and so many players were stricken that the series was cancelled with no winner declared.

Building a Following

Interest in NHL hockey grew appreciably through the 1920s and 1930s, but the popularity curve was far from smooth.

In 1919, the Mount Royal Arena was built as the home of the Montreal Canadiens and five years later, the Montreal Forum was constructed to house the Maroons, the other NHL team in that hockey-mad city. In Ottawa, Frank Ahearn built a 10,000-seat arena called the Auditorium in 1923. And in Toronto, Maple Leaf Gardens was completed in 1931.

When Ottawa met the Canadiens in the 1923-24 playoffs, 11,000 jammed into the Auditorium to see the Canadiens, with Howie Morenz, defeat the Senators 4-2. The Canadiens went on to defeat Vancouver to win the Stanley Cup, the first of 23 they would win in the NHL's 80-plus years.

The Forum, the Canadiens' home for most of the century, was actually built as the home of the Maroons. But a warm spell spoiled the natural ice at the Mount Royal Arena in the fall of 1924, so the Canadiens asked to play at the Forum, which had artificial ice. So it was that the Canadiens opened the Forum on November 29, 1924, whipping the Toronto Maple Leafs 7-1.

The 1924-25 season witnessed the first labor-management dispute when the players of the Hamilton Tigers, where the Quebec Bulldogs had shifted in 1920, went on strike before the playoffs. They wanted to be paid an extra $200 Cdn. per player for work during the playoffs, a seemingly reasonable request since Hamilton had made a record profit.

Fans' Target: NHL president Clarence Campbell enraged Montreal fans in March 1955 when he suspended their hero, Maurice (Rocket) Richard.

League president Calder, though, acted in support of the owners, in the belief that giving in to the players would put at risk the owners' "...large capital investment in rinks and arenas, and this capital must be protected."

Accordingly, Hamilton was disqualified from the playoffs, and the players were suspended and fined $200 Cdn. each. The Hamilton players' stand on playoff pay would be echoed in a similar stand later in the century by all NHL players, but at the time it seemed a minor obstacle on the league's pathway to success.

By the 1927-28 season, the NHL had grown from three teams to ten, split into two divisions: the Canadian and American. The Canadian division included the Toronto St. Patricks, the Ottawa Senators, the New York Americans, the Montreal Maroons and Montreal Canadiens. The American division consisted of the Boston Bruins, the New York Rangers, the Pittsburgh Pirates, the Chicago Blackhawks and the Detroit Cougars. This two-division alignment remained intact for 12 seasons, although this era was hardly immune from franchise shifts.

After winning the Stanley Cup in 1927, the Ottawa Senators, increasingly cashstrapped as the Great Depression approached, slid downhill. In 1930, the Senators sold star defenseman Frank (King) Clancy to the Toronto Maple Leafs for $35,000 Cdn., the largest sum ever paid for a hockey player. But even that cash infusion couldn't staunch the financial hemorrhage and, after suspending operations for the 1931-32 season, the Senators moved to St. Louis. The Eagles, as they were called, staggered through one season, before folding. Franchises also sprung up, struggled and folded or moved, in Pittsburgh and Philadelphia.

There was no shortage of star players in this era, which featured the scoring exploits of Nels Stewart, Cy Denneny, Aurel Joliat, Babe Dye, Montreal's incomparable Morenz, Harvey (Busher) Jackson, Charlie Conacher, Bill Cook and Cooney Weiland.

The game was evolving, finding itself, through the NHL's early days. Forward passing of the puck was not permitted at all until the 1927-28 season, when a rule change legalized this radical change in the defensive and neutral zones. When another rule change in 1929-30 gave players the green light to pass the puck ahead to a teammate in all three zones, goalscoring doubled. Ace Bailey led the league with 22 goals in 1927-28, compared to 43 goals for the league-leading Weiland the following season.

Play in the NHL was often vicious in the early days, but no incident horrified fans quite like Eddie Shore's attack on Ace Bailey on December 12, 1933 at the Boston Garden. Shore had been bodychecked into the boards by Red Horner and got up seeking revenge. He skated up to Bailey, who had his back to him, and knocked his feet out from under him. Bailey's head smacked against the ice and he went into convulsions. Horner responded by knocking Shore out with one punch, opening up a seven-stitch cut. Surgeons had to drill a hole in Bailey's skull to remove a blood clot that had formed near his brain. He remained unconscious, near death for 15 days and never played again.

The NHL of the 1930s produced many sublime evenings, also, but none like the Longest Game, a playoff encounter that began March 24 and ended March 25 in 1936.

That night, the Montreal Maroons and the Detroit Red Wings faced off in a Stanley Cup semifinal series opener that lasted 176 minutes 30 seconds. The only goal was scored by Detroit's Modere (Mud) Bruneteau at 16:30 of the sixth overtime period, provoking momentary stunned silence among the 9,000 fans at the Montreal Forum, followed by a huge ovation of relief. The game that began at 8:34 pm had ended at 2:25 am the following morning and all in attendance were utterly exhausted. None deserved a rest more than Detroit goaltender Norm Smith, a Maroons castoff, who stopped 90 shots in his first NHL playoff game.

The Forum was also the scene for one of the saddest days in NHL history—the funeral of Canadiens great Howie Morenz on March 10, 1937. Morenz had died from complications arising from a broken leg. More than 25,000 fans filed past the coffin at center ice in the Forum.

As the 1930s progressed, teams began to die as well, as the NHL shrank from a ten-team, two-division league to a one-division league with seven teams by 1940.

The War Years

In the early 1940s, a rule change introduced a center red line to the NHL ice surface. The idea was to speed up play and reduce offside calls. The change marked the onset of the league's so-called Modern Era.

As the NHL moved into this new phase, one player dominated the transition—Maurice (Rocket) Richard. Playing

Mr. Hockey: Gordie Howe's marvellous career stretched over five decades. His legendary longevity permitted him to play in the NHL with his sons, Mark and Marty.

Russian Bear: Anatoli Tarasov has been called the father of Soviet hockey. In fact, he studied the hockey writings of Toronto's Lloyd Percival.

right wing with center (Elegant) Elmer Lach and left winger Hector (Toe) Blake, Richard was the scoring star for the Montreal Canadiens, a symbol of competitive excellence for all French-Canadians and one of the most fiery, combative athletes ever to play any professional sport.

In the 1944-45 season, Richard scored 50 goals in 50 games, setting the standard for scoring brilliance for years to come. Lach (80 points), Richard (73) and Blake (67) finished 1-2-3 in the scoring race, earning the nickname, the 'Punch Line'.

Richard set a single-game scoring record that season, too, by scoring five goals and adding three assists as the Canadiens whipped the Red Wings 9-1 in Montreal on December 28.

The Stanley Cup highlight of the World War II period had to be the Toronto Maple Leafs' dramatic comeback victory in 1942, the only time in NHL history that a team overcame a 3-0 deficit in games to win a seven-game final series.

The Maple Leafs, second-place finishers during the 48-game regular season, found themselves in that predicament against the Detroit Red Wings, who had finished fifth in regular-season play.

At that point in the series, Maple Leafs' manager Conn Smythe, the man who built Maple Leaf Gardens and whose hockey credo was: "If you can't beat 'em in the alley, you can't beat 'em on the ice," took extreme measures.

Smythe benched right winger Gordie Drillon, the Leafs' top scorer, provoking outrage among Maple Leafs' supporters.

ICE TALK

"I HAVE NEVER SEEN A BETTER PLAYER THAN RICHARD FROM THE BLUE LINE IN."

TOMMY GORMAN, MONTREAL CANADIENS GENERAL MANAGER (1940-41, 1945-46), SPEAKING OF MAURICE (ROCKET) RICHARD

Rubbing salt in the fans' wounds, he replaced Drillon with Don Metz, a raw rookie, putting him on a line with Nick Metz, his brother, and Dave (Sweeney) Shriner. The trio dominated the rest of the series as the Leafs, who got spectacular goaltending from Turk Broda, did the seemingly impossible and won the Stanley Cup. Drillon never played for the Leafs again.

Many NHL stars of this era enlisted in the Canadian armed forces and served in the war, including Broda, Syl Apps, Bob Goldham, the Metz brothers, Jimmy Orlando, Sid Abel, Mud Bruneteau and Bucko McDonald. The league operated throughout the wartime era, but the quality of competition was thinned by military service.

It was in the 1940s, too, that the NHL stabilized as a six-team league, its constituent members coming to be known as the 'Original Six.' The general managers, the sporting architects of those teams, became as legendary as the players: Frank J. Selke in Montreal; Toronto's Smythe; Jack Adams, who built the great Detroit Red Wings teams of the 1950s; Tommy Ivan with the Chicago Blackhawks.

The Richard Riot

Sports journalist Rejean Tremblay once said: "The Rocket once told me that when he played he felt he was out there for all French Canadians."

Accordingly, all of French Canada was outraged in March 1955 when NHL president Clarence Campbell suspended Richard from the final three regular-season games and the entire playoffs for slugging a linesman in a fracas during a game in Boston.

Campbell, who embodied Anglophone dominance for many French-Canadians, attended the Canadiens' next game, against Detroit, at the Montreal Forum and quickly became a target for the irate Montreal fans seeking revenge for what they perceived as unjustly severe treatment of their hero.

At the end of the first period, a young man approached the NHL executive, extending his hand. But when Campbell held out his for an expected handshake, the man slapped his face. Moments later, a tear-gas bomb was set off behind one of the goals and soon after, the city's fire chief stopped the game, which was forfeited to Detroit.

The 15,000 fans filed out onto Ste-Catherine Street and a procession of pillaging unfolded along the street for several blocks.

The next day, Richard went on radio and television to appeal for calm in Montreal. The incident resonates to this day in Quebec. Many cite it as the spark that touched off the so-called Quiet Revolution, a period of profound and peaceful social change in the early 1960s.

The league entered the 1950s with its depth of talent restored, its membership rock solid and the quality of play impressive.

The Rocket and Mr. Hockey

If the overall quality of play was high, two teams stood out head and shoulders above the pack — the Detroit Red Wings and the Montreal Canadiens. Between them the Red Wings and Canadiens won ten of 11 Stanley Cups from 1950-1960. From 1951 through to 1960, the Canadiens made the Stanley Cup finals ten straight times, winning the Cup six times, including five in a row from 1956-60.

Beginning with the 1948-49 season and ending with the 1954-55 campaign, the Red Wings finished first in the regular season seven straight times, topping things off with a Stanley Cup victory four times during that run of excellence.

The Red Wings were constructed around Gordie Howe — Mr. Hockey, a prolific scorer and physically powerful player with a legendary mean streak he often expressed by delivering a pile-driver elbow to an opponent.

The Canadiens' leader was Maurice (Rocket) Richard, a passionate star with a burning desire to win at all costs. Richard's eyes, it was said, lit up like a pinball machine as he crossed the opposition blue line and homed in on the net to score.

In the Stanley Cup semifinals against Boston in 1952, Richard scored one of his most memorable goals. After a thunderous check by Boston's Leo LaBine, Richard left, semi-conscious, for the Forum clinic to have a nasty gash to the head stitched. He returned to the game late in the third period, with the score tied 1-1. His head bandaged, still groggy, Richard fashioned an end-to-end rush that he completed by fending off defenseman Bill Quackenbush with one hand and shovelling a one-handed shot past goaltender Sugar Jim Henry.

ICE TALK

"It was Bobby Clarke who brought them through. With the series tied, 3 to 3, he called the Flyer players together, put them all in a motel last night and laid it on the line.

"Then he went out on the ice and showed them how to do it. He deserved to be the star of the game before he even stepped on the ice."

Islanders Gerry Hart on the final game of the 1975 Stanley Cup Playoffs Semi final

With two spectacular stars like Howe and Richard, the NHL's popularity soared, and television broadcasts of NHL games only added to its appeal.

It was a period of consistently fat profits for the club owners: Conn Smythe in Toronto; the Norris family, which owned or controlled the Detroit Red Wings, Chicago Blackhawks and New York Rangers; Weston Adams in Boston; and the Molson family in Montreal.

Some of the players, notably Ted Lindsay of Detroit and Doug Harvey of Montreal, did some figuring and estimating and concluded that they were reaping a small slice of a revenue pie that was much larger than the owners let on.

In 1957, Lindsay was the driving force behind the formation of the National Hockey League Players' Association. The group wanted to take control of the players' pension fund, and channel broadcast revenues from the All-Star game directly into the fund.

The owners were, to say the least, hostile to the players' efforts. Jack Adams, the Red Wings' GM, traded Lindsay and goaltender Glenn Hall, both first-team All-Stars, to the Chicago Blackhawks. The Canadiens, unwilling to lose their best defenseman, waited three years before trading Harvey to the New York Rangers. Ownership battled the players every step of the way and in 1958 the players dropped their attempt to form a legally recognized association.

The exciting on-ice wars between the Red Wings, Canadiens, Bruins and Maple Leafs obscured the decade-ending labor-management skirmish. Far more prominent in the public imagination was the dominance of the Canadiens, who won a record five straight Stanley Cups to close the decade.

The Canadiens of that era were so proficient on the power play they forced a rule change. In 1956-57, the NHL ruled that a penalized player could return to the ice if the opposing team scored a goal in his absence. Previously, a player had to sit out the full two minutes, during which time the potent Canadiens power-play unit sometimes scored two or even three times.

As the league moved into a new decade, Richard retired, but another brilliant player emerged with the Chicago Blackhawks — Bobby Hull. Actually, it was Bernie Geoffrion, one of Richard's ex-teammates, who became the second player to score 50

The Fog: Fred Shero coached the Philadelphia Flyers to two straight Stanley Cups in the 1970s but couldn't rekindle that magic as coach of the New York Rangers.

Skill Set: Anders Hedberg, who played for the Winnipeg Jets as well as the New York Rangers, helped to change the way hockey is played in North America.

ICE TALK

"THERE IS NO WAY (THE CANADIENS) CAN BEAT US WITH A JUNIOR B GOALTENDER,"

GEORGE (PUNCH) IMLACH, TORONTO MAPLE LEAFS' GENERAL MANAGER AND HEAD COACH ON ROOKIE MONTREAL GOALIE ROGATIEN VACHON ON THE EVE OF THE 1967 STANLEY CUP FINAL SERIES

goals in a season. Of course, Geoffrion recorded the feat in the 1960-61 season, a 70- not a 50-game season. Hull recorded the first of his five 50-plus goal seasons the following year.

Hull and teammate Stan Mikita were at the top of an impressive list of 1960s scoring stars that included Frank Mahovlich, the still-impressive Howe, Jean Beliveau, Andy Bathgate, Red Kelly, Alex Delvecchio, Rod Gilbert, Ken Wharram, John Bucyk and Norm Ullman.

The Toronto Maple Leafs supplanted the Canadiens as the dominant team in the early 1960s, winning three straight Stanley Cups from 1962-64, but the Canadiens won four in five years from 1964-69. They might have won five straight, except for Toronto's stunning upset victory over Montreal with an aging team in 1967.

That Stanley Cup final was truly the last of an era, because the NHL was preparing for unprecedented growth as the decade wound down.

A Victory for the Aged—Toronto's 1967 Stanley Cup Win

The Montreal Canadiens had won two straight Stanley Cups and seemed a solid bet to win a third as they prepared to meet the Maple Leafs in the final pre-expansion final series.

The Maple Leafs, third-place finishers during the season, had surprised lots of people by knocking off the first-place Chicago Blackhawks in the semifinals, but the younger, speedier Canadiens had swept the New York Rangers in four games, going with rookie goalie Rogatien Vachon.

The Maple Leafs' lineup had an average age of more than 31 years that included 42-year-old goalie Johnny Bower, and 41-year-old defenseman Allan Stanley. Twelve members of the roster were over 30—seven of them over 35.

When the Canadiens won Game 1, 6-2, with Henri Richard recording the hat-trick and Yvan Cournoyer scoring twice, it seemed to confirm the experts' analysis—the younger, quicker Canadiens were simply too good for the aging Leafs.

Then the ageless Bower went out and shut out the Canadiens as Toronto won Game 2, 3-0. The Leafs won Game 3 in overtime 3-2, with Bower brilliant again, making 60 saves. But when he strained his groin in the Game 4 pre-game warm-up, Maple Leafs' coach Punch Imlach had to insert Terry Sawchuk in goal.

The Canadiens seemed to solve Sawchuk, winning 6-3 to even the series 2-2. But Sawchuk only gave up two goals in the final two games—as Toronto stunned the hockey world by winning the series 4-2. The ageless wonders had turned back the clock and rediscovered their prime.

"I felt sick for a month afterwards," said Montreal defenseman Terry Harper. "To lose the Stanley Cup, that was horrible, but to lose to Toronto and have to live in Canada afterwards, oh man—everywhere you'd go you'd run into Leafs' fans, well, that was like losing twice."

ICE TALK

"A MISTAKE HAS BEEN MADE."

NHL PRESIDENT CLARENCE CAMPBELL, AFTER MISTAKENLY ANNOUNCING THAT THE EXPANSION VANCOUVER CANUCKS WOULD SELECT FIRST OVER THE BUFFALO SABRES IN THE 1971 ENTRY DRAFT

Broad Street Bounty

"We take the shortest distance to the puck and arrive in ill humor." That was the Philadelphia Flyers credo, as enunciated by head coach Fred Shero. He wasn't kidding.

The Flyers were constructed around a core of stellar players: goaltender Bernie Parent; defensemen Jim Watson and Bob Dailey; centers Bobby Clarke and Rick MacLeish; and wingers Bill Barber and Reggie Leach.

The supporting cast included some honest checkers like Bill Clement, Terry Crisp and Ross Lonsberry and a platoon of enforcers like Dave (The Hammer) Schultz, Bob (Houndog) Kelly, Don (Big Bird) Saleski, Jack McIlhargey and Andre (Moose) Dupont.

The blend of goaltending brilliance, team defense, toughness and scoring punch helped make the Flyers the first expansion club to win one Stanley Cup, let alone two.

Shero was nicknamed 'The Fog' by his players because he was given to cryptic sayings.

On the day of Game 6 in Philadelphia's Stanley Cup victory over the Boston Bruins in 1974, Shero wrote this message on the chalkboard in the dressing room: "Win together today and we'll walk together forever."

The Flyers won, and carved their names into the Stanley Cup.

So Long, Original Six, Hello Expansion

The success—artistic and financial—of the Original Six had attracted interested investors as early as the mid-1940s. In 1945-46, representatives from Philadelphia, Los Angeles and San Francisco had applied for franchises. The Original Six owners, jealously guarding their rich profit margins, were hostile to the notion for years.

But envious of the lucrative TV contracts U.S. networks were signing with the National Football League, American Football League and Major-League baseball, and recognizing that such riches were definitely beyond the grasp of a six-team, Canadian-based league, the league governors decided to proceed with expansion. The decision was spurred, in part, by aggressive efforts by the Western Hockey League, a development league, to push for major-league status.

The NHL governors received 15 applications for new franchises and in February, 1966, granted teams to Los Angeles, San Francisco, St. Louis, Pittsburgh, Philadelphia and Minnesota. The new franchises cost $2 million U.S. each.

The new teams were grouped together in the West Division, which enabled them to be competitive amongst themselves, even if they weren't really competitive with the six established teams in the East Division. The first three years of expansion, the St. Louis Blues, coached by Scotty Bowman, and staffed with aging stars like Glenn Hall, Jacques Plante, Doug Harvey, Dickie Moore and others, advanced to the Stanley Cup final. Each year, the Blues lost in four straight games.

The third of those three four-game sweeps of the Blues was administered by Bobby Orr and the Boston Bruins. Orr had become the first defenseman in NHL history to record 100 points in 1969-70, when he scored 33 goals and added 87 assists for 120 points to win the scoring championship. Many thought it was the first Stanley Cup of a Boston dynasty, but Orr's career was foreshortened by a series of knee injuries. He left the NHL before he was 30, with just two Stanley Cup rings—1970 and 1972.

Expansion coincided with the establishment of the NHL Players' Association—ten years after Ted Lindsay's effort had failed. A Toronto lawyer named Alan Eagleson had helped striking players on the minor-league Springfield Indians win their dispute with Eddie Shore, the club's miserly, ogre-like president and manager.

That victory helped him win the players' support when, led by a core group of Toronto Maple Leafs players, the association was established in 1967, with Eagleson as its executive director.

King of Kings: After Wayne Gretzky was traded to Los Angeles in 1988, it suddenly became chic to be seen at an NHL game in La-La Land.

Players' salaries, kept artificially low for decades, were about to increase dramatically, but it was a rival league—the World Hockey Association—far more than the Eagleson-led NHLPA that would be responsible.

The Winnipeg WHA franchise provided instant credibility for the rival league by signing Bobby Hull for $1 million Cdn. Then they borrowed Hull's nickname—The Golden Jet—to name their own club. Other high-profile players who followed included J.C. Tremblay, Marc Tardif, Gerry Cheevers and Derek Sanderson.

Many clubs signed players to lucrative contracts rather than lose them to WHA teams.

To combat the upstart league, the NHL kept on expanding, adding Vancouver and Buffalo in 1970. That year, the great Gilbert Perreault was the prize available for the expansion club fortunate enough to choose first in the entry draft. To decide between the Sabres and Canucks, the league brought in a wheel of fortune apparatus, the kind popular at country fairs. The Sabres were assigned numbers one through ten, with the Canucks getting 11-20. The wheel was given a spin and came to rest at the number 1—or so it seemed. Clarence Campbell, the league president announced that the Sabres had won, prompting elation among the Buffalo supporters. But the wheel had stopped at 11. Campbell stepped back to the microphone and uttered this phrase: "A mistake has been made."

Perreault played 17 seasons for the Sabres and scored 512 goals, while Dale Tallon, selected by the Canucks, had a solid, but unspectacular career with Vancouver, Chicago and the Pittsburgh Penguins. Expansion continued in 1972, when Atlanta and the New York Islanders were added, and in 1974 the Kansas City Scouts and the Washington Capitals joined the league. The NHL had tripled in size in just seven years, severly depleting the talent base.

The dilution was made more apparent by the 1972 Summit Series between Canada and the Soviet Union. Canadians expected their pros, who had been banned for years from competing in World Championships or Olympic competitions, to drub the Soviets, but were stunned when the Soviets beat Canada 7-3 in the opening game at the Forum. The Soviet game, with legendary coach Anatoli Tarasov directing its development, had caught up to and, in many areas, passed the Canadian style. That realization stunned a country which prided itself on producing the best hockey players in the world.

Canada, playing on pride, guts and determination, won a narrow series victory with four victories, three losses and one game tied. But the game had changed forever.

On the expansion front, meanwhile, not all the franchises took root where they were first planted. The California Golden Seals moved to Cleveland in 1976, then merged with the struggling Minnesota North Stars in 1979. The Kansas City Scouts moved to Denver, Colorado in 1976 and then in 1982 to East Rutherford, New Jersey, where they remain as the Devils.

In the early expansion days, Montreal general manager Sam Pollock took advantage of expansion to build a 1970s dynasty in Montreal. The Canadiens, rich in solid talent throughout their farm system, swapped good young players, and sometimes established but aging players, to talent-starved expansion clubs for high draft picks.

Super Mario: The Pittsburgh Penguins won the Stanley Cup in 1991 and 1992 when Mario Lemieux—whose career was sadly shortened by illness and injury—was hockey's dominant player.

In this fashion, the Canadiens obtained Guy Lafleur, Steve Shutt, Bob Gainey, Doug Risebrough, Michel Larocque, Mario Tremblay—the building blocks of the six Stanley Cup champions during the 1970s.

Many complained that the rapid expansion drastically diluted the talent in the NHL. The Philadelphia Flyers, the first post-expansion club to win the Stanley Cup, certainly weren't overloaded with talent. Their canny coach, Fred Shero, made the most of a small nucleus of excellent talent, led by goalie Bernie Parent, center Bobby Clarke, and wingers Bill Barber and Reggie Leach, and a belligerent style of play that intimidated the opposition.

That formula led the Flyers to back-to-back Stanley Cup championships in 1974 and 1975. By 1976, the Canadiens load of drafted talent—particularly Guy Lafleur—had matured, and Montreal rolled to four straight Stanley Cup championships to close out the 1970s.

ICE TALK

"I REALLY LOVED EDMONTON. I DIDN'T WANT TO LEAVE. WE HAD A DYNASTY HERE. WHY MOVE?"

WAYNE GRETZKY, ON HIS BEING TRADED TO THE LOS ANGELES KINGS IN 1988, A TRANSACTION THAT SENT ALL OF CANADA INTO A STATE OF MOURNING

The turn of the decade also saw the ten-year war with the WHA resolved, when the only four surviving teams from the rival league—the Quebec Nordiques; Hartford Whalers; Edmonton Oilers; and Winnipeg Jets joined the NHL. The teams were stripped of the talent they had recruited, often in bidding wars with NHL clubs, and denied access to TV revenue for five years after joining the NHL.

As a result, the Jets lost stars Anders Hedberg and Ulf Nilsson, both of whom played for the New York Rangers thereafter. The Oilers were permitted to keep Wayne Gretzky, who had signed a personal services contract with Oilers owner Peter Pocklington. And the Whalers iced a lineup that included 50-year-old Gordie Howe, playing with his sons, Mark and Marty.

The Nordiques' response was be to creative in its recruiting efforts. Club president Marcel Aubut arranged for Slovak stars Peter and Anton Stastny to defect from Czechoslovakia, and the pair were joined one year later by older brother Marian. The Stastnys, especially Peter and Anton, became the scoring stars on the rebuilt Nordiques.

The success of the Stastnys helped convince NHL managers that there were rich veins of talent in Europe that had to be tapped. Communism was one major obstacle to doing so immediately, however.

There were few large impediments to importing Scandinavian talent, though, as the New York Islanders found out. They won four straight Stanley Cups, beginning in 1980, with some talented Scandinavians, like Tomas Jonsson, Stefan Persson, Anders Kallur and Mats Hallin, playing important roles.

The European influence really took hold in the NHL, though, with the Edmonton Oilers, who supplanted the Islanders as the NHL's pre-eminent team in 1984, when they won the first of five Stanley Cups in seven years.

Glen Sather, the Oilers' general manager and coach, sprinkled some talented Europeans like Jari Kurri, Esa Tikkanen, Reijo Ruotsalainen, Kent Nilsson and Willy Lindstrom around the Edmonton lineup, with good results.

But Sather went one step further, borrowing much from the flowing, speed-based European style and adapting it to the NHL. Sather once described the Oilers' style as the Montreal Canadiens (of the 1970s) updated for the 1980s.

The style of play—executed by great players like Gretzky, Mark Messier, Glenn Anderson, Paul Coffey and Kurri—helped Sather construct a Canadiens-like 1980s dynasty.

Thinking Globally

As the NHL moved toward the 1990s the governors began to develop a larger vision. This was not an easy process. The traditions and mind-set of the Original Six had continued to dominate the league well after expansion had transformed a small, regional league into a continental one, albeit a weak sister compared to major-league baseball, football and basketball.

The NHL had evolved into a 21-team league but was controlled by the triumvirate of league president John Ziegler, Chicago Blackhawks owner Bill Wirtz and NHLPA executive-director Alan Eagleson.

The league had traditionally been gate-driven, dominated by shrewd entrepreneurs like Smythe, the Norrises, the Wirtz family and the Molsons, who owned their own arenas and knew how to fill them but had little feel for or interest in marketing the league as a whole.

A series of linked events began to change this. By the summer of 1988, Wayne Gretzky had led the Edmonton Oilers to four Stanley Cups and established himself as the best player in hockey. But to Oilers owner Peter Pocklington he was a depreciating asset whose value had peaked.

Pocklington traded Gretzky to the Los Angeles Kings—sending Edmontonians, and Canadians in general, into mourning, and stunning NHL ownership.

Bruce McNall, then the Kings' owner, promptly raised Gretzky's salary. He reasoned that Gretzky would generate far greater revenues for the Kings, both at the gate and through advertising and he was proved right.

Two years later, the St. Louis Blues used similar logic when they signed Brett Hull, their franchise player, to a three-year contract. Then they signed restricted free agent defenseman Scott Stevens to a four-year deal.

While salaries were rising, there were other parts of the hockey business taking off as well. In the United States more people watched NHL hockey on Fox and ESPN than ever before. In Canada, Saturday became a double dream as *Hockey Night in Canada* began running doubleheaders. And in the U.S. and Canada the NHL found success in five new markets. Anaheim, Ottawa, San Jose, Miami Florida and Tampa Bay all greeted the game with excitement and big crowds. The value of an NHL franchise rose and the level of people wanting to own a team grew.

As the economics of major professional hockey changed, the NHL realized that the old, gate-driven model would not work anymore. Hockey entrepreneurs began to build new, larger arenas, which featured scores of so-called luxury suites, hotel-plush boxes designed to enable corporate executives and guests to enjoy a game in high style.

Across the Continental divide: Edmonton GM/coach Glen Sather had his high-flying Oilers play a European style, which led to five Stanley Cups in a seven-year span.

Labor Man: Under executive-director Bob Goodenow (right), the NHL Players' Association has become more proactive about getting its share of the NHL revenue pie.

New forms of advertising opportunities—on scoreboards, rink boards, even on the ice itself—were deployed to generate more money. And the NHL, long a marketing luddite among major professional leagues, got into the merchandising business in a concerted way.

As the hockey business grew more sophisticated, the players became more assertive about their interests, also. Dissatisfaction with the now-disgraced NHLPA executive-director Alan Eagleson's autocratic, company-union style had been growing and, in 1990, the players selected former agent Bob Goodenow, the man who had negotiated Brett Hull's blockbuster contract, as their new director.

At the end of the 1992 season, the players staged an 11-day strike, demanding, among other things, the marketing rights to their own likenesses. They wanted a chunk of the revenue pie, in other words, and were prepared to fight to get it. The players also sought more relaxed free agency guidelines enabling them to sell themselves on the market.

As the league adjusted to a new economic and labor reality, it sought new leadership capable of achieving peace with the players and the league's on-ice officials, and proactively directing its newly ambitious business aspirations.

In 1992, a search committee selected Gary Bettman, a lawyer and former executive with the marketing-slick National Basketball Association to become the league's first commissioner.

Early in his tenure, Bettman made a business statement by recruiting two powerful new partners to set up NHL franchises—the Disney Corporation and Blockbuster Entertainment.

Michael Eisner, the Disney CEO, named his company's team the Mighty Ducks of Anaheim, after a commercially successful movie of the same name. Wayne Huizenga, head of Blockbuster, established a second team in Florida, the Panthers, based in Miami.

It had long been a cliché that pro sports was an entertainment business, but recruiting the likes of Eisner and Huizenga suggested that NHL head office had actually begun to believe this maxim.

One team—the Ottawa Senators—misread the market and grossly overestimated the promotional opportunities available to young stars when they signed untried No. 1 draft pick Alexandre Daigle to a five-year contract in June 1993. The deal included a marketing component that was unrealistically generous for an unproven rookie.

If the Gretzky, Hull and Stevens contracts had lifted the salary ceiling, the Daigle deal significantly raised the entry level and helped cause an ownership backlash. The notion of a rookie salary cap took hold and a second owner-player showdown in three years loomed.

The result was a lockout that cancelled 468 games from October 1, 1994 to January 19, 1995, shrinking the regular season to 48 games with no inter-conference play. The deal finally struck included a rookie salary cap and provided somewhat greater freedom of movement for older players.

The new, five-year deal couldn't help franchises stuck with outmoded arenas, however, and two Canadian teams, the Quebec Nordiques and Winnipeg Jets, moved south to Denver and Phoenix, respectively—Quebec for 1995-96, Winnipeg for the 1996-97 season. The move proved successful for Colorado when they won the Stanley Cup in their first year. A small-market American franchise also packed its bags for the South, as the Hartford Whalers became the Carolina Hurricanes in 1997.

The Next One

Eric Lindros was so dominant as a junior hockey player that he was dubbed 'The Next One'—Wayne Gretzky being 'The Great One'—well before he was drafted No. 1 overall by the Quebec Nordiques in 1991.

He was also supremely confident in his ability and secure in the knowledge that his extraordinary skill and potential as a marketing vehicle gave him unprecedented leverage to negotiate.

He warned Nordiques president Marcel Aubut, with whom he did not get along, not to draft him, saying he would refuse to report if he were selected. Sure enough, Quebec drafted him and Lindros, true to his word, did not report. He played another year of junior and for Canada's Olympic team at the 1992 Olympics in Albertville, France.

In June 1992, Aubut invited a bidding contest for Lindros and thought he had made a blockbuster deal with the New York Rangers. But the Philadelphia Flyers also had an offer on the table that included $15 million U.S., six players and two first-round draft picks.

An arbitrator was called in and he awarded Lindros to the Flyers in one of the most bizarre transactions in NHL history.

First Commish: On NHL commissioner Gary Bettman's watch, the NHL has expanded into new U.S. markets, and built the fan base.

Going For Gold

The 1997-98 season was an historic one for the NHL, which, for the first time ever, suspended operations to enable the stars from all participating countries to join their respective national teams to compete at the 1998 Winter Olympics in Nagano, Japan. The result was the first-ever best-on-best men's hockey tournament and the Czech Republic won the gold medal, beating Russia 1-0 in the final.

The Olympic Games gave the NHL a great chance to move further away from its parochial Original Six mentality and further establish itself as a major force in the international sporting market.

As the league's vision continues to expand globally, so does its roster of franchises. The Nashville Predators and Atlanta Thrashers launched their franchises in 1998 and 1999, respectively, and this season sees the league ranks swell to 30 teams with the addition of the Minnesota Wild and the Columbus (Ohio) Blue Jackets. Unlike previous expansion efforts, the NHL, under Bettman, is deploying its considerable marketing forces not just to ensure that individual franchises succeed, but to implant a hockey culture across the United States.

Through its state-of-the-art website, grassroots programs such as the NHL's involvement with In-Line and Street hockey, as well as its growing involvement with women's hockey, the league is, in fact, raising the profile of the NHL as well as the sport of hockey itself.

As the NHL heads into the next century, the marketing momentum is building; the league and the sport are growing. Its future has never been more exciting.

Mightiest Duck: Disney Company CEO Michael Eisner transposed cinematic marketing techniques to help sell the sport of hockey in Southern California.

Teams in the NHL

With the growth of the National Hockey League in North America and the influx of bright international stars like Jaromir Jagr, Sergei Fedorov and Peter Forsberg, the NHL is showcasing more individual talent than it ever has. Yet the team concept continues to endure as the bedrock principle of the sport. It's a cliché in hockey that no player—no matter how spectacular his contribution—is bigger than his team.

Consider Eric Lindros, one of the true superstar talents in the NHL. Lindros entered the NHL with Philadelphia in the 1992-93 season, loaded down with achievements. He had helped the Oshawa Generals win the Memorial Cup as Canada's best junior team, helped Canada's National Junior Team win the World Junior Hockey Championship, helped Team Canada win the 1991 Canada Cup (now the World Cup of Hockey) tournament, and helped Canada's Olympic team win a silver medal at the 1992 Winter Olympics in Albertville, France.

He has continued to pile up awards in the NHL, winning the Hart Trophy as the league's most valuable player in 1995. But Lindros and his growing number of followers had to wait while the Flyers surrounded their awesomely talented star with the right supporting cast before seeing their hero lead Philadelphia into the Stanley Cup Finals for the first time in his era in 1997.

The ultimate standard

Successful hockey teams are an amalgam of coaching acumen, solid team defense, great goaltending, timely scoring, leadership, fan support and the most elusive factor of all—team chemistry.

Coaches set the tone for success and none was more successful than Hector (Toe) Blake, the legendary coach of the Montreal Canadiens in the 1950s and 1960s.

In his first meeting with his team, in October 1955, Blake told his players: "There are some guys in this room who play better than I ever did. I have nothing to teach them. But what I can show you all is how to play better as a team."

Blake obviously succeeded. In 13 years as coach of the Canadiens, the team finished first in the regular season nine times and won eight Stanley Cups, including five straight from 1956-60.

Scoring titles and individual awards may be the measure of a player's excellence, but NHL teams are measured by one standard only—their ability to win the Stanley Cup.

Doom Trooper: Big, offensively skilled John LeClair won a Cup with Montreal in 1993, but as a Flyer he has yet to claim the sport's ultimate prize.

An entire generation of Toronto Maple Leafs fans has grown to adulthood without seeing their club win the Cup, yet the legend of an aging Leafs club that did win it in 1967 lives on.

In the early 1970s, the New York Islanders entered the NHL as an expansion club and were carefully crafted into a formidable group by general manager Bill Torrey. The validation of Torrey's genius in drafting Denis Potvin, Mike Bossy, Bryan Trottier, Clark Gillies and others was the four straight Stanley Cups the Islanders won, beginning in 1980.

As great as those stars were, though, the Islanders championship chemistry didn't click until Torrey traded for Butch Goring, a speedy, gritty, centerman. Goring checked the opposing team's top center and, a keen student of the game, designed the Islanders' penalty killing system.

The Edmonton Oilers of the 1980s were loaded with offensive firepower, boasting the likes of Wayne Gretzky, Jari Kurri, Glenn Anderson, Paul Coffey and Mark Messier. But they didn't become champions until coach Glen Sather had taught them to play solid, if not necessarily brilliant, team defense.

Mario Lemieux led Pittsburgh to two straight Stanley Cup triumphs in the early 1990s, but a key member of both teams was Trottier, who brought invaluable playoff experience to those Pittsburgh teams.

New York fans of a certain age have fond memories of stars like Jean Ratelle, Rod Gilbert and Vic Hadfield, the famous GAG (Goal-a-game) line of the 1970s. But none of those players ever won a Stanley Cup.

The Rangers faithful had to wait until 1994, after Messier, who learned how to be a champion with the Oilers, had moved to New York and instilled team values in his new teammates.

Fair Trade: When Colorado Avalanche traded Owen Nolan to the San Jose Sharks for defenseman Sandis Ozolinsh they acquired one of the most offensively talented defensemen in all of the National Hockey League.

Saving goals

And no team can succeed without great goaltending: the Islanders' Billy Smith; Grant Fuhr of the Oilers; the Rangers' Mike Richter; Tom Barrasso of the Penguins.

No goalie can boast a Stanley Cup performance chart quite like Patrick Roy of the Colorado Avalanche. He led the Canadiens to a Stanley Cup as a rookie in 1986 and backstopped them to another in 1993, when he cooly closed the door on the opposition as Montreal won 10 games in overtime.

In 1996, Roy's stingy netminding was central to Colorado winning the Stanley Cup. In that four-game sweep of the Florida Panthers, Roy gave up just four goals total—one per game. In 1995-96, the talent-rich Red Wings won a record 62 regular-season games, breaking the old record for most victories in a season (60) set in 1976-77 by the Canadiens. But that Montreal team was in the process of winning four straight Stanley Cups.

The Red Wings' berths in the 1997 and 1998 Stanley Cup finals were, for them, further chances to measure themselves against the other great teams in NHL history by the only yardstick that matters—Stanley Cup championships.

And in 1998-99, the Stanley Cup finally was won by a team from the sunny southern United States. The Dallas Stars had the best regular season record and went on to win the Cup in six games.

MIGHTY DUCKS® OF ANAHEIM

®&© Mighty Ducks

With the Kariya-Selanne partnership still lacking adequate support, the Ducks missed out on a playoff berth in 1999-2000.

It figures that a team based so close to Hollywood would have not one, but two leading men. Speedy wingers Paul Kariya and Teemu Selanne provide the Ducks with the most dynamic one-two offensive punch in the NHL. They have been teammates for four full seasons (plus another partial season), and in three of those seasons both players finished among the league's top five scorers. Last year, Kariya was fourth in the league with 86 points and Selanne was fifth with 85.

Unfortunately, so far in the Kariya-Selanne era, their supporting cast has not been supportive enough. In fact, in the seven years the franchise has been in operation, Anaheim has finished out of the playoffs in five of them, including 1999-2000.

The 1999-2000 season looked promising, however Anaheim finished the year with 83 points, the same total as the 1998-99 playoff season but four points back of the final postseason berth in a tougher Western Conference. Special teams played a prominent role in the disappointing season. The Ducks had the worst penalty kill in the league (79.1 percent) and the formerly potent power play was only average.

Optimistic outlook

As the Ducks look to rebound from a disappointing season, they take comfort in the fact that the scoring of Kariya and Selanne is not the team's only strength. The defense is solid. Oleg Tverdovsky was a hit in his return season to Anaheim. He collected 51 points to rank ninth among NHL defensemen. Vitaly Vishnevski and Niclas Havelid turned in encouraging rookie seasons, with the former providing a physical element.

Fredrik Olausson will be missed. The steady, veteran blueliner quietly retired at season's end and the Swede was a locker room leader for the younger defensemen. In goal, the team is looking for Guy Hebert to rebound from a season in which he slumped. The usually reliable netminder was not as crisp as he has been, though a neck injury in December may have been a factor.

The Ducks froze ticket prices for the first time this off-season. After being a huge draw in their first five seasons, the Ducks' attendance has slipped the past two seasons. But GM Pierre Gauthier said there would be no payroll-cutting to compensate. His top priorities in the off-season were giving coach Craig Hartsburg a two-year contract extension, getting some help for Kariya and Selanne up front and adding players who have experienced playoff success, something the incumbent Ducks know little about.

Celluloid birth

The NHL's Mighty Ducks probably wouldn't exist if it hadn't been for Emilio Estevez and a rag-tag bunch of skaters who turned a low-budget Disney production into a celluloid success.

"Finnish Flash" Teemu Selanne is a fixture in the league's scoring race. He finished fifth last year.

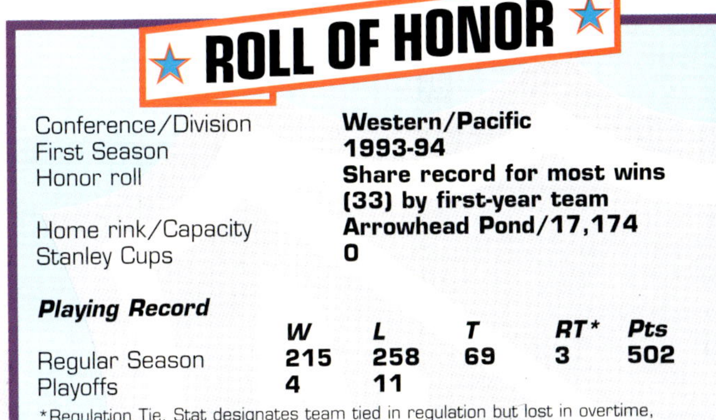

ROLL OF HONOR

Conference/Division	**Western/Pacific**
First Season	**1993-94**
Honor roll	**Share record for most wins (33) by first-year team**
Home rink/Capacity	**Arrowhead Pond/17,174**
Stanley Cups	**0**

Playing Record

	W	L	T	RT*	Pts
Regular Season	215	258	69	3	502
Playoffs	4	11			

*Regulation Tie. Stat designates team tied in regulation but lost in overtime, therefore receiving one point in a losing game.

"The movie was our market research," recalls Disney chairman Michael Eisner, who approached the NHL about an expansion franchise after the screen version of the Mighty Ducks grossed almost $60 million.

In the fall of 1993, the real-life Mighty Ducks became the NHL's third California-based member, joining the Los Angeles Kings and San Jose Sharks, and were the league's big surprise that first year, tying an NHL first-year team record with 33 victories, including 19 road wins, the most ever by a first-year club.

In the strike-shortened 1994-95 season, they developed their first star players, such as Kariya and Tverdovsky, who was then traded, along with center Chad Kilger, to obtain the high-scoring Selanne from the Winnipeg Jets on February 7, 1996.

The Mighty Ducks are equally powerful at the marketing and merchandising level. Their logo—a goalie mask resembling an angry duck—and team colors of purple, jade, silver, and white are big sellers well beyond the Magic Kingdom.

Gretzky's Heir: Many hockey observers believe that the speedy Paul Kariya is the 1990s version of Wayne Gretzky, combining speed, skill and an uncanny ability to anticipate how plays will develop.

Atlanta Thrashers®

It took 19 years for the hockey fans of Georgia to have their own team to cheer again in 1999, but wins were hard to come by.

The old saying is that Rome wasn't built in a day. The Atlanta Thrashers can certainly relate to that. The expansion franchise is experiencing the growing pains associated with being the new kid on the block.

In the Thrashers' first season, they led the league in several categories. Unfortunately, all were negative, and most by a wide margin. Atlanta had the fewest wins (14; the next closest team had 19), fewest points (39; next closest was 54), fewest goals for (170; next closest was 194), most goals against (313; next closest had 310), biggest goal differential (minus-143; next closest was minus-106). You get the idea.

Atlanta won just four games in the final 40, and had losing streaks of 12 and 10 games. The season ended on a familiar note, with four straight losses. But, of course, it was expected that the Thrashers would struggle. And the immediate goal is not the Stanley Cup. The immediate goal is simply improvement. "We had to get through this year," coach Curt Fraser said after the season. "We didn't have 14 wins by accident. We've got to make some changes. We need to improve."

Building a foundation

There are several building blocks in place. Andrew Brunette responded to his second expansion team in as many seasons (he was with Nashville in 1998-99) by having a career year. At age 26, he set career highs with 23 goals and 27 assists for a team-high 50 points. GM Don Waddell made several midseason trades which boosted the team's speed and offensive punch, acquiring forwards Hnat Domenichelli, Steve Guolla, Donald Audette and Shean Donovan. Rookie Frantisek Kaberle, another player obtained via trade, flashed potential as a defenseman who can run the power play and start the breakout.

The biggest area of concern for the Thrashers is goaltending. When healthy, former Senator Damian Rhodes, playing in front of an inexperienced defensive corps, had his moments, but they weren't consistent enough. And Rhodes missed nearly four months of action due to injury. One of the biggest items Waddell planned to address in the off-season was the backup position, which was disappointing in year one.

Still lacing them up: Ray Ferraro gave veteran leadership.

Veteran forward Ray Ferraro has a career as a broadcaster waiting for him when he decides to hang up the skates, but he proved that there's still some hockey left in his aching knees. He was second on the team with 19 goals and 44 points for his best season in three years, plus he provided steady leadership.

The season was clearly a learning experience for the youngster the Thrashers hope will develop into their franchise player, Czech forward Patrik Stefan. He had just five goals.

Hockey returns

Atlanta was the NHL's original Deep South team when the expansion Flames debuted in 1972 with legendary Bernie "Boom Boom" Geoffrion as coach. The Atlanta Flames toiled in the league for eight years without achieving much success, then bolted in 1980 to become the Calgary Flames.

The NHL's return to the home of the Braves began on June 25, 1997, when Atlanta was awarded an NHL expansion team. Like the baseball Braves and NBA Hawks, the Thrashers are a division of Turner Sports, Inc., a Time Warner Company. Famed head honcho Ted Turner supposedly liked the name Thrashers because the state bird is the Brown Thrasher.

Quite a draw

With so many transplants in the area from traditional hockey hotbeds, the sport is growing rapidly in Georgia and the city was excited to see the NHL return. A billboard hovering above a downtown freeway counted down the days until the Thrashers' first game and the enthusiasm remained throughout year one, despite a tough season on the ice.

Atlanta broke the record for average attendance by a first-year team, drawing 17,205 per game to top the mark of 16,989 set by the 1993-94 Mighty Ducks of Anaheim.

Expanding stats: Andrew Brunette led the Thrashers in scoring with 23 goals and 50 points, both career highs.

ROLL OF HONOR

Conference/Division	**Eastern/Southeast**
First Season	**1999-2000**
Honor roll	**Set attendance record for an expansion team: 705,398**
Home rink/Capacity	**Philips Arena/18,750**
Stanley Cups	**0**

Playing Record

	W	*L*	*T*	*RT*	*Pts*
Regular Season	**14**	**61**	**7**	**4**	**39**
Playoffs	**0**	**0**			

BOSTON BRUINS®

A disappointing 1999-2000, made worse by a sickening incident, means that for Boston fans the only way to go is up.

They are no longer the Big, Bad Bruins of yore. In fact, they are among the most gentlemanly teams in the game, averaging the third-fewest penalty minutes per game in the league in 1999-2000. But the team has been stained by an infamous big, bad incident that took place in February.

With time running out in a 5-2 loss, veteran tough guy Marty McSorley blindsided Vancouver tough guy Donald Brashear, who had gotten the best of him in a fight earlier in the game, with a two-handed swing of his stick to the head, knocking out Brashear and giving him a concussion. The incident touched off a lot of talk about violence in hockey and the role of goons. The NHL responded with the longest suspension in league history: the rest of the season (23 games) plus the playoffs.

The McSorley affair isn't the only dark cloud the Bruins are trying to get out from under. After advancing to the second round of the playoffs in 1999, the Bruins won just 24 games last season, the franchise's lowest total in more than three decades. The Bruins lost 328 man-games to injuries and forwards Dmitri Khristich and Tim Taylor held out and were not re-signed.

Making a bad season worse was parting with a legend. With the Bruins' hopes of making the playoffs fading rapidly, the team dealt Ray Bourque, "the franchise" for 20 years, to Colorado, giving the star defenseman a shot at his first Stanley Cup.

Harmony in the front office

As the season wound down, it looked as if coach Pat Burns' tenure was over. The poor communication between Burns and the front office of Harry Sinden and Mike O'Connell improved with some postseason discussions, and they have a rejuvenated relationship.

One agreement that was reached regards style of play. Expect Boston to loosen things up, to forecheck more aggressively and not be so defensive-minded. Bolstering the defensive corps was a top off-season priority, and Burns will want to improve the special teams too. Boston ranked 27th out of 28 in penalty killing and 22nd on the power play last year. Injury-plagued No. 1 center Jason Allison played just 37 games, and goalie Byron Dafoe, who slumped after a stellar 1998-99, are looking for bounce-back seasons.

The next franchise player appears to be on his way to living up to expectations. Forward Joe Thornton, the top overall draft pick in 1997, had a breakthrough season, leading Boston with 23 goals and 60 points.

Awesome Orr

Boston's last Cup triumph was in 1972. That Cup, like the one in 1970, featured the uplifting play of young defenseman Bobby Orr, who first arrived on the scene in 1966-67, after the Bruins had missed the playoffs for seven straight seasons.

On May 10, 1970, Orr, arguably the best defenseman ever until his knees gave out after ten years with Boston, left his personal imprint on the team's first Cup win in 29 years, scoring the winning goal against St. Louis.

With Ray Bourque now in Colorado, it's Joe Thornton's chance to become the new franchise player.

Storied franchise

One of the original six NHL teams, the Bruins started play in the 1924-25 season. They were fortunate to have had several glittering performers grace their roster in ensuing years—notably the tough guy defenseman Eddie Shore, right winger Dit Clapper and center Milt Schmidt. But despite these talents they had only three Stanley Cups to their credit before Orr, slick center Phil Esposito and (Chief) Johnny Bucyk combined their talents for the two Cups in the early 1970s.

Orr was the first NHL defenseman to win the scoring title, achieving the feat in 1969-70. Esposito won five scoring titles in just over eight seasons with Boston. In 1968-69, he became the first NHL player to amass more than 100 points in a single season.

Byron Dafoe (right) was a Vezina Trophy finalist in 1998-99, allowing less than two goals per game.

ROLL OF HONOR

Conference/Division	**Eastern/Northeast**
First Season	**1924-25**
Honor roll	**29 straight winning seasons**
Home rink/Capacity	**FleetCenter/17,565**
Stanley Cups:	**5 (1929, 1939, 1941, 1970, 1972)**

Playing Record

	W	*L*	*T*	*RT*	*Pts*
Regular Season	**2408**	**1899**	**751**	**6**	**5573**
Playoffs	**236**	**252**	**6**		

Buffalo Sabres®

After suffering a first round playoff defeat to the Flyers, the Sabres, still anchored by Hasek, look to bounce back in style.

The Sabres are an example for the rest of the NHL to emulate. The scrappy, small-market team can't afford a big payroll, so they draft well, develop their talent in a quality minor-league affiliate (the Rochester Americans) and, at least for the past few seasons, have been considered a serious Stanley Cup threat.

In 1998, the team made it to the conference final. In 1999, Buffalo won the Eastern Conference and in the Stanley Cups Finals lost to the Dallas Stars in six games, with the final goal in triple overtime earning a spot as one of the most controversial in Finals history. Last year, the Sabres didn't secure a playoff spot until the season's last day, then they lost to Philadelphia in the first round.

The 1999-2000 season was supposed to be the last for superstar goalie Dominik Hasek, a two-time league MVP. But then he suffered through an injury-plagued season in which he played just 35 games, so rather than go out under such circumstances, he decided to play one more season. While the Dominator was hurt, the Sabres discovered they have a ready replacement in Martin Biron, who notched five shutouts and allowed less than two and a half goals per game.

Peca performance: Buffalo captain Michael Peca won the 1997 Selke Trophy and was a finalist for the award in both 1998 and 1999.

Power outage

One of the main contributors to the Sabres' subpar season was the league's worst power play at 10.5 percent. In fact, of the 16 playoff teams, only Dallas scored fewer regular season goals than the Sabres' 213. Miroslav Satan followed up his breakthrough 40-goal season with 33, tied for 16th in the league. But until veteran star Doug Gilmour was brought in at the trade deadline, Satan didn't get much offensive help. With sickness limiting Gilmour's playing time in the postseason, Buffalo managed just eight goals in five games.

Russian rookie Maxin Afinogenov showed offensive flair, but as the season wore on he wore down. Besides getting Gilmour at the trade deadline, the Sabres also acquired centerman Chris Gratton, who gives the team size and skill in the pivot. The best center, captain Michael Peca, is looking to bounce back from a subpar season by his high standards.

The 2000 playoffs were not only disappointing, there also was a feeling of déjà vu in game two, when Philadelphia scored a phantom goal in winning 2-1. It came courtesy of a John LeClair blast past Hasek, who look stunned that the puck had beaten him. Not until a few minutes later did replays show the puck had ripped through the twine on the side of the net. It wouldn't have counted had the replay been seen sooner, but since play had resumed, the goal stood.

Flashy past

The Sabres were once one of the NHL's flashiest offensive teams. The franchise scored a major coup months before it took to the ice for the first time in the 1970-71 season. Through a stroke of luck—the spin of a numbered wheel—the Sabres got the first draft pick ahead of their expansion cousin, the Vancouver Canucks.

George (Punch) Imlach, the wily former Toronto Maple Leafs coach who was the Sabres first coach and general manager, plucked a rangy, swift-skating magician named Gilbert Perreault from the junior ranks. The high-scoring center was an anchor for more than a decade, especially when teamed with youngsters Rick Martin and Rene Robert to form the French Connection line. Perreault and Martin still rank 1-2 in club history for goals scored, with 512 and 382, respectively. The trio powered the Sabres to the Stanley Cup final in 1975, where they lost to Philadelphia in six games: a sobering end to their best season—they had a franchise-high 113 points in winning their first Adams Division title. Until last season, the Sabres had never been closer to a Stanley Cup title, despite the promise of the Scotty Bowman era in the early 1980s.

But Bowman did become the winningest NHL coach while in Buffalo. He passed Dick Irvin's 690 career coaching wins in 1984.

The Dominator: Dominik Hasek delayed his retirement for a season after an injuries limited him to just 35 games in 1999-2000.

ROLL OF HONOR

Conference/Division — **Eastern/Northeast**
First Season — **1970-71**
Honor roll — **Stanley Cup Finalists, 1975, 1999**
Home rink/Capacity — **HSBC Arena/18,595**
Stanley Cups — **0**

Playing Record

	W	L	T	RT	Pts
Regular Season	1112	890	376	4	2604
Playoffs	92	104			

Calgary Flames®

The Flames hopes of recreating their 1996-97 form were extinguished when they missed the playoffs once more.

The Calgary franchise hopes it has re-stoked its Flames after four straight years of missing the playoffs. There is a new regime in place. GM Al Coates was replaced by Craig Button, former director of player personnel for the Dallas Stars. He vowed never to say the words "small market" when talking about the Flames or use it as an excuse for a lack of success.

Button didn't wait long to make a major move. On draft weekend, he bolstered the goaltending position with a familiar face. Brought in to take over retired Grant Fuhr's role as proven veteran was Calgary native and former Flames hero Mike Vernon. The 1989 Stanley Cup winner will compete for playing time with Fred Brathwaite, who established himself as a reliable starter last year after Fuhr got hurt.

The defense in front of them is solid. The resurgent Phil Housley sets the tone offensively from the blue line. Derek Morris is a future all-star, while Tommy Albelin is a steady veteran and Denis Gauthier a bone-crusher who sets the physical tone when he's healthy.

Jarome Iginla is one of the game's top young power forwards.

No longer the "other" Bure

Since Valeri Bure arrived in Calgary from Montreal in 1998, he has emerged from the shadow of his superstar brother Pavel of the Florida Panthers. Valeri scored 26 goals in 1998-99, and last season he became a star in his own right with 35 goals (tied for 11th in the NHL) and 75 points (tied for 14th). Fellow 20-somethings Marc Savard and Jarome Iginla are also dynamic offensive performers. Cory Stillman, who sat out half of last year with a bad shoulder, is a potential 30-goal man.

But after that crew, the offensive contributions are scant. In the Western Conference, only Nashville had fewer goals than the Flames' 211 last year. Besides the draft and dealing with 20 free agents and settling into a new job, Button was looking to find more scoring on his roster. Speedster Rico Fata has shown potential for a couple years, but hasn't yet translated it into reliable production.

After the season-ticket base dropped below 9,000, there were fears the franchise would be sold. The good news is that fan confidence seems to be returning and the Flames made the 14,000 level it needed for the team not to be sold. Now ownership has pledged that it will raise the budget by $6 million, or 25 percent.

Heading South

Exciting was a word used in 1972, when the Flames' franchise got its start—in Atlanta. It was a bold move by the NHL, as it was their first venture into the Deep South of the United States, an experiment that lasted seven years after Georgia businessman Tom Cousins was granted a franchise.

Former Montreal Canadiens star and legend Bernie "Boom Boom" Geoffrion, served as coach and showman in the early years, wooing fans in their thousands in an accent every bit as sweet as a Georgia peach. Excited fans would flock to the 15,000-seat rink known as The Omni to watch Geoffrion direct a stunning ice symphony with awesome performers such as dynamic goaltender Daniel Bouchard and flashy forwards Jacques Richard, Eric Vail and Guy Chouinard.

Moving Flames

Alas, the novelty soon wore off. Geoffrion was gone by 1975, and so was the franchise five years later, purchased by Vancouver real-estate magnate Nelson Skalbania, and transferred to Calgary.

It was a humble beginning in the Flames' new abode, the 7,000-seat Stampede Corral, where the club remained until moving into the 20,000-seat Saddledome in 1983.

The Flames would win one Stanley Cup, two Conference titles and two best-overall crowns over the next 15 years. (Badger) Bob Johnson arrived from the University of Wisconsin to coach the Flames in 1982 and took them to the Stanley Cup final in 1985-86.

Three years later, with wisecracking Terry Crisp at the helm, Calgary won its first Cup, becoming the first visiting team to do so against the Canadiens at the Montreal Forum. Fittingly, it was the final bow for Lanny McDonald, the bushy-lipped co-captain who had come to epitomize the heart and soul of the team.

Comeback king: Since returning to the Calgary Flames, Phil Housley has enjoyed back-to-back 50-point seasons.

ROLL OF HONOR

Conference/Division	**Western/Northwest**
First Season	**1972-73 (Atlanta); 1980-81 (Calgary)**
Honor roll:	**First overall in 1987-88, 1988-89**
Home rink/Capacity	**Canadian Airlines Saddledome/17,139**
Stanley Cups:	**1 (1989)**

Playing Record

	W	*L*	*T*	*RT*	*Pts*
Regular Season	**1012**	**878**	**332**	**5**	**2361**
Playoffs	**69**	**87**			

CAROLINA HURRICANES™

Finally settled, the Hurricanes are hoping they can continue to build a loyal fan base by turning in some outstanding displays.

The Carolina Hurricanes are finally settling into life in the South. The 2000-01 season is the former Hartford Whalers' fourth in North Carolina, but it's really only their second season home, as they played their first two seasons in far-flung Greensboro. Last year was the Canes' first in the Raleigh Entertainment and Sports Arena.

For most of the 1990s, the Whalers/Hurricanes were also-rans, but things began to change in 1999. The Canes won the Southeast Division and earned the No. 3 seed in the Eastern Conference playoffs. Last season, Carolina finished above .500, but fell one point shy of the playoffs. Still, it was the first time in 11 years the franchise had strung together back-to-back plus-.500 seasons.

For the first two years the Hurricanes were in Carolina, the cornerstone player was big center Keith Primeau. But he was involved in a long contract squabble last season and was eventually traded to Philadelphia in January. In return, the Canes got backup goalie Jean-Marc Pelletier and center Rod Brind'Amour. The latter is one of the best two-way players in hockey, though the Canes never got to see his best last season. Brind'Amour and future Hall of Famer Ron Francis give Carolina a top-notch twosome in the pivot.

Ron Francis is the league's quietest superstar. Including his days in Hartford, Francis is the Whalers/Hurricanes' leader in games, goals, assists and points.

Scoring speedsters

The Canes spread the scoring around. Speedy Jeff O'Neill can fill up the net, as can even quicker Sami Kapanen, who won the fastest skater title at the All-Star Game. Re-signing free agent Gary Roberts, a rugged presence as well as a goal scorer and fan favorite, was the Canes' top priority in the off-season.

Acrobatic Arturs Irbe enjoyed a solid second season in Carolina's goal, though he was overworked (75 games) and the Canes need to find him some reliable backup. The defense is unspectacular. Glen Wesley is a steady influence, but the best two-way defenseman is Sean Hill, who went into the off-season as an unrestricted free agent. The Canes don't play a particularly physical brand of hockey, and they were the league's least penalized team last year (9.7 minutes per game).

ROLL OF HONOR

Conference/Division	**Eastern/Southeast**
First seasons	**1979-80 (Hartford); 1997-98 (Carolina)**
Honor roll	**Southeast Division title, 1998-99**
Home rink/Capacity	**Raleigh Entertainment & Sports Arena/ 19,000**
Stanley Cups	**0**

Playing Record

	W	L	T	RT	Pts
Regular Season	638	815	213	0	1489
Playoffs	20	35			

Frustrating misses

Hartford was one of four WHA teams to join the NHL in 1979—along with Winnipeg, Quebec and Edmonton. The Whalers fans were loyal to the end, although the lack of a winning tradition was often a source of frustration. The team finished first in its division only once—in 1986-87—and, that season aside, it never ended higher than fourth place. The Whalers missed the playoffs 10 times in their 17 years in Hartford. Only once did they advance beyond the first playoff round.

Hartford's first NHL season featured the awe-inspiring Howe family, the legendary Gordie—whom the Whalers had signed to a WHA contract in 1977—and sons Mark and Marty. Gordie, a 50-year-old grandfather, played in all 80 games in 1979-80, scoring 15 goals and collecting 41 points, inspiring his young and adoring teammates to the playoffs before retiring at the end of the season.

The player who has most marked the Whalers' history is Francis. He spent all of the 1980s with the club and remains the leader in most of the franchise's offensive categories. Francis collected 821 points and 264 goals in 714 games as a Whaler.

A new beginning

The Compuware group had a successful formula with their youth and junior hockey operations, and they have been trying to adhere to the same blueprint with the Hurricanes. General manager Jim Rutherford and head coach Paul Maurice were both members of that Compuware program.

In fact, it was Maurice who became the youngest head coach in pro sports when he replaced Paul Holmgren behind the Hartford bench in 1995. He had been highly successful with the Detroit Junior Red Wings, where he compiled a 86-38-8 record in two years.

Art for Arturs' sake: Irbe enjoyed a solid season between the pipes.

and
KOHO

ROLL OF HONOR

Conference/Division	**Western/Central**
First season	**1926-27**
Honor roll	**28 straight playoff berths 1969-70 to 1996-97**
Home rink/Capacity	**United Center/20,500**
Stanley Cups	**3 (1934, 1938, 1961)**

Playing Record

	W	*L*	*T*	*RT**	*Pts*
Regular Season	**2056**	**2167**	**769**	**2**	**4883**
Playoffs	**187**	**214**	**5**		

Chicago Blackhawks®

Three years after their 28-year postseason streak ended, the Chicago Blackhawks are looking to return to the playoffs in 2001.

A streak of 28 straight playoff apperances ended when the Blackhawks missed the postseason in 1998. Now Chicago is in the midst of a new streak, three straight non-playoff seasons, and the team is looking to put an end to that run post haste.

In fact, the Hawks are beginning to earn a reputation for too little, too late. In 1998-99, they went 13-6-4 down the stretch and closed the season with six straight wins, only to miss the playoffs by eight points. Last year, they closed 9-3-3, including wins in the final three, to finish nine points out of the last playoff spot. This resulted in yet another coaching change.

The new coach is a groundbreaker. Alpo Suhonen, a native of Finland, is the first European-bred head coach in NHL history. It's no surprise that although the Hawks were one of the last franchises to embrace the European influence, they would now be the first to hire a European head coach. This is because manager of hockey operations Mike Smith, the man who did the hiring, has long been at the forefront of the European invasion.

Up-tempo hockey

Both Smith and Suhonen, a former Toronto Maple Leafs assistant, believe in a fast-tempo style of play, so expect the Hawks to open things up. No more dump and chase hockey. That suits speedy Tony Amonte, one of the most consistent goals scorers in the league, just fine.

"A wide-open game? I'm smiling about that," said Amonte, who scored 40 goals in three of the past four seasons.

The Hawks have some weapons to play that style. Waiver-wire steal Steve Sullivan, plucked from Toronto last year, plays well with Michael Nylander, who had a career year as a first-year Hawk.

The defense hasn't had a cornerstone since Chris Chelios left in 1999. Boris Mironov has the tools, but more will be expected this year after an injury-plagued 1999-2000 campaign. Kevin Dean is as solid as they come on the Hawks' blue line.

Muldoon's curse

Despite their playoff streak, actually getting their hands on the Stanley Cup has been a different proposition for Chicago. Victories have been few and far between for the Blackhawks, who joined the NHL way back on September 25, 1926.

Their first head coach was a man named Pete Muldoon, who lost the job after one only season in charge. However, it was a season spiced with intrigue. Muldoon was fired after a woeful display by the Blackhawks. But he didn't go gently. He is alleged to have placed a curse on the team, saying it would never finish first because it had treated him so ignominiously. The Muldoon curse lasted 40 years. Chicago didn't finish first until the 1966-67 season. In Stanley Cup play, the Blackhawks have managed to escape the curse only three times—when they won in 1934, 1938 and 1961.

Eric Daze has two 30-goal seasons and three 20-goal seasons in his five years as a Hawk.

Super sniper: Right winger Tony Amonte has been Chicago's most reliable player and his tally of 43 goals in 1999-2000 was third-best in the NHL.

A history of talent

Yet, it is a franchise which has been blessed with some wonderful talent who, before moving into the spacious United Center in the 1994-95 season, played at raucous Chicago Stadium.

Bobby Hull, the 'Golden Jet' who shellshocked goaltenders with his patented slap shot, became the first NHLer to score more than 50 goals in a season, in 1966. Stan Mikita, the gifted Hockey Hall of Fame center, sparkled for 21 seasons, scoring 541 goals, second to Hull's 604. Both Hull and Mikita are regarded as the unofficial 'inventors' of the curved stick.

Then there was 'Mr. Goalie', Glenn Hall, who introduced the butterfly style of goaltending much in vogue today. After Hall, it was Tony (O) Esposito making some history—his 15 shutouts in 1969-70 are a modern-day single-season NHL record.

ROLL OF HONOR

Conference/Division	**Western/Northwest**
First Season	**1979-80 (Quebec); 1995-96 (Colorado)**
Honor roll	**107-point season in 1996-97**
Home rink/Capacity	**Pepsi Center/18,129**
Stanley Cups	**1 (1996)**

Playing Record

	W	*L*	*T*	*RT*	*Pts*
Regular Season	**718**	**731**	**217**	**1**	**1654**
Playoffs	**86**	**76**			

Colorado Avalanche®

In 2000, the Avalanche came up one game short of a place in the Stanley Cup finals; next season they hope to go one better.

In the midst of winning six straight division championships, the Colorado Avalanche have done the amazing—pulled off a youth movement. Without dropping from the NHL's elite, the 1996 Stanley Cup champions have added several impact youngsters in the past couple seasons. Every team would love to have a nucleus which includes forwards Chris Drury, Milan Hejduk and Alex Tanguay and defenseman Martin Skoula. Drury was the 1999 NHL Rookie of the Year. Expect the Avalanche to seriously compete for the Stanley Cup for the foreseeable future.

Then there are the superstars. The heart and soul of the franchise since its pre-Colorado days has been center Joe Sakic. The quiet sniper became the captain in 1992 and was the Conn Smythe Trophy winner as playoff MVP during the 1996 Cup run. He had a subpar 1999-2000 season, especially in the playoffs, and entered the off-season as a restricted free agent.

Many hockey people consider the Avs' other center, Peter Forsberg, the best all-around player in the game. Three-time Stanley Cup winner Patrick Roy enters the season three wins short of Terry Sawchuk's all-time record for wins by a goaltender.

New ownership

The Avs made a serious bid for the 2000 Stanley Cup by aquring veterans Dave Andreychuk and Ray Bourque in a late-season trade. But, as in the 1999 playoffs, Colorado was stopped in the Western Conference finals by Dallas in seven games. To help get to that next level, the Avs have re-signed Bourque, the future Hall of Fame defenseman, for at least one more year.

The franchise is entering a new ownership era. The new money man is Stan Kroenke, a Wal-Mart hier who owns 40 percent of the Super Bowl champion St. Louis Rams. His $450 million bid for not only the Avalanche, but also the Denver Nuggets and the Pepsi Center trumped the offer of a group that included Denevr Broncos legend John Elway.

Checkered history

This is NHL Part 2 in Colorado, and, it's been a spectacular sequel thus far. Unlike 1976-77, when Colorado inherited the mediocre Kansas City Scouts, the region managed to entice the Quebec Nordiques, a rising NHL power, whose owners felt they could no longer financially survive without a revenue-generating new rink in Quebec City.

Nordiques president Marcel Aubut and his ownership group sold the franchise to COMSAT, an entertainment company headed by Charlie Lyons, in the summer of 1995. That returned the NHL to Colorado, without a franchise after the Rockies moved and they became the New Jersey Devils in 1982.

Quiet Superstar: Joe Sakic quietly, unassumingly accumulates his points every season, like clockwork.

As a player in the Swedish Elite League, Peter Forsberg was known as the best player not in the NHL. Now he's one of the best players in the league.

One of four World Hockey Association teams absorbed by the NHL in 1979, the Nordiques made the playoffs for seven straight years after their initial season. But as star players aged and key draft picks failed to deliver the goods, lean times arrived for the Nordiques. Quebec missed the playoffs for five straight seasons much to the chagrin of the fans.

In 1991, No. 1 draft pick Eric Lindros refused to sign with the Nordiques, setting off a year-long battle that culminated in Quebec trading him to both the New York Rangers and Philadelphia Flyers. An arbitrator had to intervene, awarding him to the Flyers. This trade appears to have been a turning point for the franchise. Among the players Quebec acquired was Forsberg, who is becoming as much a part of the Colorado scenery as the Rocky Mountains.

ROLL OF HONOR

Conference/Division	**Western/Pacific**
First season	**1967-68 (Minnesota); 1993-94 (Dallas)**
Honor roll	**Finished with franchise-best 114 points in 1998-99**
Home rink/Capacity	**Reunion Arena/16,962**
Stanley Cups	**1 (1999)**

Playing Record

	W	*L*	*T*	*RT*	*Pts*
Regular Season	**1034**	**1160**	**410**	**6**	**2484**
Playoffs	**129**	**121**			

DALLAS STARS™

The Dallas Stars came oh so close to retaining the Stanley Cup in 2000, but they found just one team better than them.

The Dallas Stars' reign as Stanley Cup champion is over. It lasted one glorious season, and the feeling was so sweet that the Stars made a strong run at extending their rule one more year. Dallas made a return trip to the Stanley Cup Finals this past spring, but rather than hoisting the Cup, the team watched a visiting squad celebrate the championship right there in Reunion Arena. That feeling wasn't any fun, so the Stars players are determined to get that sweet feeling of victory back.

Dallas was built for the playoffs, built to dethrone the Stars' predecessor as champion—the Detroit Red Wings. Mike Modano, the first overall pick in the 1988 draft by the then-Minnesota North Stars, is the heart of the roster. Modano has developed into one of the best two-way centers in hockey. Last season, he tied for eighth in the league with 81 points and was named to the NHL Second All-Star Team. He ranked second in the 2000 playoffs in points with 23, one behind teammate Brett Hull.

Other Dallas players with a long history of putting the puck in the net include forwards Hull and Joe Nieuwendyk and defenseman Sergei Zubov. The Stars don't score a lot of goals but they don't let many in their own net. Only Philadelphia and St. Louis gave up fewer goals than Dallas in the entire NHL last season.

Eddie Belfour was brilliant in the regular season and even better in the Stanley Cup Finals after a dose of flu laid him low in Game One.

Eddie the Eagle

While the Stars play a stellar brand of defense, a huge factor in their defensive success is the play of goalie Eddie Belfour. Belfour led the league in save percentage last year (.919) and his four playoff shutouts was a league-best total.

The captain sets the physical tone for Dallas. Defenseman Derian Hatcher makes sure no one gets a second crack at goals around Belfour's crease. Zubov is the power-play quarterback and one of the best in the league at leading the play out of his own end. Darryl Sydor also provides offensive flair from the point.

Another strength for the Stars is face-offs but they will miss the retired Guy Carbonneau, a three-time Selke Trophy winner who won three Stanley Cups in his 18-year NHL career. But there are young faces ready to take a bigger role in Dallas, including Jamie Langenbrunner and Brenden Morrow.

Tragic start

The franchise, which has operated in Dallas since 1993, burst on the NHL scene in 1967-68, along with five others: the Seals (with whom the Stars would later merge), Kings, Flyers, Penguins and Blues. They were the Minnesota North Stars then, but an early on-ice tragedy made star-crossed a more appropriate description.

On January 13, 1968, about halfway through the North Stars' inaugural season, a helmetless Bill Masterton struck his head violently on the ice and died in hospital from brain injuries two days later. It was the first and, thankfully, to this day, the only NHL on-ice death.

Bill Goldsworthy was the North Stars' first big goal-scorer. He was the first player from a post-1967 team to score 250 goals, 48 of which came in the 1973-74 season.

Lone Star Star: In center Mike Modano, the Dallas Stars have an outstanding player; he and they are Stanley Cup winners in 1999.

On the move

The North Stars made the Stanley Cup final in both 1981 and 1991, losing to the New York Islanders and Pittsburgh Penguins, respectively. The North Stars' tremendous playoff run in 1991 temporarily revived lagging fan interest in Minneapolis but in 1993 Norm Green, who had become the team owner three years earlier, moved the franchise to Dallas.

Dropping the North from their nickname, the Stars were the first NHL club in Texas and the sixth franchise to be based in the United States 'Sun Belt'. Six years later, the Stars became the first of these teams to have the Stanley Cup shining upon them.

Detroit Red Wings®

For the Detroit Red Wings, after another disappointing exit to Colorado in the playoffs, it's time for its young players to step up.

The Detroit Red Wings were the team of the 1990s. Only the Pittsburgh Penguins won as many Stanley Cups as Detroit's two, and 100-point seasons were a routine matter for the Wings. The new millennium brought much of the same—108 points in 1999-2000, second best in the league. But the Wings lost in the second round of the playoffs for the second straight year, and for the second straight year to arch-rival Colorado. Now the motivation is to show that Detroit's time hasn't passed.

For sheer star power, the Wings lineup reads like a future roster of the Hall of Fame. Up front, Steve Yzerman, Brendan Shanahan, Sergei Fedorov provide the fireworks for one of the most explosive offenses in the league. Detroit led the league with 278 goals last year.

Nicklas Lidstrom and Chris Chelios anchor a stingy defensive corps. And then there are other possible Hall of Famers—forward Igor Larionov and defenseman Larry Murphy—who went into the off-season unsure of whether they'd be back in a winged wheel jersey.

In the past few years, Detroit has sacrificed the future to remain in the hunt for the cup, giving up young players and draft picks for veterans. With two straight second-round straight second-round playoff ousters, that philosophy is changing. The Wings are now having to think about the future as well as the present.

Another run

The core group, although getting gray around the temples, is still capable of another run at the title. Detroit won the championship in 1997 and 1998 with a complete team effort, rolling four lines and playing with heart. The engine driving the team is Yzerman, who has been the captain since 1986 and who shows no signs of slowing down. He leads by example.

Coach Scotty Bowman is the winningest coach in NHL history. He has eight Stanley Cups as a coach, tied with his idol Toe Blake. Bowman has forgotten more hockey than anyone else knows. His tactics are often times maddening to his players, but he gets positive results.

If Detroit is to remain in the elite, young players such as defenseman Jiri Fischer and forward Yuri Butsayev must develop quickly. And a huge key to the success of the team is Chris Osgood. Although Osgood has posted impressive stats playing on very good teams, his role has generally been to not hurt the team. Now, he must take on more responsibility and help carry the team.

Red hot past

The Red Wings were the NHL powerhouse in the first half of the 1950s, winning four Stanley Cups in six years.

That was the era of the Production Line of (Gordie) Howe, (Ted) Lindsay and (Sid) Abel, defensive stalwarts Red Kelly and Bob Goldham, icy-veined Terry Sawchuk in goal and Jolly Jack Adams at the managerial helm.

First Among Equals: The flashiest player on Detroit's roster is undoubtedly Sergei Fedorov, a two-way superstar.

Until Wayne Gretzky came along a few decades later, Howe was the NHL's leading career goal-scorer with 801, all but 15 of them coming with Detroit. His linemate Lindsay is regarded by many as the toughest customer of all time. Abel, who went on to coach the Red Wings, was the set-up man on the line.

Sawchuk was impenetrable in goal, recording 85 shutouts with Detroit and an NHL record 103 in his career. The numbers brought Sawchuk an election to the Hockey Hall of Fame, one of nearly 50 people associated with the Red Wings who have earned such an honor.

Stevie Y: Yzerman may be Detroit's elder statesman, but his Red Wings career points total is second only to Gordie Howe.

ROLL OF HONOR

Conference/Division	**Western/Central**
First season	**1926-27 (Cougars); 1930-31 (Falcons); 1932-33 (Red Wings)**
Honor roll	**Seven straight regular-season titles (1948-49 to 1954-55)**
Home rink/Capacity	**Joe Louis Arena/19,983**
Stanley Cups	**9 (1936, 1937, 1943, 1950, 1952, 1954, 1955, 1997, 1998)**

Playing Record

	W	*L*	*T*	*RT*	*Pts*
Regular Season	**2163**	**2054**	**775**	**2**	**5103**
Playoffs	**233**	**215**	**1**		

ROLL OF HONOR

Conference/Division	**Western/Northwest**
First season	**1979-80**
Honor roll	**5 Cups in first 11 seasons**
Home rink/Capacity	**Skyreach Centre/17,100**
Stanley Cups	**5 (1984, 1985, 1987, 1988, 1990)**

Playing Record

	W	*L*	*T*	*RT*	*Pts*
Regular Season	**791**	**660**	**215**	**8**	**1805**
Playoffs	**133**	**82**			

Edmonton Oilers®

The Edmonton Oilers didn't produce a playoff surprise in 2000, but they may go far in this year's postseason.

The Edmonton Oilers have almost always been synonymous with Glen Sather. That is no more. The legendary president and GM has bolted for the bright lights of Broadway, taking over the helm of the New York Rangers. In Sather's place? The man everyone always assumed would succeed him: Kevin Lowe.

Lowe was the Oilers' first-ever draft pick (selected, of course, by Sather) and he scored the franchise's first NHL goal. Now he has the daunting task of following a legend. But Lowe has the confidence of the organization and its players.

"With Glen leaving, Kevin was the guy everyone trusted with the team," said winger Mike Grier.

To fill the posititon he vacated as head coach, Lowe has turned to his longtime Edmonton teammate, Craig MacTavish, famous as the last NHL player to not wear a helmet.

There have been 10 captains in Oilers history. Lowe and MacTavish were two of them. The leader now is center Doug Weight, who has consistently been the team's best offensive player since coming from the Rangers in 1993. Weight's desire to win was on display during the Oilers' brief 2000 playoff run. He played with badly bruised ribs, taking much punsihment in that sensitive area, but still finished with five points in five games.

A solid core

The captain doesn't have to carry the whole weight in the scoring department. Ryan Smyth came into the league as a sniper, scoring 39 goals in his second season, and it looks as if he has regained his shooting eye. He scored a team-high 28 goals last season after netting just 33 in the two previous seasons combined. He plays with a lot of energy, as does penalty-killer extraordinaire Todd Marchant. Boyd Devereaux and Dan Cleary offer hope for the future.

The MVP of the team in 1999-2000 was goalie Tommy Salo. He became a workhorse, playing in 70 games. He has a good group of defensemen in front of him. Jason Smith was a steal from the Maple Leafs. The Oilers also have some flash at the blue line with the likes of Tom Potti and Janne Niinimaa. Highly regarded, defenseman Eric Brewer was brought in during the off-season.

After posting first-round upsets in the 1997 and 1998 playoffs, the Oilers have been bounced out in round one by Dallas each of the past two seasons. It has been a long time since Edmonton has gone into the playoffs as a serious contender, but the GM and the coach still remember what that felt like.

Camelot on ice

The Edmonton franchise didn't join the NHL until 1979—one of four World Hockey Association franchises to do so—but it surely made up for lost time. In five years, the Oilers built a powerhouse that produced five Stanley Cups in seven years, between 1983-84 and 1989-90. They were successful because a superb nucleus of players came of age together, and Sather displayed a green thumb in developing the vast talent on hand. "In the 1980s it was Camelot," recalls ex-Oilers owner Peter Pocklington. "It was almost surreal. We were always on a roll."

The supporting cast sometimes changed but the main actors did not. There was Wayne Gretzky, arguably the finest player to lace on skates, menacing Mark Messier, crafty Jari Kurri, multi-dimensional Glenn Anderson, the steady Lowe on defense and the unflappable Grant Fuhr in goal.

The shock trade of Gretzky to the Los Angeles Kings in 1988 signalled the impending demise of Camelot, but it wasn't the end of the Oilers' spring skate with the Stanley Cup. Messier, Anderson, Kurri, Fuhr and Lowe were around for one last hurrah, in 1989-90.

Carrying the Weight: Center Doug Weight has been the Oilers' best offensive player since coming from the Rangers in 1993.

Meltdown: Edmonton's gritty winger Bill Guerin chipped in a combined 54 goals in 1998-99 and 1999-2000.

ROLL OF HONOR

Conference/Division	**Eastern/Southeast**
First season	**1993-94**
Honor roll	**Most points (83) by first-year team (1993-94)**
Home rink/Capacity	**National Car Rental Center/19,200**
Stanley Cups	**0**

Playing Record

	W	*L*	*T*	*RT*	*Pts*
Regular Season	**226**	**225**	**91**	**6**	**549**
Playoffs	**13**	**18**			

Florida Panthers®

For the Panthers, 2000 ended in a disappointing playoff defeat. A year wiser, the new campaign seemingly holds more promise.

Things are looking quite sunny in South Florida. Just two years removed from a 63-point season, second-worst in the league in 1997-98, the Panthers posted 98 points last season, ninth-best in the NHL. The 35-point leap over that two-year span was biggest improvement in all of the NHL.

Armed with a new multiyear contract, GM Bryan Murray is looking to continue that improvement. At the center of all the team's plans is dynamic winger Pavel Bure, arguably the most exciting offensive player in the league.

He came to the Panthers midseason in 1998-99, after holding out from the Vancouver Canucks, and made an immediate impact, scoring 13 goals in 11 games. Then he blew out his knee. But Bure came back stronger than ever and scored 58 goals last season, 14 more than anyone else in the league.

The Panthers' lack of playoff experience was a factor in their four-game sweep at the hands of New Jersey in round one. Murray was expected to get some veteran help in the off-season, including perhaps a player or two from the European leagues. But improvement also is expected to come from within.

Young sniper Mark Parrish has combined for 50 goals in his first two seasons and he appears to only be getting better. Twenty-five-year-old Viktor Kozlov had a team-record 53 assists last year.

Offensive punch

Florida plays a more wide-open style than most teams, which puts pressure on the Robert Svehla-led defense and the goaltender, whether it be Trevor Kidd or Mike Vernon. The Panthers acquit themselves well, ranking ninth in the league in goals against last year.

Only two teams in the Eastern Conference scored more than the Panthers last year. At the trading deadline, Murray made a deal for veteran Mike Sillinger which sparked a late-season resurgence.

He seems to thrive playing setup man for Bure and he was outstanding in the playoffs. Ray Whitney is good for around 30 goals per season.

By the time the 2000-01 season begins, the Rob Niedermayer era may be a memory. The franchise's first-ever draft pick tallied just 10 goals last season, and he entered the 2000 off-season as an unrestricted free agent—and an expensive one at that. It seemed very possible that one way or another, Niedermayer will begin the 2000-01 campaign in another uniform.

Rob Niedermayer became the original Panther when he was selected as the team's first-ever draft pick in 1993.

Pavel Bure led the league in goals in 1999-2000 with 58, 14 more than any other player.

Brash rats

Owned by Wayne Huizenga of the Blockbuster Video empire, the Panthers were something of a blockbuster themselves in 1993-94, the season they joined Tampa Bay as the NHL's expansion entries from the Sunshine State.

Under renowned hockey tactician Roger Neilson the Panthers became the most successful first-year NHL team, collecting 83 points and narrowly missing a spot in the Stanley Cup playoffs.

The Panthers came achingly close to a playoff berth in the strike-shortened 1994-95 season, adhering to the same smothering style and solid goaltending by John Vanbiesbrouck, the first pick in the 1993 expansion draft.

But Panthers management, headed by Bill Torrey, who shaped the New York Islanders' dynasty in the early 1980s, decided a coaching change was required and Neilson was replaced by Doug MacLean, a product of the Detroit Red Wings system.

MacLean modified the neutral-zone trap during the 1995-96 season, favoring a mix of offense and defense, and it vaulted the Panthers to a dramatic seventh-game Conference final triumph over Pittsburgh and a hard-fought six games before succumbing to Colorado in the final.

Los Angeles Kings®

Still waiting on their Hollywood ending, the Kings will be looking to continue their upswing in form in 2000-01.

In a town that creates movie magic, the Los Angeles Kings are still looking for their happy ending. While it hasn't happened yet, at least the script appears to be getting better. The Kings are on the upswing after a mostly forgettable second half of the 1990s. In the last six years of that decade, Los Angeles missed the playoffs five times. Last season, the Kings turned things around with a 94-point season (a 25-point improvement from the previous season) and earned a No. 5 seed in the playoffs. Unfortunately, that got them a first-round date with the Detroit Red Wings. The series ended in a Detroit sweep.

Rob Blake is the barometer for this team. The big defenseman struggled through several injury-plagued seasons during the 1990s playoff drought. When he had a healthy season in 1997-98, a Norris Trophy-winning season, Los Angeles reappeared in the postseason. He missed 20 games in 1998-99, another non-playoff campaign, before bouncing back strong last year, playing 77 games and finishing third among defensemen with 57 points. He was a Norris Trophy finalist again and the Kings were back in business. His health, as always, is crucial.

Offensive firepower

Los Angeles wins by unleashing its potent offense. The leader of the pack is ageless wonder Luc Robitaille, who had his first 40-goal season in La-La Land in 1986-87. Last year the sniper poster 36 goals, which tied him for ninth in the league. Glen Murray and Ziggy Palffy added 29 and 27 goals, respectively. The two top centers, Jozef Stumpel and Bryan Smolinski, entered the off-season as restricted free agents.

The Kings power play was average during the regular season, but if the Kings are going to make any noise in the playoffs this year, they are going to have to do a lot better in this area. Against Detroit, L.A was 0-for-23 with the man advantage. The Wings, conversly, scored seven power-play goals.

In Stephane Fiset and Jamie Storr, Los Angeles has a pair of capable goalies. Neither has been able to claim the No. 1 job, however, which might be needed if the Kings are to be a serious contender. Top teams almost always have an undisputed top goalie. Andy Murray is in his second season as head coach. He hopes his predecessor, Larry Robinson, left behind some good luck. Robinson went on to win the Stanley Cup with the New Jersey Devils this spring.

LA stars

The franchise has had its share of jewels. One of them was Marcel Dionne, a diminutive but Houdini-like center who was acquired in a trade with Detroit after the 1974-75 season. He skated his way into the Hall of Fame, scoring 550 of his 731 career goals—third-best in NHL history—as a member of the Kings. Along the way, Dionne inherited Charlie Simmer and Dave Taylor as linemates, and the Triple Crown Line, as they were dubbed, were the scourge of the league for several seasons.

Luc Robitaille has been the sniper of old since returing to L.A, scoring 39 and 36 goals, respectively, the past two seasons.

The Dionne era ended in 1987, when he was dealt to the New York Rangers. But in true Hollywood fashion another superstar arrived on the set just over a year later—Wayne Gretzky. The NHL's marquee player arrived from Edmonton in a blockbuster trade. While Gretzky revived sagging hockey interest in Los Angeles, the Kings got no closer to their first Stanley Cup triumph than the dramatic 1992-93 final against the Montreal Canadiens.

Rob Blake (below) won the 1998 Norris Trophy, and was a finalist for the award in 2000.

ROLL OF HONOR

Conference/Division	Western/Pacific
First season	1967-68
Honor roll	Reached Stanley Cup final 1992-93
Home rink/Capacity	Staples Center/18,500
Stanley Cups	0

Playing Record

	W	L	T	RT	Pts
Regular Season	1022	1204	378	4	2426
Playoffs	55	95			

ROLL OF HONOR

Conference/Division	**Eastern/Northeast**
First season	**1917-18**
Honor Roll	**Record for most consecutive Stanley Cup titles (5)**
Home rink/Capacity	**Molson Centre/21,273**
Stanley Cups	**24 (1916, 1924, 1930, 1931, 1944, 1946, 1953,1956, 1957, 1958, 1959, 1960, 1965, 1966, 1968, 1969,1971, 1973, 1976, 1977, 1978, 1979, 1986, 1993)**

Playing Record

	W	*L*	*T*	*RT*	*Pts*
Regular Season	**2714**	**1702**	**802**	**4**	**6234**
Playoffs	**381**	**249**	**8**		

Montreal Canadiens®

A lack of goals and injuries to key players left the 1999-2000 Canadiens an agonizing two points shy of the playoffs.

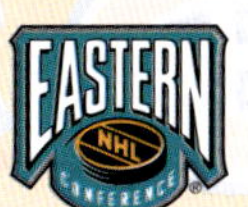

No franchise has boasted as many offensive superstars as Montreal, but in recent years the Canadiens' offense has been populated mostly by Hab-nots. Two seasons ago, Montreal scored the second-fewest goals in the league; last year there were two teams below the Habs in the scoring column, one being the expansion Thrashers.

The hope is that the offensive woes can be cured by good health. Last season the Montreal training staff was the busiest in the league as the Canadiens lost nearly 550 man-games to injury. Captain Saku Koivu suited up just 24 times and his durability has become a concern. Trevor Linden, a six-time 30-goal scorer, was out 32 games last year, and Brian Savage, a three-time 20-goal man, was on the shelf for 44 games. Enigmatic defenseman Vladimir Malakhov missed most of the season with knee injuries before being dealt to New Jersey in March.

The M*A*S*H unit that was the Canadiens locker helps explain why coach Alan Vigneault was a finalist for the Jack Adams Award as the league's top coach despite Montreal missing the postseason. The team was in contention until the final weekend and finished two points out of the final playoff spot.

Ray of light: Netminder Jeff Hackett helped the Canadiens to become of the top penalty-killing teams in the league.

Dynamic duo

For a team that doesn't score much, it helps to have stellar goaltending, and the Habs' talented tandem of Jeff Hackett and Jose Theodore provide just that. Only three teams allowed fewer goals than Montreal's 194 last year. The Canadiens' penalty-killing is among the best in the league thanks in large to the puck stoppers.

Hackett and Theodore benefit from a solid-but-unspectacular group of defensemen, led by steady shot-blocker extraordinaire Eric Weinrich. Sheldon Souray, a promising banger, was obtained in the Malakhov trade.

Missing the playoffs was not the hardest blow to the Habs faithful in the year 2000. Forward Trent McCleary took a slap shot to the throat in January that required emergency surgery and a month after the season ended, legendary right winger Maurice "The Rocket" Richard died after a long battle with cancer.

Great expectations

No team has to deal with higher expectations from its loyal followers than the Canadiens—and that's because of the winning tradition of the Club de Hockey Canadien. With 24 Stanley Cups, Montreal has experienced more excellence than any other major North American pro sports franchise except the New York Yankees, who have 25 World Series titles. The Canadiens have 11 more Cup triumphs than their closest pursuer, the Toronto Maple Leafs.

Saku Koivu led Montreal in scoring last season with only 44 points.

Torch of Glory

Little did J. Ambrose O'Brien realize, when he founded the team on December 4, 1909, that it would gain world-wide renown for its hockey prowess. In fact, he sold the club just one year later. But by 1926 Canadiens players such as Edourard "Newsy" Lalonde, Aurel Joliat, Joe Malone, Georges Vezina and Howie Morenz were stars.

The late 1950s saw an unmatched five consecutive Stanley Cups, as the team responded to an excerpt from the John McRae poem *In Flanders Fields*—"To you from failing hands we throw the torch. Be Yours to Hold it High" which has been a fixture in the dressing room since 1952. No one grabbed the torch with as much gusto as Richard, the team's career goal-scoring leader with 544. An icon in Quebec, Richard's suspension for striking a linesman touched off a riot by fans at the Forum on March 17, 1955.

The string of Stanley Cups started the following the year as Jean Beliveau, Dickie Moore, Boom Boom Geoffrion, Doug Harvey, Jacques Plante and Maurice's kid brother Henri led a star-studded cast coached by Toe Blake, who would win eight Cups in 13 seasons behind the bench.

With Scotty Bowman at the helm, the Canadiens added four straight Stanley Cups between 1975-76 and 1978-79.

NASHVILLE PREDATORS™

With the experienced David Poile at the helm, the Predators have every reason to believe that success is around the corner.

So far in its short life, the Nashville franchise has yet to live up to its nickname of Predator. Goals have been tough to come by. In Nashville's inaugural season, it scored 190 times, once-more than L.A.'s Western Conference-worst total. Last year, the Predators were the lowest scoring bunch in the conference.

But building an expansion franchise is a slow and steady process, and most people in the hockey world recognize that with David Poile running the show, it's only a matter of time before the Predators become a perennial playoff team. Previously Poile helmed the Washington capitals, and in his 15 years as the GM of the Caps, Washington was a mainstay at the top of the standings.

The Predators believe they drafted their franchsie player when they took center David Legwand with the second overall pick in 1998. Legwand showed some promise in his rookie season by scoring 13 goals, tied for 13th among NHL newcomers in that category last year. Nashville provides a great environment for the speedy youngster to do his apprenticeship, what with it being new to the sport of hockey and thus relatively low-pressure.

Ronning keeps going and going

Legwand would do well to pay close attention to Cliff Ronning. The 5'8" forward is probably the team's MVP. He moved from center to wing last season to make room for Legwand, and he led the team offensively for the second straight year, this time with 26 goals and 62 points. The seemingly ageless one will be 35 this season. Patric Kjellberg is the only other Predator coming off a 20-goal season. He also brings size (6'2") and a defensive conscience to the table. Greg Johnson is a reliable two-way center and Vitali Yachmenev is a battler in his own zone. They will be counted on to pick up their offensive game this season.

The defense can be solid but unspectacular. The Predators need a full, healthy season from ace blueliner Kimmo Timonen, an All-Star Game selectee who played just 51 games. The power play is a sore point with Nashville. The Predators were fourth-worst in the league with a mere 13.5 percent conversion rate, though a healthy Timonen would undoubtedly have helped boost that percenatge. Defenseman Drake Berehowsky is coming off a strong year in which he recorded career highs in goals, assists, points and games. The 6'2", 211-pound workhorse, who led the Predators in average ice time last season with 22.40 minutes, was rewarded in June when Poile chose to exercise his contract option for the upcoming 2000-2001 season.

Mike Dunham heads into his third year as a No. 1 goaltender. His numbers got better across the board vs. the Predators' inaugural season, but there is still room for improvement. His backup, Tomas Vokoun, will push for more playing time.

A backup to Martin Brodeur in New Jersey for a couple of seasons, Mike Dunham is showing more and more confidence.

Hockey Tonk USA

The team was embraced by the country music industry right from the beginning. Barbara Mandrell had the entire squad over her house for dinner before the 1998-99 season began. Others who bought Panther season tickets included Reba McEntire, Deana Carter and Garth Brooks.

There was a Hockey Tonk Jam in March of 1998 to raise awareness for the Predators, with performances from Faith Hill, Tim McGraw and others. The event included Delbert McClinton's debut performance of Hockey Tonk (The Predators Song). McGraw even rewrote one of his hit songs, "I Like It, I Love It," to have a Predators bent and it served as an anthem for the club.

Vince Gill was once spotted banging on the penalty box glass and giving the choke sign to Theo Fleury. The ultimate blending of hockey and country music came when singer Mindy McCready started dating Berehowsky.

Center Greg Johnson provides steady two-way play for the Predators.

ROLL OF HONOR

Conference/Division	**Western/Central**
First NHL Season	**1998-99**
Home Arena/Capacity	**Gaylord Entertainment Center/17,500**
Former Cities/Nicknames	
NHL Championships	**0**

Playing Record

	W	*L*	*T*	*RT*	*Pts*
Regular Season	**56**	**94**	**14**	**7**	**133**
Playoffs	**0**	**0**			

NEW JERSEY DEVILS®

New Jersey Devils: Stanley Cup champion. It has a nice ring to it, but now comes the tough part: trying to repeat.

The Devils players basked in a championship glow all summer long. They took turns hosting the Stanley Cup for a couple days at a time and had their backs slapped nearly everywhere they went.

The old sports saying is that it's even more difficult to defend a championship than it is to win a first one. New Jersey found that out after winning the 1995 Cup. The following season, the Devils didn't even make the playoffs. This current Devils lineup seems too good to let something like that happen. The 1995 version wasn't very talented offensively and was somewhat gimmicky in relying on the stifling neutral-zone trap defense. These Devils still play conscientious defense, but they have a wealth of skill too.

New Jersey has long had a no-star, low-offensive system, so it would surprise a lot of hockey fans to know that the Devils led the Eastern Conference and were second overall in the league in goals last year. There were no New Jersey players in the top 20 in points, but there were several lurking just below that level, and this season some of those players will become recognized as bona fide offensive stars. The No. 1 line of Jason Arnott (56 points) and Czechs Patrik Elias (72 points) and Petr Sykora (68 points) has become dominant, and it was especially effective in the 2000 playoffs. Elias tied for 11th in the league last year with 35 goals.

Franchise Defenseman: Scott Stevens won the Conn Smythe Trophy as playoffs MVP.

Rookie of the Year

The Devils organization is second to none is developing players and Scott Gomez is the latest gem. Rookie Gomez stepped right into a prominent role on the team, notched 19 goals and 70 points, good enough to earn the 2000 Calder Trophy. His teammate, the Calder winner in 1994, Martin Brodeur, was brilliant in backstopping his team to the title. Brodeur is on his way to a Hall of Fame career.

The heart of the team is captain Scott Stevens, who is a wrecking ball on the ice. The hard-hitting defenseman picked up the Conn Smythe Trophy as playoff MVP thanks to the physical tone he set. Behind the bench is another person with impressive credentials as a championship defenseman. Larry Robinson, the former Canadiens star, was promoted from assistant coach to head coach in March when Robbie Ftorek was fired. New Jersey had just eight games left in the regular season. It was a bold move by management, but it paid off in the end. This season Robinson has control from day one. He has new bosses, though, as a group led by New York Yankees owner George Steinbrenner takes control.

From funnies to champs

Few remember that the New Jersey Devils were once the Kansas City Scouts, and only vaguely that they were the Colorado Rockies. John McMullen and his group purchased in 1982 and moved to the New Jersey Meadowlands. The Devils were almost as dreadful as the Scouts and Rockies in their early years in New Jersey. In fact, after a 1983 game in which Edmonton routed New Jersey 11-4, Oilers superstar Wayne Gretzky likened the Devils to Mickey Mouse.

Until 1988, the Rockies-Scouts-Devils had qualified for a playoff berth only once in 13 seasons, and had one playoff-game victory—by Colorado in 1977-78.

But the first taste of post-season play as the Devils was memorable as they reached the Wales Conference championship before losing to Boston in seven games. The Devils did not make the conference final again until 1994. That ended in heartbreak, when Stephane Matteau's seventh-game overtime goal sent the New York Rangers, not New Jersey, to the Stanley Cup final.

But under Lemaire, part of eight Stanley Cup championships as a player with Montreal, the Devils embarked on a 1994-95 playoff run in which it lost only four of 20 games, culminating in a four-game sweep of the favored Detroit Red Wings for the first Stanley Cup in the history of the

New Jersey goaltender Martin Brodeur was brilliant in the Stanley Cup Finals.

ROLL OF HONOR

Conference/Division	**Eastern/Atlantic**
First season	**1974-75 (Kansas City); 1976-77 (Colorado); 1982-83 (New Jersey)**
Honor Roll	**Allowed only seven goals in four-game 1994-95 Stanley Cup final sweep of Detroit**
Home rink/Capacity	**Continental Airlines Arena/19,040**
Stanley Cups	**2 (1995, 2000)**

Playing Record

	W	*L*	*T*	*RT*	*Pts*
Regular Season	**756**	**1025**	**285**	**5**	**1802**
Playoffs	**73**	**50**			

ROLL OF HONOR

Conference/Division	**Eastern/Atlantic**
First season	**1972-73**
Honor roll	**Four straight Stanley Cups, 1979-80 to 1982-83**
Home rink/Capacity	**Nassau Veterans Memorial Coliseum/16,297**
Stanley Cups	**4 (1980, 1981, 1982, 1983)**

Playing Record

	W	*L*	*T*	*RT*	*Pts*
Regular Season	**976**	**936**	**310**	**1**	**2263**
Playoffs	**128**	**90**			

New York Islanders®

The Islanders are hoping that new owners and a slew of fresh faces will kick start their revival.

If you go to a New York Islanders game this season, make sure you buy a program. Otherwise, you might have a tough time recognizing the players. GM Mike Milbury made some drastic roster moves during the off-season. The newcomers include goalies John Vanbiesbrouck and Rick DiPietro, defenseman Roman Hamrlik, and forwards Mark Parrish and Oleg Kvasha.

There is another pair of important newcomers: owners Charles Wang and Sanjay Kumar. The Islanders go through ownership changes the way most teams go through hockey tape, but this time there is cause for optimism. These software moguls have deep pockets and are committed to the community. Wang and Kumar bought a team that hasn't made the playoffs since 1994 and that last year had the league's lowest payroll. But the new owners have expressed a willingness to spend on a winner.

Milbury took a big risk in selecting DiPietro with the first overall pick in the draft. DiPietro, from Boston University, became the first goalie ever picked No. 1. Three years ago, Milbury had made Roberto Luongo the highest-drafted goalie ever when Luongo was taken fourth overall. In with a new goalie of the future and out with the old goalie of the future. Luongo was dealt with forward Olli Jokinen to Florida for Parrish and Kvasha. The Isles' crease has becoming a revolving door: last year's top netminder, Kevin Weekes, was traded away the same weekend as Luongo, as they followed Tommy Salo and Felix Potvin out of town. Vanbiesbrouck, obtained from Philadelphia for a fourth-round draft pick, is 37.

Hamrlik time

In trading for Hamrlik, the Isles acquired a much-needed power-play quarterback. The flashy Czech has great offensive skills. He came over from Edmonton for defenseman Eric Brewer, a promising 21-year-old who slumped as an NHL sophomore last year, and forward Josh Green. He will take some pressure off captain Kenny Jonsson, who suffered through concussion and migraine problems last season.

The forward ranks are filled with promising youngsters, good news for a team that scored the second-fewest goals in the league last year. New York is extremely high on teenager Tim Connolly. Mariusz Czerkawski busted out with 35 goals last year, giving the Isles the sniper to replace Ziggy Palffy. There's a long way to go, but the Islanders hope they are back on the path to glory.

Torrey magic

The Islanders managed only 12 victories and 30 points in their fledgling season but they improved dramatically from then on, as astute general manager Bill Torrey, who'd been an executive with the expansion California Seals, started weaving his magic. Torrey hired Al Arbour as head coach following the 1972-73 season. One week later, he drafted Denis Potvin, a gifted young junior defenseman. At the draft table the following year, Torrey grabbed a bruising forward named Clark Gillies, and a shifty center named Bryan Trottier.

The combative Billy Smith, a little-known goaltender Torrey had selected in the 1972 expansion draft, suddenly became a key component in the building process. In the 1977 draft, Torrey plucked a wiry, high-scoring forward named Mike Bossy from the Quebec Major Junior League and the last building block was virtually in place.

By the 1979-80 season, these five players led an Islanders charge that displaced the Montreal Canadiens as the dominant NHL force. The Canadiens were seeking a fifth straight Cup when the upstart Islanders breezed through four series, including a six-game victory over Philadelphia in the final, for the first of four consecutive Stanley Cup championships.

The Islanders narrowly missed matching the Canadiens' record five straight Cups. They reached the final in 1983-84, only to lose to the Edmonton Oilers.

Kevin Weekes proved to be a solid goalie but was traded away to make room for No.1 pick Rick DiPietro.

Mariusz Czerkawski is coming off a huge season in which he tied for 11th in the league in goals despite his team's offensive woes.

ROLL OF HONOR

Conference/Division	**Eastern/Atlantic**
First season	**1926-27**
Honor roll	**Ended 54-year Stanley Cup drought in 1993-94**
Home rink/Capacity	**Madison Square Garden/18,200**
Stanley Cups	**4 (1928, 1933, 1940, 1994)**

Playing Record

	W	*L*	*T*	*RT*	*Pts*
Regular Season	**2103**	**2107**	**782**	**3**	**4991**
Playoffs	**183**	**195**	**8**		

New York Rangers®

New York have made big changes as they bid to halt their run of three straight seasons of missing the playoffs.

There's a new sheriff in town. His name is Glen Sather, which is exciting news for fans in the Big Apple. No hockey man has a reputation or track record to surpass Sather's. He was the architect of the Edmonton Oilers dynasty of the 1980s and he kept the small-market, small-payroll Oilers competitive in recent years despite the financial limitations of that franchise. The Rangers have missed the playoffs the past three seasons despite a seemingly limitless budget, and expectations will be high right off the bat for the new GM.

Sather quickly made a number of moves, the biggest of which involved a man very familiar to both Sather and Rangers fans. He re-signed the most popular Ranger of recent times—Mark Messier. The 39-year-old legend won five Stanley Cups with Sather in Edmonton before moving to the Rangers—practically willing New York to the Cup in 1994—then joining Vancouver in 1997.

The man who became captain after Messier left town, Brian Leetch, has been a fixture on the Rangers blue line since 1988. He'll benefit from Messier taking on some of the leadership burden. Leetch has won both his Norris Trophies as the NHL's top defenseman while Messier was his teammate (1992, 1997).

A need to spend wisely

Last year's Rangers were a prime example of money not buying success. New York had the highest payroll in league history yet still finished 12 points out of a playoff spot. Big spending on such free agents as Theo Fleury and Valeri Kamensky backfired. The team seemed to tune out coach John Muckler, who was fired in late March. Entering July, a new coach had not been appointed

Mike Richter is looking to bounce back from a season in which he had a hot start, then suffered a knee injury in the All-Star skills competition. He might not be ready at the start of the season, but he can still be one of the best goalies in the league.

The Rangers need Fleury to have the kind of season this year he was expected to have last year. The NHL's shortest superstar is certainly capable of more than 15 goals, which was his disappointing total last year. Manny Malhotra should get a chance to develop his young offensive skills. Gritty forward Adam Graves experienced tragedy at home last year, when one of his prematurely born twin sons died.

From Cup to Cup

Success in the playoffs hasn't been a Rangers hallmark. No NHL team has won a Stanley Cup one year after joining the league, as the Rangers did in 1928, but no team has gone without a Stanley Cup for 54 years, as the Rangers did before making up for lost time and striking paydirt in 1993-94.

In the early years, Madison Square Garden echoed with exhortations for scoring star Frank Boucher, brothers Bill and Bun Cook and Lester Patrick, the club's first coach and general manager. In the second game of the 1928 Stanley Cup finals, the 44-year-old Patrick was pressed into service as the team's goaltender. He allowed only one goal, the Rangers won in overtime, and Patrick was forever etched in the club's history as a Rangers' hero.

Another brother combination—Mac and Alex Shibicky—joined with future Hall of Famer Neil Colville to lead the Rangers to their 1940 Cup triumph. While the Rangers' Cup drought continued, the club made the playoffs nine straight years, starting in 1966-67.

The Rangers, who lost to Montreal in the 1978 final, wouldn't get another chance for nearly 20 years until 1994 in the final against Vancouver. The Cup-clinching goal in Game 7 of the final came from Messier, a five-time Cup winner with Edmonton and one of several acquisitions made by Rangers general manager Neil Smith in building his championship squad.

Little Mess: Rugged and skillful, Adam Graves has learned his NHL lessons well from his mentor, past and present team-mate Messier.

Goaltender Mike Richter is coming off a knee injury. When healthy and on his game, he is still one of the league's best.

Ottawa Senators®

The Senators took a small step back in 1999-2000, but there is much for hockey fans to look forward to in Canada's capital city.

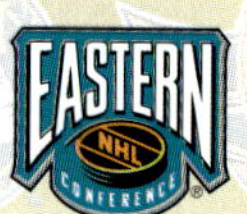

The good news is that Ottawa is one of the better teams in hockey after a long indoctrination in the league as a cellar dweller. The better news is that the Senators are still the Ottawa Senators, not the Portland Something-or-others. Owner Rod Bryden threatened to sell the team to a destination south of the border because his losses were approaching eight figures. But the fans of Ottawa came through in a season ticket drive, and there was some tax relief provided on the Corel Centre, so the Senators are staying put.

Next on the agenda—learning how to win in the playoffs. After four years of spectacular futility upon entering the NHL in 1992, Ottawa has rebounded nicely to make the postseason each of the past four seasons. The Sens even won the division in 1998-99 with an impressive 103 points. But so far, Ottawa has won just one playoff series—an upset of top-seeded New Jersey in 1998. In 1999-2000, the sixth-seeded Sens bowed out in six games vs. Toronto, a year after being swept by the Buffalo Sabres in round one.

This is still a young team, almost a necessity for small-market Canadian teams, since the older players get and the more success they achieve, the more salary they require. The line of Radek Bonk, Marian Hossa and Selke Trophy finalist Magnus Arvedson flourished last year, until the playoffs, and they range in age from 21 (Hossa) to 28 (Arvedson). Daniel Alfredsson, who suffered a knee injury which limited him to just 57 games, managed an impressive 21 goals in his limited action. The 1996 rookie of the year hasn't played as many as 60 games since his sophomore campaign, but he's still just 27.

Super Shawn: Shawn McEachern has been an offensive force for Ottawa over the past three seasons, scoring 84 goals during that span.

The Yashin issue

The team's superstar center, Alexei Yashin, didn't play one shift for the Senators last season. He held out despite having a contract, and things got ugly. The team sued Yashin, who hung out in Europe and dated a supermodel, and it won. The result of the team suit, as ruled by an arbiter, is that Yashin still owes the team a year of service. The soap opera continued to roll into the middle of July and it wasn't clear if Yashin would return to the Senators, be traded away, or keep on sitting out.

Shawn McEachern didn't feel the loss of Yashin as much as many people expected. The gritty winger tied Hossa for the high-flying Senators' team lead in goals with 29. His fractured thumb in the playoffs hurt the club's offensive punch. Stalwart blueliner Wade Redden's broken foot didn't help matters either. Patrick Lalime, who had been out of the NHL for two years prior to last season, should get a serious shot at being the everyday goalie.

Walking the plank

While the past few seasons have been filled with regular season success, there have been plenty of stormy moments in their brief history. Mel Bridgman, the club's first general manager was fired immediately after the Senators' maiden season of 24 points—second-lowest in NHL history for a minimum 70-game schedule. The first-year Senators also tied an NHL record with only one road victory.

The abysmal record gave Ottawa the first draft choice in 1993, and the Senators grabbed Quebec Junior League scoring whiz Alexandre Daigle. Signed to a whopping five-year, $12 million contract, Daigle never lived up to expectations and has become an NHL journeyman.

Yashin has a long history of contract squabbles. He missed three months in 1995-96 before that dispute was settled. In the interim, the popular Rick Bowness—Ottawa's head coach from Day One—was fired, and key administrative personnel left the organization in frustration.

Ottawa's current general manager, Marshall Johnston, is the club's fifth. With a more secure future, things now look brighter.

Daniel Alfredsson has had some injury setbacks, but when healthy he sets an example for his teammates with his strong work ethic.

★ ROLL OF HONOR ★

Conference/Division	**Eastern/Northeast**
First season	**1992-93**
Honor roll	**Northeast Division title, 1998-99**
Home rink/Capacity	**Corel Centre/18,500**
Stanley Cups	**0**

Playing Record

	W	*L*	*T*	*RT*	*Pts*
Regular Season	**201**	**346**	**79**	**2**	**483**
Playoffs	**10**	**18**			

★ ROLL OF HONOR ★

Conference/Division — **Eastern/Atlantic**
First season — **1967-68**
Honor roll — **Consecutive Stanley Cups, 1974-75**
Home rink/Capacity — **First Union Center/19,519**
Stanley Cups — **2 (1974, 1975)**

Playing Record

	W	*L*	*T*	*RT*	*Pts*
Regular Season	**1298**	**898**	**408**	**3**	**3007**
Playoffs	**158**	**140**			

PHILADELPHIA FLYERS®

The Flyers came very close to returning to the Stanley Cup Finals, but the talent is there for a charge in 2000-01.

The Flyers finished the season as the Eastern Conference's No. 1 seed despite entering the playoffs with an interim coach behind the bench and their best player, Eric Lindros, sidelined by yet more concussion problems. Craig Ramsay took over for coach Roger Neilson, who was undergoing cancer treatment. During the off-season, Ramsay was given the permanent gig. Despite leading 3-1, New Jersey toppled Philly in a thrilling Conference finals series.

Lindros' off-season looked a little rockier. He was a restricted free agent and the team made a qualifying offer, but he was still suffering from effects of his concussions by midsummer. There were plenty of bad feelings between Lindros and GM Bobby Clarke. Lindros had been stripped of his captaincy in favor of stalwart defenseman Eric Desjardins.

Power forward Rick Tocchet re-upped with the team in the off-season. He is still an irritant to opponents and tough to move from the crease. The Flyers have one of the highest-flying offenses and dynamic power plays, led by Mark Recchi—third in the league last year with 91 points—and John LeClair—seventh with 40 goals.

Goaltending sensation

The brightest spot for the Flyers last year was the emergence of rookie sensation Brian Boucher in net. He led the league in goals-against average (1.91) and was brilliant in the playoffs, outdueling Dominik Hasek in the first round. The man whose job Boucher took, John Vanbiesbrouck, went to the Islanders in the off-season. Other rookies also brightened the Flyers' future. Simon Gagne showed some flair up front and Andy Delmore showed potential as an offensive defenseman.

Keith Primeau and Daymond Langkow give the Flyers strength up the middle regardless of Lindros' status. Primeau, a big, strong center in the mold that Clarke so likes, was part of a blockbuster trade last season that saw popular Rod Brind'Amour dealt to Carolina. In a controversial move, Clarke signed power forward Kevin Stevens in the off-season. Stevens, a former All-Star who is good buddies with Tocchet and Recchi, had been involved in a crack cocaine scandal in 1999-2000.

Intimidating force

There's always been something special about the Flyers, one of the six expansion teams to join the NHL for the 1967-68 season. Six years later, they became the first expansion team to win the Stanley Cup, an exploit repeated in 1974-75. The Flyers of that era were tough and talented, attributes exemplified by acknowledged on-ice leader Bobby Clarke, who today is the Flyers' president and general manager.

Enforcers Dave (The Hammer) Schultz, Bob (Hound Dog) Kelly and Don Saleski did plenty of body-thumping. The Flyers' bruising defense corps of Andre (Moose) Dupont, the Watson brothers—Joe and Jim—and Ed Van Impe dished out more bitter medicine.

But the Flyers, under coach Fred Shero, were much more than brawn. They had a 50-goal man in Rick MacLeish, another in Reggie Leach, who in 1975-76 notched 61 goals, only the second NHLer to reach that mark. And they had Bill Barber, whose 420 goals in 903 games as a Flyer remain the career best on the club.

In goal, Bernie Parent, traded to Toronto in 1971 and re-acquired two years later, won the Conn Smythe Trophy as the most valuable performer in the Stanley Cup playoffs in both 1974 and 1975, the first player to accomplish the feat. Amid the triumphs, there was also tragedy. Barry Ashbee, one of the Flyers' best defensemen, had his career ended in 1974 after being struck in the eye by a puck, and Vezina Trophy winner Pelle Lindberg was killed in an automobile accident at the height of his goaltending career in 1985.

Eric Lindros suffered more worrying concussions in 2000 and he also lost the captaincy.

The arrival of Brian Boucher made former No. 1 goaltender John Vanbiesbrouck expendable and he will suit up for another team.

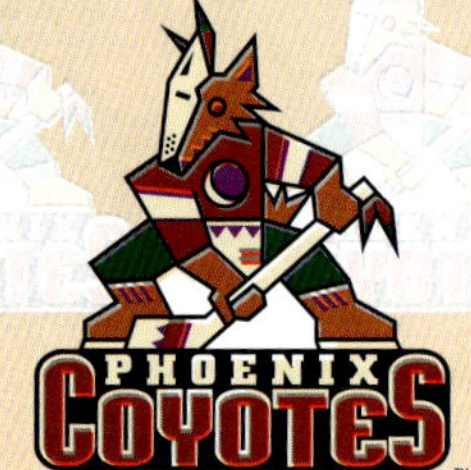

PHOENIX COYOTES®

The Phoenix Coyotes hope the 2000-01 season will end later than the first round of the playoffs.

Phoenix got Wayne Gretzky. Unfortunately, they didn't get Gretzky the player, they got Gretzky the owner. Like Pittsburgh's Mario Lemieux, Gretzky has joined the ownership ranks even though he could still probably center his team's top line. The Great One is in the new ownership partnership headed by Steve Ellman. Gretzky has control over hockey operations.

The Coyotes are still looking to break their first round playoff jinx. The franchise has won just two playoff series in its 21 years, the last coming in 1987 as the Winnipeg Jets. In the 2000 playoffs, the sixth-seeded Coyotes were bounced in the opening round by Colorado.

There were a lot of question while the new ownership settled in as to what the Phoenix roster would look like this season. As of midsummer, the goaltending situation was the most unclear. Nikolai Khabibulin sat out the entire 1999-2000 season (sniper Robert Reichel also sat out the season) and incumbents Sean Burke and Bob Essensa were restricted free agents.

Two of the biggest stars on the team—forwards Keith Tkachuk and Jeremy Roenick—were rumored as possible trade bait. Tkachuk played just 50 games last year (he still managed to score 22 goals) and then had off-season surgery on both his right ankle and left knee. Roenick tied for 11th in the league with 78 points.

Phoenix captain Keith Tkachuk scored 22 goals but injuries limited his season to just 50 games.

Hot start

The Coyotes hope they get off to the same hot start they did last year, when they led the league after 29 games with 18-8-3 record, but sustain it rather than swoon. Phoenix lost seven straight down the stretch. Another area in need of improvement is the power play. The Coyotes had the second-worst unit in the league last year at a mere 11.9 percent success rate.

Defenseman Lyle Odelein (Columbus) and wingers Dallas Drake (St. Louis, via Columbus) and Mikael Renberg (Sweden) left town during the off-season, the first two in the entry draft. Skillful Joe Juneau and tough-guy Brad May were traded for to fill the voids left by Renberg and Drake.

The defense is mediocre. Teppo Numminen is the anchor and he is one of the better blueliners in the league. Fellow veterans Jyrki Lumme and Keith Carney are also tied up to long-term deals.

Shaping influence

The Coyotes' NHL roots are in Winnipeg, where the Jets entered the league in 1979. While not very proficient in the NHL, the club was instrumental in the evolution of European players and, so, had much to do with shaping the style and substance of the game.

While Swedish stars Ulf and Kent Nilsson, and Anders Hedberg from Winnipeg's WHA years didn't accompany the Jets to the NHL, European stars such as Willy Lindstrom and Lars-Erik Sjoberg carried the torch successfully. The Jets also had NHL scoring great Bobby Hull for 18 games that first season, before trading him to Hartford.

As the 1980s unfolded, two players emerged to become the cornerstones of the Jets franchise. Dale Hawerchuk, a rangy center who was the No. 1 overall pick in the 1981 NHL draft, was the team's leading scorer for the next nine years, a remarkable stretch of form that catapulted him to the team's all-time leader in goals (379) and points (929).

Thomas Steen, of Sweden, wasn't a prolific scorer. But he combined toughness, speed and grace for 14 seasons with the Jets, making him the club's longest-serving player. There wasn't a dry eye in the Winnipeg Arena when the Jets retired Steen's No. 25 in a ceremony following the 1995 season.

Wily Coyote: Jeremy Roenick (right) finished tied for 11th in the league with 78 points in the 1999-2000 season.

ROLL OF HONOR

Conference/Division	**Western/Pacific**
First season	**1979-80 (Winnipeg); 1996-97 (Phoenix)**
Honor roll	**Club record 43 wins and 96 points in 1984-85**
Home rink/Capacity	**America West Arena/16,210**
Stanley Cups	**0**

Playing Record

	W	*L*	*T*	*RT*	*Pts*
Regular Season	**657**	**798**	**211**	**4**	**1529**
Playoffs	**28**	**59**			

PITTSBURGH PENGUINS®

Pittsburgh may have a different style in 2000-01 with the Czech Republic's Olympic gold medal-winning coach directing the team.

When you have arguably the world's greatest player on your roster—and the Pittsburgh Penguins do with winger Jaromir Jagr—it's always a good idea to make him as comfortable as possible. Jagr's former linemate, Mario Lemieux, is in the owner's box, and now Jagr's former Czech Olympic coach, Ivan Hlinka, is behind the bench as the successor to Miracle on Ice hero Herb Brooks. Hlinka, brought on as an associate coach in February, became the second born-and-bred European head coach in NHL history, named shortly after Chicago tabbed Finland native Alpo Suhonen right after the 1999-2000 season.

Jagr isn't the only Penguin to have played for Hlinka. On a roster that boasts a large immigrant population, Robert Lang, Jiri Slegr, Martin Straka and Josef Beranek also won the 1998 Olympic gold under Hlinka's direction. Jagr won his second straight Lester B. Pearson Award (MVP as voted by the players) in 2000 and he won his third straight scoring title, scothering 96 points despite missing 19 games.

The Penguins have perhaps the most skillful set of forwards in the league in the likes of Jagr, Alexei Kovalev, Lang, Straka and Jan Hrdina. The enigmatic Kovalev had his most productive regular season with 66 points, though he didn't have his usual big playoff run. Matthew Barnaby adds the agitator quality to the forward corps.

Aubin is the man

For many years, Tom Barrasso ruled the Pittsburgh crease. But there is a changing of the guard in the Penguins net. Barrasso was traded to Ottawa last season for Ron Tugnutt, and Tugnutt signed in the off-season with Columbus.

That gives Jean-Sebastien Aubin the No. 1 spot. Aubin saw action in 51 games as a rookie and played well, then got hurt just prior to the playoffs, which opened the door for Tugnutt to lead the team to a first-round upset of Washington.

The defense is solid if unspectacular for Pittsburgh. Darius Kasparaitis is the ultimate warrior, Bob Boughner is tough, and Janne Laukkanen and Jiri Slegr are good two-way players.

Things are looking up for the franchise since Lemieux took ownership in 1999. The team broke even financially on an operating basis after working it way out of bankruptcy and reaching the second round of the playoffs too. Ticket sales increased, naming rights to the arena were sold and there is no more popular owner in sports.

The Penguins will open the new season in a sort of home from home, a venue dear to the hearts of at least the Penguins' Czech Olympians Hlinka, Jagr, Straka, Slegr and Lang, as well as Russians—silver medalists—Aleksey Morozov and Darius Kasparaitis. It will be in Japan, the country which hosted the1998 Winter Olympics, in a two games series against Nashville.

Lemieux said, "We are excited about taking our team and our organization to Japan to start the 2000-2001 regular season."

Leading from the front: Jaromir Jagr was an inspirational captain, winning his second straight Lester B Pearson Award (MVP voted by the players) as well as his third straight scoring title.

Bolstering a center

The history of the Penguins did not start on June 9, 1984, the day they selected Lemieux as the top pick in the NHL entry draft — but the fortunes of the franchise improved dramatically as of that date. Gradually, general manager Patrick assembled strong support for Lemieux. Jagr, a gifted Czechoslovakian, was grabbed in the 1990 entry draft, two-way center Francis was obtained in a trade with Hartford, and rangy Larry Murphy was added to the defense corps to clear the goal crease for netminder Tom Barrasso.

Two great hockey minds joined the Penguins for the 1990-91 season—(Badger) Bob Johnson as coach and Scotty Bowman as director of player development. Together, the former Stanley Cup-winning duo made the Penguins, out of the playoffs in seven of the previous eight seasons, into sudden Stanley Cup champions.

Bowman made it two straight Cups in 1992 when he relieved Johnson as coach at the start of that season. Johnson died of cancer several weeks later and fans honored his memory in a candlelight ceremony at the Civic Arena.

Martin Straka finished with a +24 rating for the 1999-2000, second best on the Pittsburgh team, despite missing 11 games.

★ ROLL OF HONOR ★

Conference/Division	**Eastern/Atlantic**
First season	**1967-68**
Honor roll	**Five division titles, two Stanley Cups in last 10 years.**
Home rink/Capacity	**Mellon Arena/16,958**
Stanley Cups	**2 (1991, 1992)**

Playing Record

	W	*L*	*T*	*RT*	*Pts*
Regular Season	**1079**	**1173**	**352**	**6**	**2516**
Playoffs	**100**	**90**			

ROLL OF HONOR

Conference/Division	**Western/Pacific**
First season	**1991-92**
Honor roll	**Upset first-round playoff opponent 1994, 1995, 2000**
Home rink/Capacity	**San Jose Arena/17,483**
Stanley Cups	**0**

Playing Record

	W	*L*	*T*	*RT*	*Pts*
Regular Season	**227**	**399**	**80**	**7**	**541**
Playoffs	**20**	**29**			

San Jose Sharks®

Beware any playoff team going to San Jose for a playoff series: these are Shark-infested waters.

The Sharks have become known as first-round playoff predators. San Jose made a reputation for opening-round upsets in the mid-1990s and it rekindled that spirit in the 2000 tournament, shocking top-seeded St. Louis, which had recorded 114 regular-season points, six more than any other team in the league. A second-round elimination at the hands of Dallas was closer than a five-game series might lead one to believe.

There are many signs pointing to continued improvement in San Jose. The Sharks are the kind of hard-working, blue-collar team that does well in the playoffs. The biggest story last season was the reemergence of Owen Nolan as a dominant force. The power forward had seemingly fallen off the radar screen the previous couple seasons, but he roared back with a career-high 44 goals and he followed that up with a gritty playoff performance in which he displayed leadership despite a painful abdominal strain.

There are other character players, including Mike Ricci, the wild-haired center who never goes less than 100 percent. Vincent Damphousse, in his first full year as a Shark, posted 70 points and was a big reason for Nolan's rebirth.

Youth brigade

The Sharks have relied on players who look as if they don't yet have to shave every day. Jeff Friesen, Niklas Sundstrom, Patrick Marleau, Alexander Korolyuk and Marco Sturm have all played several seasons in the NHL even though they all were born between 1975 and 1979. Their games are still on the upswing.

The precocious one in the defensive corps is Brad Stuart. The player who was drafted third overall in 1998 had a stellar rookie campaign for San Jose. He played in all 82 games and led the team's blueliners with 10 goals and 36 points. The top defensive pairing of Mike Rathje and Marcus Ragnarsson is one of the best in the league at shutting down an opponent's top line.

Last season, Mike Vernon was traded away and Steve Shields got the No. 1 goaltending gig for the first time. The results were inconsistent, but he apprenticed under Dominik Hasek in Buffalo so he learned from the best.

One interesting off-season signing was left wing Scott Thornton, from the Dallas Stars. He earned a suspension last year for cold-cocking a player who is now a teammate, Sturm. San Jose is looking for Thornton to provide a veteran presence.

Coach Darryl Sutter signed a new two-year contract in the off-season. So far, he has the program moving in a continuous upward direction. He is one of just nine coaches in the past 50 years to guide his team to a better record in three consecutive seasons. Last year, San Jose had a franchise-record 35 wins.

San Jose center Mike Ricci, who will complete his 11th season in the league in 2000-01, doesn't need the letter 'C' on his uniform to provide veteran leadership for the Sharks.

Jeff Friesen matched his career high seven game-winning goals in 1999-2000 and equaled his best-ever points tally with 35.

Killer sharks

San Jose joined the NHL for the 1991-92 season, 17 months after the league granted permission to George and Gordon Gund to sell the Minnesota North Stars in return for the rights to an expansion team in San Jose.

A first order of business was to come up with a suitable nickname for the new club that would appeal to the fans. A competition was held and the Sharks emerged as the favorite.

The nickname is fitting for a franchise that has frequently struck without warning and shattered the Stanley Cup aspirations of the old guard. Ask the Detroit Red Wings, a strong Cup contender in 1993-94 who were ripped apart by the Sharks in the first round, losing in an emotion-charged seventh game. San Jose was in only its third season at the time, and had managed only 11 victories in an 84-game schedule the previous year.

The Sharks, whose team colors of Pacific teal, gray, black and white were an instant merchandising hit with the fans, pulled another major surprise in 1994-95, eliminating the second-seeded Calgary Flames in seven games in the opening round of the Western Conference playoffs.

ST. LOUIS BLUES®

After winning the Presidents' Trophy in 2000, St. Louis learned you can take nothing for granted in the playoffs.

The Blues led the league with 114 points in 1999-2000 to earn the Presidents' Trophy. But they didn't even get close to the much more coveted trophy—the Stanley Cup—bowing out to San Jose in the first round of the playoffs.

The Blues got young defenseman prospect Mike Van Ryn when an arbitrator ruled him a free agent, and signed veterans Sean Hill (defense) and Dallas Drake (forward). The defense needs to give Al MacInnis and Chris Pronger more rest-time in games. Drake is the prototype forward for the Blues' system; he has good speed and he loves to hit. Van Ryn has the potential to be a star.

Pronger and MacInnis give St. Louis arguably the best one-two punch at defense in the league. Pronger won the Hart Trophy as league MVP after leading the league in minutes per game (30:14), finishing second among defensemen in scoring (14 goals, 48 assists, 62 points), and winning the plus-minus title (plus-52). Pronger also won the Norris Trophy as top defenseman, succeeding MacInnis.

St. Louis' All-Star defenseman Al McInnis was awarded the Norris Trophy for the best defenseman in the league in 1998-99.

MacInnis wins the Norris

The special teams are something special in St. Louis. Last year, the Blues were second in the league in killing penalties and seventh with the man advantage. Much of the credit in both cases goes to MacInnis and Pronger, but they certainly get plenty of help. Michal Handzus was tied for third in the league with four short-handed goals and he was a finalist for the Selke Trophy.

Pronger isn't the only reigning trophy winner. Coach Joel Quenneville won the 2000 Jack Adams Award as top coach and sniper Pavol Demitra (28 goals, eight penalty minutes) took home the Lady Byng Memorial Trophy as the league's most sportsmanlike player. Pierre Turgeon also had just eight penalty minutes to go with 26 goals. Turgeon had 66 points in just 52 games and he had some heroics in the playoffs despite torn thumb ligaments.

Goalie Roman Turek enters his second season as the No. 1 guy after coming over from Dallas. He had a great regular season, finishing second in the league in both goals-against average (1.95) and wins (42), but he couldn't sustain that level in the playoffs. Forward Jochen Hecht had a strong postseason in his rookie campaign (10 points in seven games) and he should be a dandy.

Sentimental favorites

In their early years, the Blues, a product of the NHL's 1967 expansion, provided every hockey fan with a trip down memory lane, drafting or signing many of the heroes of their youth—Glenn Hall and Jacques Plante in goal, Doug Harvey, Al Arbour and Jean-Guy Talbot on defense, center Phil Goyette and diminutive forward Camille Henry. The first year, the Blues even managed to coax the former Montreal Canadiens great Dickie Moore out of retirement.

Teaming up with young snipers such as Red Berenson, Gary Sabourin and Frank St. Marseille, the old-timers were sprightly enough to get the Blues into the Stanley Cup final in each of the club's first three seasons, winning the West Division regular-season title in two. They were sentimental favorites in all the Stanley Cup finals but, despite a gritty effort, they were swept two straight years by Montreal and by Boston in 1969-70. Scotty Bowman, launching a Hall-of-Fame coaching career, was behind the Blues' bench those last two seasons.

The Blues haven't returned to the Stanley Cup final since those halcyon days, despite a number of talented performers passing through their ranks. Brett Hull, acquired in a 1988 trade, emerged from virtual obscurity to become the Blues' career goal-scoring leader, including 86 goals in 1990-91, a single-season output topped only by the great Wayne Gretzky. The latter became Hull's teammate for the last few weeks of the 1995-96 season, after the Blues obtained his services in an unsuccessful bid to reach the Stanley Cup final.

Pierre Turgeon's overtime goal in Game 7 of the 1999 playoffs against Phoenix had the Coyotes singing the Blues.

ROLL OF HONOR

Conference/Division	**Western/Central**
First season	**1967-68**
Honor roll	**Made Stanley Cup final first three years in NHL**
Home rink/Capacity	**Kiel Center/19,260**
Stanley Cups	**0**

Playing Record

	W	*L*	*T*	*RT*	*Pts*
Regular Season	**1122**	**1092**	**390**	**1**	**2635**
Playoffs	**120**	**146**			

ROLL OF HONOR

Conference/Division	**Eastern/Southeast**
First season	**1992-93**
Honor roll	**NHL single-game attendance record: 28,183 (1996)**
Home rink/Capacity	**Ice Palace/19,500**
Stanley Cups	**0**

Playing Record

	W	*L*	*T*	*RT*	*Pts*
Regular Season	**195**	**360**	**71**	**7**	**468**
Playoffs	**2**	**4**			

Tampa Bay Lightning®

Although results remained disappointing in 1999-2000, things have started to look up for Tampa Bay.

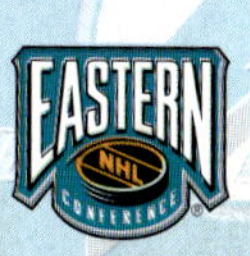

NHL life has been tough for the Tampa Bay Lightning. The team has been competing for nearly a decade now, yet it has made the playoffs just once, in 1996. That was the team's only winning season and it was eliminated in the first round by the Philadelphia Flyers. Last season, the Lightning's 54 points was better than only the expansion Atlanta Thrashers. Tampa's 1998-99 total of 47 points was the worst in the league, as was its 44 points in 1997-98.

It seems clear that there is only one way for the Lightning to go—up. And they will do so on young legs. Tampa was the league's youngest club last year, regularly playing 10 rookies. It was the first year of the Bill Davidson ownership. Davidson, the Detroit businessman with experience in both championships (NBA's Pistons) and hockey (IHL's Vipers), has finally brought stability to the franchise's top level. His top hockey people are familiar to him—former Vipers GM Rick Dudley and former Vipers coach Steve Ludzik. They were a successful combo in the IHL. Dudley was also a former Ottawa Senators GM.

The future of the franchise is dynamic forward Vincent Lecavalier. The top overall pick in the 1998 draft had an exceptional sophomore NHL season, leading the team with 25 goals and 67 points. He seems capable of living up to the hype that surrounded him in his draft year. Fellow forwards Mike Johnson and Todd Warriner seem to work well with Lecavalier. Fredrik Modin, who will be 26 this season, has found a home in Tampa. The former Maple Leaf put his lethal wrister to use for a career-high 22 goals last year. Brian Holzinger, a finesse forward who can chip in some offense, came over during the season in a deal that sent former No. 3 overall pick Chris Gratton to Buffalo.

Heartwarming comebacks

Aside from having trouble scoring, Tampa Bay also has trouble stopping other teams from scoring. They finished second-worst in the league in that category last year. Dan Cloutier struggled in his first season as a No. 1 goalie, so the Lightning obtained Kevin Weekes, played for the Vipers under Ludzik, during the off-season. Weekes was the Islanders' top goalie last year, although the Isles gave up the third-most goals in the league.

The defense has some fresh faces. First-year guys Paul Mara, Cory Sarich and Ben Clymer got valuable playing time last year and all have impressive potential Sarich was the main draw of the Gratton trade. Petr Svoboda is the steadying influence at the Lightning blue line.

Big box office

The Lightning came into the league in 1992 along with the Ottawa Senators. Because the team moved in its second season into the ThunderDome, with the largest seating capacity in the league, the team drew large crowds, including an NHL record 27,227 for its 1993-94 home opener against state-rival Florida Panthers, an expansion team that year. The Lightning left the Dome after the 1995-95 season, but not before establishing a new attendance record of 28,183 which still stands.

Goaltender Manon Rheaume made history with the Lightning in 1992. She became the first woman to play in any of the four major sports leagues when she started a preseason game for Tampa. In her one appearance, she made seven saves in 20 minutes of action. Afterward, she joined a Tampa minor league affiliate.

Phil Esposito, the Hall of Fame forward, was the driving force behind getting an expansion team for Tampa. Esposito served as general manager and alternate governor until being replaced by Jacques Demers in that role after the Lightning started the 1998-99 season 0-1-1.

Former Maple Leaf Fredrik Modin has a lethal wrister that helped him net 22 goals in his first year with the team.

Future perfect: Vincent Lecavalier is developing very nicely, leading the team in his sophomore season with 25 goals and 67 points.

ROLL OF HONOR

Conference/Division	**Eastern/Northeast**
First season	**1917-18 (Arenas); 1919-20 (St. Patricks); 1926-27 (Maple Leafs)**
Honor roll	**Only NHL team to rally from a 3-0 games deficit in Stanley Cup final to win (1942)**
Home rink/Capacity	**Air Canada Centre/18,800**
Stanley Cups	**13 (1918, 1922, 1932, 1942, 1945, 1947, 1948, 1949, 1951, 1962, 1963, 1964, 1967)**

Playing Record

	W	*L*	*T*	*RT*	*Pts*
Regular Season	**2249**	**2224**	**745**	**3**	**5246**
Playoffs	**225**	**244**	**4**		

TORONTO MAPLE LEAFS®

Toronto improved on its 1999 regular season points tally, but the Stanley Cup champion Devils ended the Maple Leafs' dreams.

Toronto is as hockey-mad a town as there is. The Leafs are the city's central attraction and a main conversation topic. Two years ago, Toronto missed the playoffs for the second straight season. But after back-to-back seasons in which the Leafs earned 97 and 100 points, respectively, expectations are soaring in the home of the Hockey Hall of Fame.

After reaching the 1999 Conference finals, the Leafs' run ended in round two at hands of rough and tough New Jersey Devils. In the final game of that series, Toronto managed a mere six shots on net. Not just for a period—for the whole game. To help shore up some offense and toughness, Toronto made a big splash in the free-agent market. They signed power forwards Shayne Corson (Montreal) and Gary Roberts (Carolina). Both players have mileage on them, but both also combine an ability to score with physical toughness.

All talk of the Leafs of the past couple seasons begins and ends with goalie Curtis Joseph, the team's MVP and a finalist for the 2000 Vezina Trophy. When Cujo arrived in town, coach Pat Quinn was able to install a more wide-open style of play that is both effective and fun to watch. Joseph cleans up most of the mistakes his aggressive teammates make.

High-flying offense

Toronto was second in the Eastern Conference in goals last year with 246. Mats Sundin was in the top 20 in the league with 73 points last year, and now he has some proven wingers (Corson, Roberts) who can help ease his burden. Steve Thomas seems to be defying age, still a threat for 30 goals at age 37. Jonas Hoglund had a breakthrough season last year with 29 goals. Nik Antropov showed enough as a rookie (12 goals) to believe that he can blossom into a first-line center. Yanic Perreault may be the best faceoff man in the league. Sergei Berezin is a dynamic offensive player who needs to produce more.

The defense is anchored by a stellar pair. Dmitry Yushkevich is a steady influence and the leader on the blue line. Tomas Kaberle has the potential to be a Norris Trophy winner some day.

The worst moment of the 1999-2000 season was not the playoff exit. It was when defenseman Bryan Berard took a stick in the face during a game in March and nearly lost his eye. Berard's career is in doubt, as are his chances of ever regaining meaningful vision in the eye. The Leafs said good-bye to a longtime favorite. Forward Wendel Clark returned to the team for his third stint in 1999-2000, then retired in the off-season.

Colorful heroes

The Leafs, who have won 13 Stanley Cups—second to the 24 hoisted by Montreal—are steeped in history, with colorful personnel such as (Happy) Day; (King) Clancy; (Turk) Broda; (Busher) Jackson; (Teeder) Kennedy; (Punch) Imlach; and Frank (The Big M) Mahovlich among those who proudly wore the Maple Leaf, emblematic of the franchise that joined the NHL in 1927.

Netminder Curtis Joseph's outstanding play helped Toronto coach Pat Quinn to go to a more wide-open and entertain style of play.

Luxury Swede: Mats Sundin will become an even more dangerous player as the quality of his surrounding cast improves.

The Leafs' most satisfying Cup was the one in 1942, when they became the only NHL club to overcome a 3-0 deficit in games in a Stanley Cup final, against Detroit. They were the first team to win three straight Cups, between 1947-49, and again won three consecutive times 1962-64; but the 1967 Cup triumph was their last.

The Cup-less interval has had great performers, notably Darryl Sittler, defenseman Borje Salming, and forward Wendel Clark.

It was Sittler who on February 7, 1976, scored six goals and added four assists in Toronto's 11-4 rout of Boston. Sittler's ten points are still a single-game NHL record.

Vancouver Canucks®

The Mark Messier era may be over in Vancouver, but the Canucks may be on the up after an improved season.

The Mark Messier era was a disappointing one. One of the greatest leaders in NHL history and a six-time Stanley Cup winner, Messier came to Vancouver in 1997 with a winning reputation, but he left having never played a single playoff game for the Canucks in three seasons with the team. But at least there's some reason for optimism. In 2000, the Canucks were part of a playoff race for the first time in a while, finishing just four points out of the last berth. They had a winning record after the All-Star break (15-10-5-2).

With Messier gone, the future may rest on a pair of twins from Sweden, forwards Daniel and Henrik Sedin, drafted second and third overall in the 1999 draft. But that's for the long-term. The Sedins have yet to play an NHL game and it will be a few years until they reach their prime.

There are some other young players already making an impact. On defense, Mattias Ohlund and Ed Jovanovski have plenty of good years ahead of them. Jovanovski, who was part of the Pavel Bure trade, may never make anyone forget the Russian Rocket, but he played great hockey down the stretch for Vancouver, rekindling memories of his promising rookie season a few years ago.

Naslund the sniper

The go-to man on offense is Markus Naslund. The Swede is now a legitimate NHL scorer, notching 27 goals last year on the heels of a 36-goal campaign. Enigmatic power forward Todd Bertuzzi looks like he's finally a consistent force (career-high 25 goals). And the Canucks have high hopes for former Hobey Baker winner forward Brendan Morrison, who came to town when Alexander Mogilny was shipped to New Jersey down the stretch. Andrew Cassels is a deft setup man who can handle No. 1 center duties.

Felix Potvin came over from the New York Islanders during the 1999-2000 season and he is set as the No. 1 goalie. He isn't quite the elite player he was early in his career with Toronto, but he showed his capability by going 11-8-4 after the All-Star break.

Burly original

One of the men who would have felt the pangs of frustration more than most was franchise torch-bearer Pat Quinn—an original Canuck, a burly defenseman selected in the 1970 expansion draft, when Vancouver, a new entry that year along with Buffalo, started to stock its franchise. As a player, Quinn left after two seasons, but he returned as general manager in 1987 and later added coaching duties. Once Quinn returned behind the bench he became the most successful skipper in team history, fashioning a .554 winning percentage from to 1992 to '95. But he has now left the team and is head coach in Toronto.

After winning a division title in 1992-93, Vancouver advanced to the Stanley Cup final for only the second time in its history the following year.The Canucks spent many of their early years in the shadow of the Sabres, their expansion cousin who, on the spin of a wheel, got the first choice in the NHL entry, and selected center Gilbert Perreault. That left Vancouver with defenseman Dale Tallon, who was not quite the impact player Perreault was. But Vancouver, with Andre Boudrias leading the team in scoring for the second straight year, won its first Smythe Division title in 1974-75, the same year Buffalo was first in the Adams Division.

The signature phrase of Frank Griffiths, the patriarch of the family who formed the Canucks and were its long-time owners, was "2 points", the number awarded to a team for each victory. The two points were easier to come by once Quinn arrived as GM in 1987.

He engineered an aggressive rebuilding plan, starting with the selection of Linden in the 1988 entry draft and adding another cornerstone—the Soviet League star Bure—in the 1989 draft.

Mark Messier may have given the Canucks veteran leadership, but his three years in Vancouver did not go as well as expected.

Defenseman Matthias Ohlund is just one of a number of promising young blue-liners who can take Vancouver forward in the future.

ROLL OF HONOR

Conference/Division	**Western/Northwest**
First season	**1970-71**
Honor roll	**Reached Stanley Cup final, 1982, 1994**
Home rink/Capacity	**General Motors Place/18,422**
Stanley Cups	**0**

Playing Record

	W	*L*	*T*	*RT*	*Pts*
Regular Season	**858**	**1170**	**350**	**8**	**2074**
Playoffs	**54**	**70**			

WASHINGTON CAPITALS®

The Capitals are a tough team to work out, improving by 34 points in 1999-2000, but failing in the playoffs.

It has been a long off-season for the Washington Capitals. The Caps had a stellar 1999-2000 regular season, finishing with 102 points and earning the No. 2 seed in the Eastern Conference playoffs. But along came the Pittsburgh Penguins and Jaromir Jagr, and in just five games the Caps were sent to the golf courses.

Washington players had a long summer to think about how to avoid a similar fate this spring. One person who had a nice break in his summer was goalie Olaf Kolzig, who stopped off in Toronto in June to pick up the Vezina Trophy as the league's top netminder. He regained his 1997-98 form, when he backstopped Washington to the Stanley Cup Finals. After slumping a bit in 1998-99, Kolzig was third in the league in wins (41) and fifth in save percentage (.917).

Peter Bondra didn't enjoy his usual success. The two-time 50-goal scorer was hampered by injuries and was reportedly on the trading block during the summer. Chris Simon had a breakthrough season and he's developed into more than just a goon. Put on Adam Oates' wing, Simon topped his previous high in goals by 13, with 29. Oates is an ageless wonder who sees the ice as well as anyone in the game. His 56 assists was second in the league last year.

Gonchar keeps Russian

Sergei Gonchar is one of the premier offensive defensemen in the NHL. His 39 goals is the most by a defenseman in the league over the past two seasons. He also led the Caps in plus-minus last year with a rating of plus-26, so he can take care of things in his own end as well. Brendan Witt adds a physical dimension to the blue line, while Calle Johansson is the calming influence at the point.

The forward ranks are filled with character guys such as Ulf Dahlen, Joe Sacco and Steve Konowalchuk. The team got tougher when forward Craig Berube, who led the Caps in penalty minutes five times during the 1990s, returned to the team during the off-season as a free agent. Defenseman Sylvain Cote, has also returned to Washington as a free agent and will add speed and depth.

Rough start

Right from the start of its NHL existence, the only way was up for the Capitals. It could not have gotten any lower for a team that joined the NHL as an expansion franchise in 1974-75 and proceeded to set all kinds of modern-day league records for futility. Most of the records are still in the book, more than two decades later.

But that first year? "It was demoralizing and depressing, but you tried not to have a defeatist attitude," remembers Doug Mohns, an NHL veteran. The 1974-75 Capitals established a record for the fewest points—21—in a 70-game season. Their .131 winning percentage remains the lowest in NHL history. They managed only one victory on the road. In one stretch they lost 17 games in a row, still a record. They went through three coaches, allowed an all-time record 446 goals and one of its goaltenders—Michel Belhumeur (which translated from French means good humor) appeared in 35 games and was the winning goaltender in none.

Olaf Kolzig returned to top form in 1999-2000 and the Capitals' netminder was awarded the Vezina Trophy as the NHL's top goalie.

Out of the pit

But climb the Capitals did—incrementally at first as Guy Charron arrived as a bonafide scorer and, finally, beyond the .500 mark and into the playoffs for the first time in 1982-83. That coincided with the arrival of the inspirational David Poile. Under Poile the Capitals had only two seasons under .500, and captured one Patrick Division title, in 1988-89.

Key draft picks such as sparkplugs Mike Gartner, Bobby Carpenter and Ryan Walter joined with defensemen Scott Stevens, Larry Murphy and Rod Langway—the latter pair coming after big trades with Los Angeles and Montreal—to continue Washington's rise from rags to respectability in the competitive cauldron of the NHL.

Peter Bondra missed 20 games through injury in 1999-2000 but still finished second on the team in goals scored with 21.

ROLL OF HONOR

Conference/Division	**Eastern/Southeast**
First season	**1974-75**
Honor roll	**Lost out to Detroit Red Wings in the 1998 Stanley Cup Final.**
Home rink/Capacity	**MCI Center/19,740**
Stanley Cups	**0**

Playing Record

	W	*L*	*T*	*RT*	*Pts*
Regular Season	**872**	**930**	**264**	**2**	**2010**
Playoffs	**65**	**77**			

NHL EXPANSION

With the arrival of expansion teams Columbus Blue Jackets and Minnesota Wild, the NHL family now has 30 members.

Just over 30 years ago, the NHL had only six teams. With the addition of the expansion Columbus Blue Jackets and Minnesota Wild this year, that number has grown fivefold. The Blue Jackets and Wild bring the NHL's roster to 30 teams, and the newcomers debut one year after the Atlanta Thrashers and two years after the Nashville Predators in the league's latest growth spurt.

An Expansion Draft was held June 23 to help stock the Columbus and Minnesota rosters. Each existing team (except Nashville and Atlanta) got to protect a certain number of its players, and the rest were thrown into a pool from which the Blue Jackets and Wild picked. Both Columbus and Minnesota picked one player from each of those 26 NHL clubs. Don't expect the Blue Jackets or Wild to compete for the Stanley Cup in the near term, but they hope to show that they're headed in the right direction. Here is a look at the NHL's newest franchises:

Columbus Blue Jackets

Columbus is the biggest city in Ohio, yet it has lacked major league professional sports until now. Support for the Ohio State University Buckeyes in Columbus is legendary, so it is clearly a great sports town. The NHL made a previous, short pit stop in Ohio in the late 1970s with the Cleveland Barons.

The Blue Jackets have local ownership led by Worthington Industries mogul John H. McConnell, who played college football at Michigan State. The man running the hockey operations is president/general manager Doug MacLean, who coached the Florida Panthers to the Stanley Cup Finals in 1996. That was the Panthers' third year in the league, so MacLean has experience in achieving early success with an expansion team. His first order of business was trading for Marc Denis, a hot goaltending prospect who was Patrick Roy's backup last year. In the Expansion Draft, Columbus took such established players as defensemen Lyle Odelein (Phoenix) and Mathieu Schneider (Rangers) and forwards Geoff Sanderson (Buffalo) and Steve Heinze (Boston).

The Blue Jackets join the Central Division of the Western Conference and will play in the brand-new Nationwide Arena, a state-of-the-art facility that seats 18,500.

Minnesota Wild

There is no place in the United States with a greater passion for hockey than Minnesota. The state's high school hockey tournament is akin to Indiana's high school basketball tournament. The NHL had a presence in the state previously with the Minnesota North Stars from 1967 to '93, before the club moved to become the Dallas Stars. Now the NHL is back after a seven-year absence.

The Wild's hockey braintrust is headed by a duo—executive vice president and general manager Doug Risebrough and coach Jacques Lemaire—who are familiar with winning. They were teammates on the dynasty Montreal Canadiens of the 1970s and they have combined to hoist 16 Stanley Cups during their careers. Lemaire coached New Jersey to the Cup in 1995.

Shortly after the Dallas Stars were eliminated from the 2000 Stanley Cup Finals, Risebrough traded for Manny Fernandez, who backed up star goalie Ed Belfour. The trade came a week before Fernandez's uncle, Lemaire, was hired as the Wild's coach. In the Expansion Draft, Minnesota stocked up with such veterans as goalie Jamie McLennan (St. Louis), tough defenseman Sean O'Donnell (Los Angeles) and forwards Darby Hendrickson (Vancouver) and Jeff Nielsen (Anaheim), native Minnesotans who were linemates at the University of Minnesota in the early 1990s.

Like the Blue Jackets, the Wild christen a new building, the Xcel Energy Center in St. Paul. Minnesota joins the Northwest Division of the Western Conference.

Wild at heart: Former Dallas Stars back-up netminder Manny Fernandez will likely be a very busy man in Minnesota.

Hockey Heroes

It's a truism in professional team sports that collective play wins championships. It's no less true that fans come out to watch the stars of the game, to marvel at their virtuosity, as much as to root for a winner.

Across its long history the National Hockey League has produced and continues to produce as richly varied a cast of sporting legends as any professional league in the world.

Each generation of fans, it turns out, has its Golden Age; each new wave of player talent leaves behind indelible memories of sporting brilliance that resonate forever in the collective imagination.

Some of the memories are passed down, like the legend of One-Eyed Frank McGee, who once scored 14 goals—eight of them consecutively—in a Stanley Cup game, a 23-2 drubbing of Dawson City by the Ottawa Silver Seven. McGee's nickname was no joke—he lost an eye when he was struck there by the butt end of a hockey stick.

Keen hockey fans, even the young ones, know of Frank Nighbor, who perfected the poke check, of Fred (Cyclone) Taylor, said to have scored a key Stanley Cup goal while skating full speed backwards, of Joe Malone, who once scored 44 goals in a 20-game season.

They certainly know the story of Lester Patrick, the coach of the New York Rangers, who in a 1928 Stanley Cup game, shed his jacket, shirt and tie and put on the goalie pads, and replaced the injured Lorne Chabot. The Rangers won the game and, later, the Cup.

Patrick was surely one of many stars of his era. The NHL of the 1920s and 1930s boasted names like Syl Apps, Ace Bailey, King Clancy, Clint Benedict, the first goalie to wear a mask, and Howie Morenz, known as the Stratford Streak, and the most electrifying player of his time.

What's my line?

The 1930s, 1940s and 1950s were famous for the marvelous forward lines that made hockey magic. The Toronto Maple Leafs had the Kid Line, with Gentleman Joe Primeau flanked by Harvey (Busher) Jackson and Charlie Conacher. The Boston Bruins featured the Kraut Line—Milt Schmidt, Bobby Bauer and Woody Dumart.

Ice Hard: The Avalanche have boasted a strong lineup of star players since arriving in Colorado in 1995, resulting in one Stanley Cup and three additional trips to the conference finals.

The Montreal Canadiens delivered the Punch Line, with 'Elegant' Elmer Lach centering for Maurice (Rocket) Richard and Hector (Toe) Blake, The Old Lamplighter. Richard was the first to score 50 goals in 50 games, the first to reach 500 goals.

And Detroit, the automobile center of America, assembled the Production Line, with Sid Abel centering for Gordie Howe and Terrible Ted Lindsay, as tough and mean a player as he was skilled.

Stars like Rocket Richard, Henri (Pocket Rocket) Richard, Jean Beliveau, Jacques Plante, Doug Harvey, Dickie Moore and Bernard (Boom Boom) Geoffrion took the Montreal Canadiens to the Stanley Cup finals for ten straight years in the 1950s. They won six Cups, including a record five in a row.

In the early 1960s, goaltender Glenn Hall, defenseman Pierre Pilotte, and fowards Stan Mikita and Bobby Hull, The Golden Jet, made the Chicago Blackhawks a feared opponent.

Stars on ice

The Toronto Maple Leafs, blending the talents of aging stars such as Bob Baun, Tim Horton and Johnny Bower with the emerging brilliance of Frank (The Big M) Mahovlich and Davey Keon, won three straight Stanley Cups.

Sublime individual feats remained a constant as the NHL expanded, first from six to 12 teams in 1968, then to 14 and 18, on up to its current—with the arrival of the Atlanta Thrashers for the 1999-2000 season—28-team membership.

Guy Lafleur's six straight 50-goal, 100-point seasons with the Montreal Canadiens in the 1970s; Mike Bossy saying he would match Richard's 50 goals in 50 games, then going out and doing it in 1981; Denis Potvin breaking the legendary Bobby Orr's goal-scoring and points records. The stars, indeed, keep on coming.

In the 1980s, sprightly Wayne Gretzky kept coming and coming, like a bad dream, his opponents thought. Here was Gretzky, scoring 92 goals, bagging 212 points, both records in 1982, winning the scoring championship by 65-point margin. There was Greztky, winning seven straight scoring titles, breaking the all-time scoring marks of Gordie Howe, leading the Edmonton Oilers to four Stanley Cups in five years.

And suddenly, The Great One had a rival—Mario Lemieux, The Magnificent One, who scored 85 goals and added 114 assists for 199 points in 1989.

As the NHL entered the 1990s, the league's galaxy of stars had become truly international, with names like Jaromir Jagr, Sergei Fedorov, Pavel Bure, Alexander Mogilny, Peter Forsberg and Teemu Selanne taking their place in the pantheon.

As spectacular as the NHL's stars have been for eight decades, the best, it seems reasonable to suggest, is yet to come.

Jaunty Jaromir: Since the retirement of the incomparable Mario Lemieux, the Pittsburgh Penguins' Jaromir Jagr has shouldered a larger burden.

RAY BOURQUE

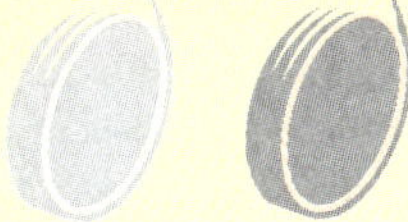
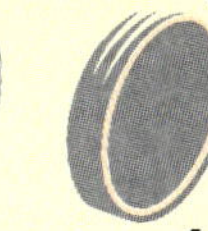

After almost 21 seasons in Boston, Bourque looks to win it all with the Avs.

Bobby Orr was the ultimate Bruin of the late 1960s and 70s, and Ray Bourque was Mr. Bruin in the 1980s and 90s. Like Orr, Bourque is a defenseman with sublime offensive skills, capable of changing the tempo of a game on his own. Like Orr, Bourque arrived in the NHL as an élite player who made an immediate impact.

In his rookie season, Bourque scored 17 goals and added 48 assists for 65 points, then an NHL record for points by a rookie defenseman. Not surprisingly, Bourque was named rookie-of-the-year in the NHL and was named a first-team NHL all-star, establishing a nearly annual NHL tradition. He has been the best defenseman of his era, winning the James Norris Trophy five times in his career.

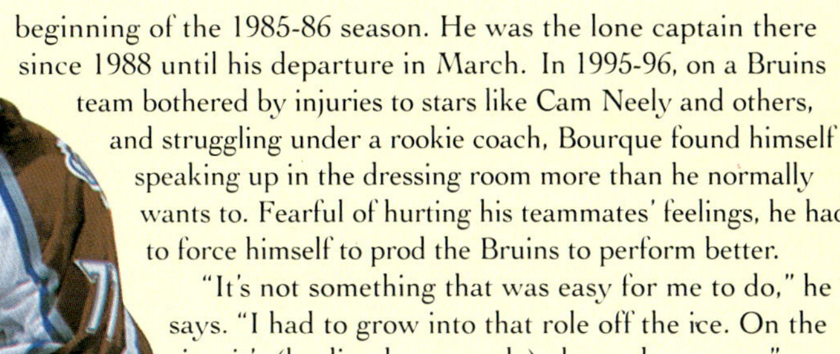

The uniform may have changed, but the steady brilliance remains the same.

Boston centerpiece leaves

In an era of unprecedented player movement—even Wayne Gretzky played for four teams—Bourque was a fixture in Boston, where he was the centerpiece player for nearly 21 seasons. That changed on March 6, when he was traded to the Colorado Avalanche. With Boston struggling and his time running out to win a Stanley Cup, Borque had requested a trade to a contending team. The Bruins obliged.

Bourque has scored 20 or more goals in a season nine times, including 31 in 1983-84, when he totaled 96 points, the most in his career. He also posted a plus-minus record that season of plus 51. That means Bourque was on the ice for 51 more goals by his own team at even strength than the Bruins' opponents scored, a barometer of his effectiveness at both ends of the ice.

A quiet leader who prefers to let his on-ice performance speak for itself, Bourque was named co-captain (with Rick Middleton) of the Bruins at the beginning of the 1985-86 season. He was the lone captain there since 1988 until his departure in March. In 1995-96, on a Bruins team bothered by injuries to stars like Cam Neely and others, and struggling under a rookie coach, Bourque found himself speaking up in the dressing room more than he normally wants to. Fearful of hurting his teammates' feelings, he had to force himself to prod the Bruins to perform better.

"It's not something that was easy for me to do," he says. "I had to grow into that role off the ice. On the ice, it's (leading by example) always been easy."

The prodding obviously helped. In danger of missing the playoffs, the Bruins lost just six of their final 19 games to qualify for the Stanley Cup tournament for the 29th straight season.

Tough times

Bourque and the Bruins had a rougher go in 1996-97, though. After leading all defensemen in 1995-96 with 80 points, Bourque slipped to 50 points and the Bruins failed to make the playoffs for the first time in 30 seasons.

It was a rare absence from the Stanley Cup tournament for the classy defenseman, yet he was back in the groove in 1997-98 as the Bruins went from the worst record in the league to fifth in the Eastern Conference. Borque's most recent quest for the Cup ended in the Conference finals with the Avs. No.77 is back with Colorado for one more season, and while he may never win the Stanley Cup, one thing is certain: As soon as he is eligible, Bourque will call the Hockey Hall of Fame home.

ICE TALK

"THERE'S NO WAY I'LL LET PEOPLE DOWN BY NOT GIVING EVERYTHING I'VE GOT OR NOT SHOWING UP AND PLAYING HARD. I FEEL EVERYONE SHOULD FEEL THAT WAY. THAT'S JUST MY MAKEUP."

RAY BOURQUE

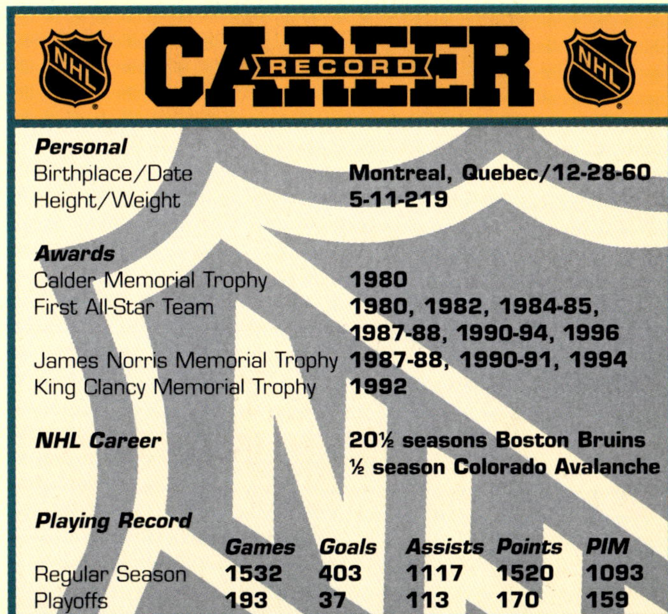

CAREER RECORD

Personal

Birthplace/Date	**Montreal, Quebec/12-28-60**
Height/Weight	**5-11-219**

Awards

Calder Memorial Trophy	**1980**
First All-Star Team	**1980, 1982, 1984-85, 1987-88, 1990-94, 1996**
James Norris Memorial Trophy	**1987-88, 1990-91, 1994**
King Clancy Memorial Trophy	**1992**

NHL Career	**20½ seasons Boston Bruins** **½ season Colorado Avalanche**

Playing Record

	Games	Goals	Assists	Points	PIM
Regular Season	1532	403	1117	1520	1093
Playoffs	193	37	113	170	159

New Jersey's Goalie of the Millennium

MARTIN BRODEUR

Brodeur has backstopped New Jersey to a pair of Stanley Cups.

Fate helped goaltender Martin Brodeur get a skate in the door as the No. 1 goaltender with the New Jersey Devils, but his stellar play and nothing but has kept him there.

Martin Brodeur has won two Jennings Trophies, awarded to the goalie(s) on the team with the fewest goals scored against it.

The year before Brodeur emerged as one of the best young goalies in the National Hockey League, the Devils' goaltending combination consisted of Chris Terreri and Craig Billington, both solid veteran goaltenders.

But Billington was shipped to Ottawa in a trade that brought Peter Sidorkiewicz to New Jersey. Sidorkiewicz, it turned out, had not recovered from a severe shoulder separation and was not ready for the 1993-94 training camp. Enter Brodeur, a promising minor-league goalie at the time.

Brodeur's play was so good as a rookie that he eased Terreri out of the No. 1 goalie's job. Brodeur played in 47 games, posted a won-lost-tied record of 27-11-8 and a regular-season goals-against average of 2.40.

As impressive as his regular-season performance chart was, Brodeur was even more brilliant in the playoffs. He posted an 8-9 won-lost mark in the Stanley Cup tournament, with a sparkling goals-against average of 1.95 as he backstopped the Devils to the Eastern Conference Finals.

Devils' Cup

By this time, Brodeur had not only supplanted Terreri as the top goalie in the Devils organization, he had staked a claim as one of the best goaltenders in the NHL—period.

Brodeur played 40 of the 48 games for New Jersey in the lockout-shortened 1994-95 season, going 19-11-6 with a 2.45 goals-against average in regular-season play.

His playoff performance was spookily brilliant. He played in all 20 of the Devils' playoff games, winning 16, with three shutouts, all in the Devils' first-round victory over the Boston Bruins, and produced this unlikely linescore for Brodeur: a 4-1 won-lost record; a 0.97 GAA and a .962 save percentage.

The wonder is that the Bruins won a game at all, facing goaltending that stingy. Brodeur remained brilliant throughout the playoffs and helped carry the Devils to their first-ever Stanley Cup championship, with New Jersey sweeping the favored Detroit Red Wings in the Finals.

Rink rat

There was a certain resonance about Brodeur playing so well and winning a Stanley Cup on a team coached by Jacques Lemaire, a brilliant center with the great Montreal Canadiens teams of the 1960s and 70s. Lots of Canadian kids are rink rats, but Brodeur grew up hanging around the Montreal Forum, where his father, Denis, was the team photographer for the Canadiens.

With 10 shutouts in the 1997-98 season, and a brilliant goals against average of 1.89 (up from 1.88 the previous year!), Brodeur collected the William Jennings Trophy for the second consecutive season. Not only is he tough to score on, he's also a great puckhandler. In the 1997 playoffs he did the nearly unthinkable—scored a goal, flipping the puck the lenght of the ice when Montreal pulled its goalie for an extra attacker.

The 2000 playoffs provided an even bigger highlight—his second Stanley Cup. Brodeur was in top form again, allowing just four goals over the last four games of the Finals. He continues to be-Devil the rest of the NHL.

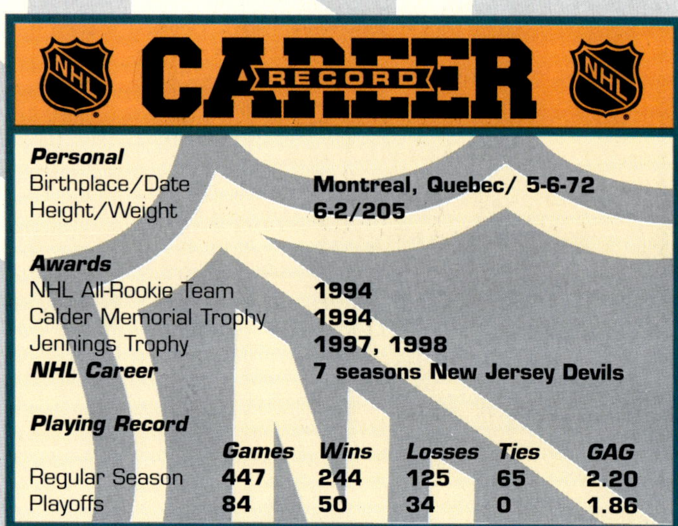

CAREER RECORD

Personal

Birthplace/Date	**Montreal, Quebec/ 5-6-72**
Height/Weight	**6-2/205**

Awards

NHL All-Rookie Team	**1994**
Calder Memorial Trophy	**1994**
Jennings Trophy	**1997, 1998**
NHL Career	**7 seasons New Jersey Devils**

Playing Record

	Games	Wins	Losses	Ties	GAG
Regular Season	447	244	125	65	2.20
Playoffs	84	50	34	0	1.86

Florida's Rocket man
PAVEL BURE

The explosive "Russian Rocket" brings fans out of their seats like no other player in hockey.

After Pavel Bure's first game with the Vancouver Canucks, the media nicknamed him the 'Russian Rocket' and his brilliant rookie season touched off Pavelmania among the long-suffering Canucks fans.

In Bure, the Canucks finally had landed a superstar to build a true contender around. The 5-foot-10, 187-pound right winger certainly arrived in Vancouver with pedigree. He first dazzled North American hockey people at the 1989-90 World Junior Championships in Anchorage, Alaska Playing on a line with Sergei Fedorov and Alexander Mogilny, Bure scored eight goals and totaled 14 points to help the USSR win the gold medal in that tournament. He was named the tournament's top forward.

The following year, he helped the Soviets win gold at the World Hockey Championships. He starred for both the junior and senior men's teams in 1990-91 also, helping the juniors win a silver medal and the senior men win the bronze.

Bure frenzy

The Canucks had drafted Bure in the sixth round of the 1989 entry draft, only to have then-NHL president John Ziegler rule him ineligible. The decision was reversed more than a year later, clearing the way for Bure to join the Canucks.

Three years after Bure was named rookie-of-the-year in the Soviet National League, he scored 34 goals for the Canucks and won the Calder Trophy as the top freshman in the NHL—and created a frenzy among Vancouver hockey supporters. In 1992-93, Bure scored 60 goals and added 50 assists for 110 points, becoming the first Canuck ever to score as many as 50 goals and reach 100 points in a season.

Bure snapped off another 60-goal season in 1993-94, slipping to 47 assists and 107 points. He then led all playoff goalscorers with 16, leading the Canucks to the Stanley Cup final, which they lost in a seven-game thriller to the New York Rangers.

He negotiated a rich new contract in the midst of the playoff run, which pushed some noses out of joint. Bure obviously had learned that leverage matters in the free enterprise system, another indicator that he was a quick study in adapting to North American life and the NHL.

Some thought the swift, creative Bure too slight to withstand the inevitable physical pounding NHL forwards are subjected to. Owing to his total commitment to his sport, Bure spent his first summers in North America adhering to a severe fitness regimen overseen by his father, Vladimir, a former swimmer and three-time Olympian for the Soviet Union.

Bure becomes a Panther

In the mid-1990s, Bure was affected by injuries. But he gritted his teeth at the start of the 1997-98 season, determined to prove he was not past his best. He scored 51 goals in what turned out to be his last season in Vancouver and carried that goal-scoring touch to the 1998 Olympics, where he netted a tournament-high nine goals for silver medalists Russia. Russia President Boris Yeltsin presented Bure with the prestigious Order of Honor during a ceremony at The Kremlin shortly after the Olympics.

He had a highly publicized standoff with the Canucks in 1998. For "personal reasons," he demanded a trade and eventually got one—to the Florida Panthers in January 1999. He made an immediate impact, scoring 13 goals in 11 games. But then he blew out his right knee.

Bure came back strong from that setback, scoring 58 goals in just 74 games in 1999-2000 and winning the Maurice "Rocket" Richard Trophy for top scorer scorer by a wide margin—14 goals.

With more tricks up his sleeve than a Vegas magician, Bure leaves many an opposing netminder scrambling.

CAREER RECORD

Personal

Birthplace/Date	**Moscow, USSR/3-31-71**
Height/Weight	**5-10/189**

Awards

Calder Memorial Trophy	**1992**
First All-Star Team	**1994**
Maurice Richard Trophy	**2000**

NHL Career — **7 seasons Vancouver Canucks**; **2 seasons Florida Panthers**

Playing Record

	Games	Goals	Assists	Points	PIM
Regular Season	513	325	263	588	348
Playoffs	64	35	34	69	74

Detroit's All-around Star

SERGEI FEDOROV

This two-time Stanley Cup champion and former league MVP is the total hockey package.

ICE TALK

"Fedorov is as good as anybody in any era skillwise. Fedorov is one of a kind."

An NHL scout

When Sergei Fedorov arrived in Detroit, the Red Wings already had a No. 1 center—veteran Steve Yzerman. So Fedorov, brilliantly talented offensively, was asked to handle a big part of the defensive load. That would seem a waste. Except Fedorov applied himself to the task and, in his second season in the NHL, he was named runner-up to Guy Carbonneau for the Frank J. Selke Trophy as the league's best defensive forward.

Two years later, in 1994, he won the trophy.

He also won the Hart Trophy that year as the league's most valuable player, was named to the first all-star team and won the Lester B. Pearson Award, voted on by his peers and awarded to the league's outstanding player.

Fedorov's skills are widely acknowledged as amongst the best in the NHL. Keeping him motivated has always been the challenge.

Russian might

He came to the league with impeccable credentials. As a junior in Russia, he centered a line with wingers Pavel Bure and Alexander Mogilny—one of the most electrifying trios ever assembled.

Fedorov played four years with Central Red Army, and helped the Soviet National team win gold medals at the World Championships in 1989 and 1990.

With his speed, improvisational moves executed at full speed, and all-around game, Fedorov made an immediate impact on the NHL, leading all rookies in goals (31), assists (48) and points (79) in 1990-91. He finished runner-up to Ed Belfour in the voting for the Calder Trophy.

As exciting as his skills are, Fedorov always has understood that even star players perform best as part of an ensemble.

Luckily, his Detroit coach, Scotty Bowman, understood this also. It was Bowman who acquired veteran Russian Igor Larionov and assembled a five-man unit with Fedorov, Vyacheslav Kozlov, Vlyacheslav Fetisov and Vladimir Konstantinov.

The unit, used selectively by Bowman, a master strategist, performed brilliantly for the Red Wings in 1995-96. Fedorov, ever the team man, moved to right wing on the unit, ceding the center

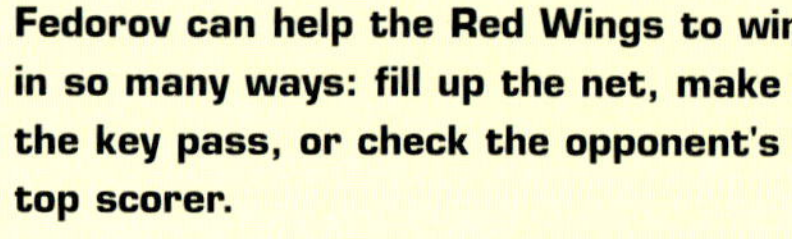

Fedorov can help the Red Wings to win in so many ways: fill up the net, make the key pass, or check the opponent's top scorer.

position on the line to Larionov, who centered the famous KLM (Vladimir Krutov, Larionov and Sergei Makarov) for the Soviet National team in the 1980s.

Like the five-man units in the Russian national teams, Detroit's unit stressed puck control and patience, preferring to circle back in the neutral zone, and to hold on to the puck in the offensive zone rather than try a low percentage play.

Russian light

Fedorov's spectacular play, sly sense of humor and good looks convinced Nike to make him their poster boy for their hockey equipment. He showcased Nike's new line of skates and is considered very worthy of attention by the newspapers.

The 1997-98 season threw up highs and lows for Fedorov. A free agent following Detroit's 1997 Stanley Cup victory, he sat out the first half of the year over terms and played his first hockey of the season for Russia at the Olympic Games in Nagano. Just after Fedorov had returned, with a silver medal, Carolina made a huge offer, which Detroit matched, so he returned to the Red Wings.

Fedorov was a key part of the Red Wings' second straight Stanley Cup championship in 1998. Now at age 30, the Russian speedster is in his prime.

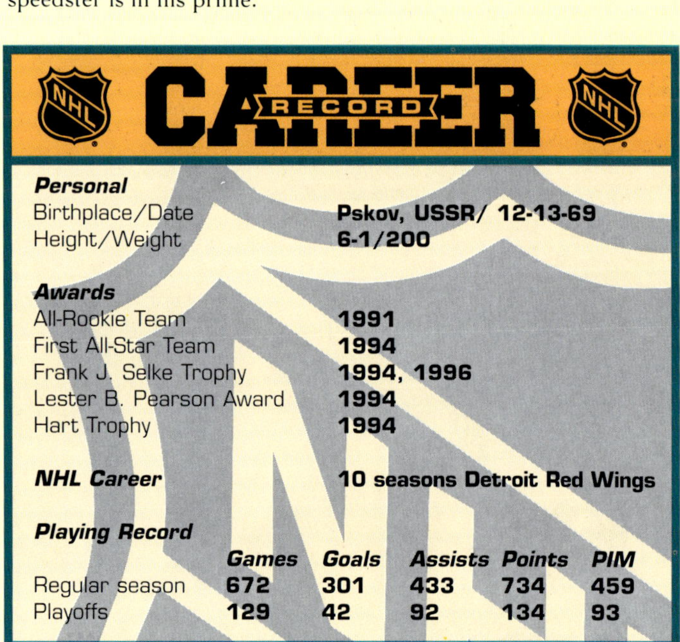

CAREER RECORD

Personal

Birthplace/Date	Pskov, USSR/ 12-13-69
Height/Weight	6-1/200

Awards

All-Rookie Team	1991
First All-Star Team	1994
Frank J. Selke Trophy	1994, 1996
Lester B. Pearson Award	1994
Hart Trophy	1994

NHL Career 10 seasons Detroit Red Wings

Playing Record

	Games	Goals	Assists	Points	PIM
Regular season	672	301	433	734	459
Playoffs	129	42	92	134	93

Big talent in a little package
THEOREN FLEURY

Fleury has proved to the size conscious NHL that small is not only beautiful, but powerful too.

In the hyper-macho world of the NHL, size is said to matter above all. Theoren Fleury's entire career has been a refutation of that cliché. Not outlandishly larger than the average thoroughbred jockey, Fleury—swift, skilled, creative and combative—has been a star at every level of hockey. He has forced hockey people, who don't let go of their stereotypes easily, to see past his stature and recognize the dazzling things he can do with the gifts he possesses, to forget about the things he cannot do.

As a junior star with the Moose Jaw Warriors, Fleury was an offensive machine, racking up 472 points in four seasons. In his final year as a junior, he produced 160 points, including 68 goals—and 235 minutes in penalties in the rough and tumble Western Hockey League. He was a member of Canada's National Junior Team in 1987 and 1988, when the team won a gold medal.

Rarely has a junior player achieved more than Fleury did. Yet he was taken 166th in the NHL Entry Draft in 1987, his low selection an obvious function of his size.

CAREER RECORD

Personal

Birthplace/Date	**Oxbow, Saskatchewan/6-29-68**
Height/Weight	**5-6/180**

Awards

NHL 2nd All-Star Team	**1995**
Co-winner Alka Seltzer Plus Award (league plus-minus leader) —with Marty McSorley	**1991**

NHL Career

10½ seasons Calgary Flames
½ season Colorado Avalanche
1 season New York Rangers

Playing Record

	Games	Goals	Assists	Points	PIM
Regular season	886	389	529	918	1425
Playoffs	77	34	45	79	116

Playing big

He began his pro career in the minors playing for Calgary's Salt Lake City farm club, but by season's end that year—1988-89—he was playing for the NHL Flames in Calgary, helping them win their first Stanley Cup championship by beating the fabled Montreal Canadiens, and in the legendary Forum, to boot.

In his first full season with the Flames, he scored 31 goals, 30 being a benchmark of excellence. The following season—1990-91—he bagged 51 goals, establishing himself as a star. He has delivered big scoring numbers every season he has played in the NHL. And playing on a team that has featured bigger, stronger players like Gary Roberts, Joe Nieuwendyk and Doug Gilmour, Fleury topped the Flames' scoring list six times from 1991 through 1998.

Dream on

Small-market Calgary faced reality in 1998-99. Fleury was due to become an unrestricted free agent, and the team wouldn't likely be able to pay what he could earn in the open market. So the Flames traded Fleury to Colorado during the season, but not before he became the team's all-time leader in points. After the trade, Fleury was once again with a contender and he was a big part of the Avs pushing Dallas to seven games in the Western Conference Finals.

Last season, free-agent Fleury signed with the New York Rangers, taking his show to North America's biggest stage. The team struggled, and by his high standards Fleury struggled right along with the rest of his teammates, but he still managed to lead the squad with 49 assists and was second with 64 points.For a guy considered too small early in his career, Fleury certainly scaled impressive heights in hockey.

The diminutive winger has taken his act to the Big Apple as a member of the Rangers.

The Simmering Swede

PETER FORSBERG

Colorado Avalanche's fiery Peter Forsberg breaks the mold of the traditionally timid European player.

The stereotype of the European player has been that of a player with great skill but no grit and determination. Colorado Avalanche center Peter Forsberg lays waste to that notion. He's got the skilled part—few players in the league can match him in that department—but he's also got a mean streak that seems hewn right out of the Canadian plains.

Forsberg is that rare combination of athlete—he is very creatively offensively, but he also has a defensive conscience. He skates back hard and is not afraid of blocking a shot. He's an intelligent player, but he also likes to get in people's faces and stir up a bit of trouble.

No retreat

"I'll tell you what sticks out in my mind isn't so much his talent level, but his toughness," said former Avalanche goaltender Craig Billington, whose role as Colorado's back-up goaltender gave him the best seat in the house on many nights to watch the gifted Swede. "He's tough," continues Billington. "When you watch him play, he's gritty and tough and he doesn't back down; and he gives it back. You get a lot of people who are skilled in this game, but who perhaps don't have the grittiness."

New Jersey Devils goaltender Martin Brodeur, perennial winner of the Jennings Trophy for lowest goals-against average, has written of Forsberg: "To me, Forsberg is the most complete hockey player in the game today. There are so many ways he can hurt you—a clutch pass, a precise slap shot or wrist shot upstairs, he does it all!"

Forsberg is an awesome combination of skill and grit. His GM wouldn't be surprised to see him win the scoring championship and the award for best defensive forward in the same season.

Peer respect

Many hockey people agree with Brodeur's assessment. In a *Toronto Sun* poll of hockey experts a few years ago, Forsberg was deemed top performer in hockey. Said an ESPN analyst, one of the panelists for the poll: "Forsberg can do so many things. But what impresses me most is the way his peers talk about him. They just shake their heads in awe at Forsberg's play, game in and game out."

Forsberg is not only a great player, he is a winner—and passionate about it. He hates losing, he can't stand it. In 1994, he scored the gold medal-winning goal for Sweden in the Olympic final versus Canada. It was in a shootout, and the unorthodox deke he used has been immortalized on a Swedish Postage stamp. Two years later, he helped lead the former Quebec Nordiques to the Stanley Cup in their first season as the Colorado Avalanche.

As for individual honors, Forsberg was the Calder Trophy winner as rookie of the years in 1995 and in 1998 he was named as First All-Star center for the first time—quite an honor at a position teeming with superstars

Forsberg's GM, Pierre Lacroix, has said: "He could win the scoring championship and at the same time win the Selke award (as best defensive forward)." Don't be surprised if the Swede one day pulls off that feat.

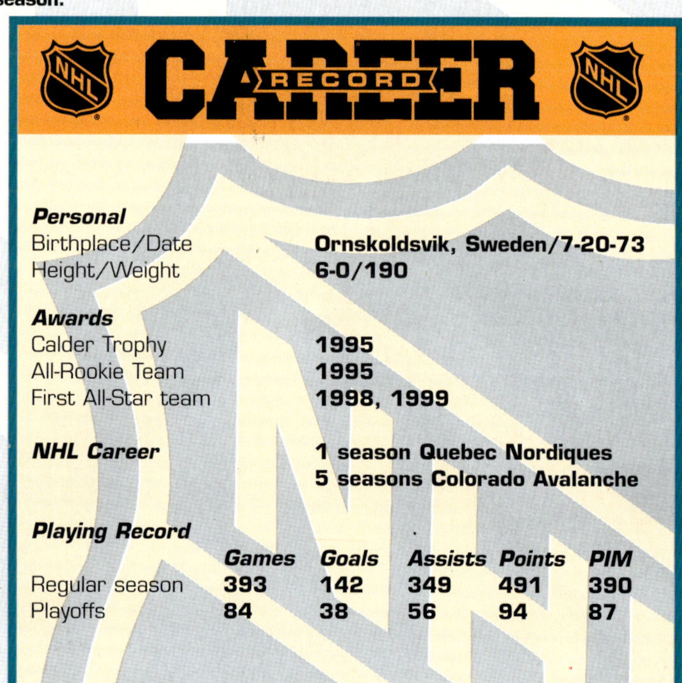

CAREER RECORD

Personal
Birthplace/Date **Ornskoldsvik, Sweden/7-20-73**
Height/Weight **6-0/190**

Awards
Calder Trophy **1995**
All-Rookie Team **1995**
First All-Star team **1998, 1999**

NHL Career **1 season Quebec Nordiques**
5 seasons Colorado Avalanche

Playing Record

	Games	Goals	Assists	Points	PIM
Regular season	393	142	349	491	390
Playoffs	84	38	56	94	87

Hockey's most dominating goalie
DOMINIK HASEK

No one has a bigger effect on a game than Buffalo's superstar netminder.

Around the time of the 1998 Olympics, Wayne Gretzky, recognized as the best player of all time in a comprehensive poll of hockey experts by the *Hockey News*, had this to say about Dominik Hasek: "I think he is the best player in the game. He's just at a level that nobody else is at right now. He's simply sensational."

In 1999, Hasek led the Buffalo Sabres to the Stanley Cup Finals for the first time since 1975.

That's a pretty ringing endorsement, considering the source. Hasek has earned such an accolade, and the awards are stacking up as proof. In 1997, he became the first goalie in 35 years to win the Hart Trophy as league MVP. He repeated his 'Hart' trick in 1998, joining immortals Wayne Gretzky, Guy Lafleur, Bobby Clarke, Bobby Orr, Stan Mikita, Bobby Hull, Gordie Howe, Eddie Shore and Howie Morenz as the only players to win consecutive Hart trophies. He is the only netminder to win the award more than once

Vezina monopoly

As for the award designed for goaltenders, the Vezina Trophy, Hasek won that five of six years from 1994-99. In 1997-98, Hasek endured early boos from the home crowd. Popular Sabres coach Ted Nolan was not brought back for the season after winning the 1997 Jack Adams Award as coach of the year. It was no secret that Hasek was not a Nolan supporter, and fans in Buffalo made Hasek into one of the villians at the start of the year. He heard boos in Marine Midland Arena and that admittedly affected his play.

Hasek was not the 'Dominator' until December, when he recorded six shutouts and got himself back on track. He eventually went on to lead the league in save percentage (.932) for the fifth straight season and his 13 shutouts were the most since Tony Esposito's 15 in 1970. Along the way Hasek took the time to lead his underdog Czech Republic to a gold medal in the 1998 Winter Olympics in Nagano, Japan, in dramatic fashion. He stoned Canada in a shootout in the semi-finals, stopping all five attempts by Canadian players in the shootout while the Czechs scored once, then shut out Russia in the gold-medal game to win 1-0.

The acrobat

In the 1998 playoffs, Hasek led the Sabres to the conference final for the first time since 1980. In 1999, he was the driving force behind Buffalo making its first Stanley Cup Finals appearance in 24 years, where the Sabres took the powerhouse Dallas Stars to six games before losing on a controversial goal in the third period of overtime. Hasek's strong play in those two postseasons has erased the unpleasant memory of the 1997 playoffs, when he got injured and then, amid a barrage of unwanted publicity, got involved in a physical confrontation with a local sportswriter that did no one much good.

When it comes to style, there is none like Hasek. He flops, he does splits, he makes sprawling saves that no one expects. One of his most famous moves is to drop his stick and grab the puck with his blocker hand — unorthodox to say the least.

One NHL scout says: "He has one of the most unorthodox styles I think I've ever seen in a goalie, but he gets the job done. The man is amazing. I've never seen anyone like him in goal."

In the summer of 1999, Hasek announced that the 1999-2000 season was to be his last. But an injury-filled regular season led him to rescind his retirement and he has vowed to play one more season. And that's bad news for shooters throughout the NHL.

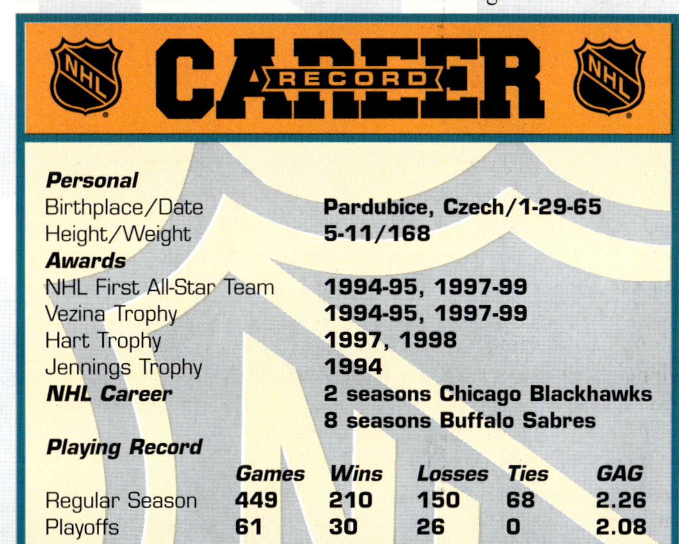

CAREER RECORD

Personal					
Birthplace/Date	**Pardubice, Czech/1-29-65**				
Height/Weight	**5-11/168**				
Awards					
NHL First All-Star Team	**1994-95, 1997-99**				
Vezina Trophy	**1994-95, 1997-99**				
Hart Trophy	**1997, 1998**				
Jennings Trophy	**1994**				
NHL Career	**2 seasons Chicago Blackhawks**				
	8 seasons Buffalo Sabres				
Playing Record					
	Games	***Wins***	***Losses***	***Ties***	***GAG***
Regular Season	**449**	**210**	**150**	**68**	**2.26**
Playoffs	**61**	**30**	**26**	**0**	**2.08**

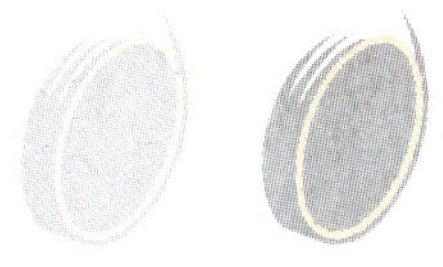

The son of a star was a legend in St. Louis but, more importantly, a Stanley Cup-winner in Dallas.

The ultimate sniper
BRETT HULL

When Bobby Hull was on the ice, all eyes were on him. Brett Hull plays a different game from his dad. A labored skater, the younger Hull moves quietly around the ice, particularly in the offensive zone, circling into spaces others have left, positioning himself to accept a setup pass. He tries to draw as little attention to himself as possible, laying in the weeds, as the hockey players say. Until, that is, he unleashes The Shot.

By the time the defenders realize it is Hull who is shooting, it often is too late. Possessed of one of the fastest, hardest slap shots in hockey, Hull is a prolific but mostly unflashy scorer. He has been called the NHL's Stealth Bomber.

Quietly to the top

Similarly, Hull insinuated himself into the NHL élite quietly. Because of his name, the NHL saw Hull coming up through the junior and college ranks, but he was not regarded as a rising star.

The Calgary Flames selected Hull in the sixth round of the 1984 entry draft, an unheralded 117th overall out of the University of Minnesota-Duluth. In his full first NHL season—1987-88—Hull scored 26 goals in 52 games for the Flames, who traded him before season's end to St. Louis.

With the Blues, Hull was paired with Adam Oates, one of the league's top playmakers. Hull and Oates quickly became a hit.

Hull scored 41 goals and added 43 assists for 84 points in his first full season with the Blues, but that was merely the warm-up.

In 1989-90, Hull scored 72 goals to lead the NHL in goal-scoring for the first of three straight seasons. The following year his quick-release shot found the net 86 times and another 70 times in 1991-92.

Along with the goal-scoring blitz came official recognition. Hull was a first-team all-star three straight times, won the Lady Byng as the league's most sportsmanlike player and the Hart Trophy as the most valuable player.

Playoff hero: The Golden Brett scored the Stanley Cup winning goal in 1999 and led the 2000 postseason in scoring (24 points).

CAREER RECORD

Personal

Birthplace/Date	**Belleville, Ontario/8-9-64**
Height/Weight	**5-10/201**

Awards

NHL First All-Star Team	**1990-92**
Lady Byng Trophy	**1990**
Hart Memorial Trophy	**1991**
Lester B. Pearson Award	**1991**

NHL Career

1/2 season Calgary Flames
10 1/2 seasons St. Louis Blues
2 season Dallas Stars

Playing record

	Games	Goals	Assists	Points	PIM
Regular season	940	610	494	1104	371
Playoffs	153	88	71	159	59

Ups and downs

He was named captain of the Blues, but he had made himself something more important to St. Louis—its franchise player.

The Blues traded Oates, the set-up man, to the Bruins in February 1992, but replaced him with Craig Janney, another able playmaker. Still, some of his fans were disappointed when Hull 'slumped' to 54 goals in 1992-93 and managed 'only' 57 goals in 1993-94. In the lockout-shortened 1994-95 season, Hull delivered 29 goals in 48 games, which pro-rates to 49 goals over an 82-game schedule. Strictly routine for the Golden Brett, some would say.

Head coach Mike Keenan stripped Hull of the captaincy in 1995-96. Nothing personal, he assured people. "The heck it's not personal," Hull said. "It's a complete slap in the face."

Gone, too, was the playmaking Janney, who had been traded to San Jose during the 1994-95 season. In March 1996, Keenan traded for Wayne Gretzky, the ultimate playmaker, but the Hull-Gretzky duo was shortlived. Gretzky left for New York as a free agent at season's end. Partway through the 1996-97 season, yet another playmaking center was brought in—Pierre Turgeon.

Then, in the summer of 1998, it was the Golden Brett himself who was involved in a move. Hull had St. Louis hockey fans singing the blues when he signed as a free agent for the Dallas Stars.

It turned out to be a great move for the Golden Brett. A man who has had his share of individual honors bought into the Stars' team-first (read defensive) style and found himself in the Stanley Cup Finals in June. A man with a penchant for offense even scored the game-winner in the Finals against Buffalo in the closing minutes of Game 2. Then, in the third period of overtime in Game 6, although his foot was in the crease, Hull scored the goal which brought the Stanley Cup to Texas.

Pittsburgh's Artist On Ice

JAROMIR JAGR

He's flashy, he's strong, he scores goals like no one else—and he picks up the odd trophy now and again

Jaromir Jagr is the closest thing the NHL has to a rock star. He's flashy, good looking and, for many years, he had long, unruly hair, too long for his helmet to contain. Jagr loves to laugh, too, and who can blame him? There seems little the 6-foot-2, 230-pound forward cannot do.

He's already a force, has been since his rookie season in 1990-91. He made the all-rookie team that year, scoring 27 goals and adding 30 assists. He added 13 points in the Pittsburgh Cup-winning playoff run.

He's the most potent force in the NHL. He's been a force from the get-go. As a rookie in 1990–91, he made the all-rookie team by scoring 27 goals and adding 30 assists. He added 13 points in the Pittsburgh Cup-winning playoff run. Jagr is a fixture as one of the top offensive players in the league. Indeed, in 1994-95, Jagr won the scoring title with 70 points, including 32 goals in the lockout-shortened, 48-game regular season.

More important, he arrived as a mature player, having to step up and shoulder the burden of being the go-to guy for Pittsburgh. Teammate Mario Lemieux took the season off to recover from his bout with Hodgkin's Disease and chronic back problems.

Record breaker

Playing the star comes effortlessly for Jagr, who has a long, fluid, deceptively swift skating stride, and he's equally fluid handling the puck. He truly creates art on ice.

"He is a master of deception," said New York Rangers goaltender Mike Richter. "If you try to anticipate with him, you'll often guess wrong. And if you just try to react, he's too fast and you get beat."

In 1995-96, Jagr lifted his artistry to new heights. He and Lemieux each scored 60-plus goals that season. But the two were friendly, complementary talents, not rivals. Jagr says he never has felt overlooked, never worried that he was playing in Lemieux's shadow.

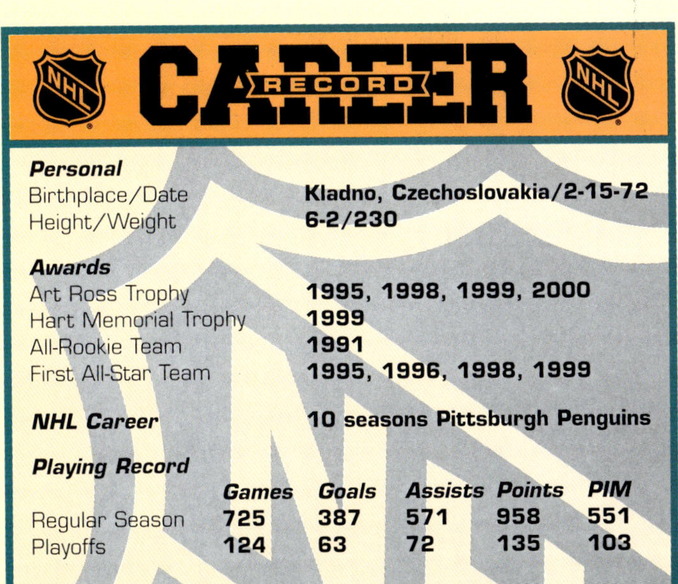

CAREER RECORD

Personal

Birthplace/Date	**Kladno, Czechoslovakia/2-15-72**
Height/Weight	**6-2/230**

Awards

Art Ross Trophy	**1995, 1998, 1999, 2000**
Hart Memorial Trophy	**1999**
All-Rookie Team	**1991**
First All-Star Team	**1995, 1996, 1998, 1999**

NHL Career — **10 seasons Pittsburgh Penguins**

Playing Record

	Games	Goals	Assists	Points	PIM
Regular Season	725	387	571	958	551
Playoffs	124	63	72	135	103

Many experts consider Jaromir Jagr the best one-on-one player in the NHL.

"No, I never looked at it that way when we were winning the Stanley Cup," said Jagr. "As long as we were winning, nothing else mattered. It's still the same now. I don't need a lot of attention."

Center Stage

He potted 47 goals and added 48 assists for 95 points in 1996-97, but improved on that in 1997-98 by becoming the only man to top the century mark (102 points—35 goals and 67 assists). The subsequent Art Ross Trophy was the second of his career and rounded off a spectacular season for Jagr that also brought him his third First All-Star appearance and a chunk of gold that was pretty unexpected.

In February 1998, Jagr was a member of the Czech Republic squad which won the gold medal at the Winter Olympics in Nagano, Japan, beating Russia 1-0 in the final.

In 1998-99, Jagr became the leader. Lemieux was busy buying the team and Ron Francis was in Carolina, so Jagr became the captain in name and substance. He was not only the best skater in the league, winning his third Art Ross Trophy by outscoring his closest competitor by 20 points, he also took an active leadership role.

Jagr won his third straight Art Ross Trophy in 1999-2000, tallying 96 points on 42 goals and 54 assists even though he missed 19 games. He has added maturity to his awesome skills, and that spells trouble for the rest of the league.

Toronto's Tornado

The Leafs' hometown hero brings both excitement and a unique style to his position.

CURTIS JOSEPH

Curtis Joseph came late to hockey. He didn't join a team until he was 10 or 11 years old, and did so then only because his cousin had paid for a spot on a team but was moving. Joseph took the place of his cousin, who happened to be goalie, which worked out great since Joseph says he couldn't skate.

NHLers who don't play for the Toronto Maple Leaf wish that cousin never would have moved. Then Joseph wouldn't have gotten into the sport and he wouldn't be making their lives so difficult now.

Joseph made up for lost time quickly after his late start in hockey. He was never drafted by an NHL team, but after a stellar freshman season at the University of Wisconsin in 1988-89 in which he was named to the conference's first all-star team, he was signed as a free agent by the St. Louis Blues. "Cujo," as Joseph is known, played only 23 games in the minors before becoming a fixture with the Blues.

Joseph displays great athleticism and makes highlight-reel saves, but he's also a master at playing the angles.

The acrobat

In the early 1990s, Joseph was an indefatigable force in the St. Louis net. He had consecutive seasons of 60, 68 and 71 games played. In St. Louis he honed his style. Or, as some observers might suggest, his lack of style.

Joseph takes a gambler's approach to the position. He is unpredictable and brazen and his acrobatic saves fill up the highlight reels. He also wanders out of net on a regular basis to play the puck. But it is controlled chaos. Joseph has great balance and he knows the percentages. His knack for starting the breakout resulted in nine assists in 1991-92, the second-highest total ever for a goaltender.

In 1995, Joseph was dealt to the Edmonton Oilers, where his reputation as a giant-killer in the playoffs soared. On the strength of Cujo's brilliant netminding, the small-market Oilers toppled heavily favored Dallas in 1997 and Colorado in 1998. He was also Canada's starting goalie in the 1996 World Cup of Hockey and also on the roster for the 1998 Olympic team.

Coming home

Cujo grew up just north of Toronto, so it was a homecoming when he signed with the Maple Leafs as a free agent in the summer of 1998. The Leafs were a mess when he arrived, having missed the playoffs two straight seasons. But with the goaltending position shored up, Toronto became an instant contender.

Over the past two seasons, the Leafs have posted 97 and 100 points and have won a combined three playoff series. Joseph was runner-up for 1999 Vezina Trophy, given to the league's best goaltender, and he was a finalist for 2000 award. His numbers are not gaudy, but his effect on the game is certainly profound.

Teammate Kris King explained it after Joseph's first season with the Leafs. "It's no coincidence we led the league in goals after not being able to score last year," said King. "The guys had the confidence to take chances on offense knowing if it didn't work out, and we ended up with an odd-man rush against us, he'd bail us out."

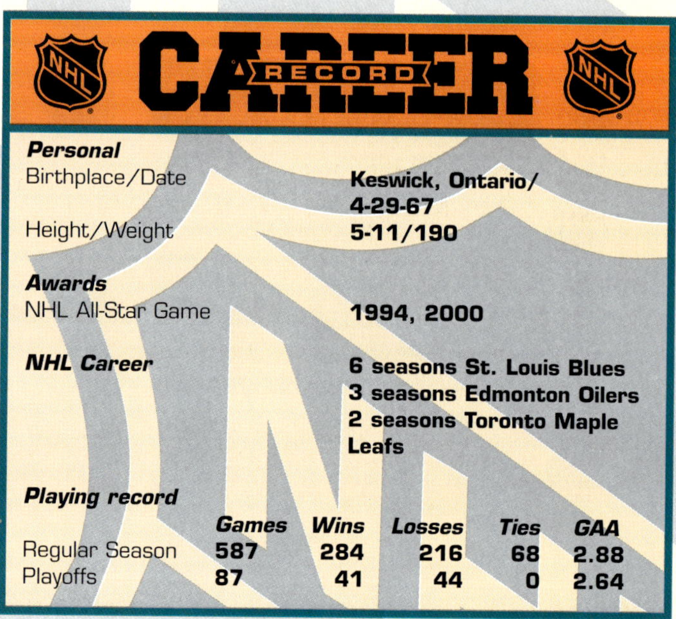

CAREER RECORD

Personal

Birthplace/Date	**Keswick, Ontario/ 4-29-67**
Height/Weight	**5-11/190**

Awards

NHL All-Star Game	**1994, 2000**

NHL Career

6 seasons St. Louis Blues
3 seasons Edmonton Oilers
2 seasons Toronto Maple Leafs

Playing record

	Games	Wins	Losses	Ties	GAA
Regular Season	587	284	216	68	2.88
Playoffs	87	41	44	0	2.64

The Mighty Duck
PAUL KARIYA

Anaheim's Paul Kariya is rated as one of the fastest men on the ice in the NHL.

When he gets his motor running, nobody in the NHL is more dangerous than Paul Kariya. At top speed, he is a blur rushing down the ice, with enough moves in his arsenal to reduce even the best defensemen in the league into pylons.

Left-winger Kariya sets the excitement meter on atomic and, teamed with linemate Teemu Selanne, he proves just how entertaining the game of hockey can be to watch. Before the 1997-98 season, Kariya was rated as the league's best player by *The Hockey News*. It pointed to his breathtaking skating, speed and quickness, puck skills, ability to raise his own play and that of his teammates and his work ethic. It also praised his hockey smarts, which is no surprise coming from a former dean's list student at the University of Maine.

Mighty Ducks' Kariya has demonstrated that if a player has the right amount of self-belief he can live with the big boys of the NHL.

Small is beautiful

The only thing Kariya doesn't have going for him is size. He is 5-11 tall and weighs 180 pounds. Too small? Scotty Bowman, the NHL's all-time winningest coach, says of him: "They said the same thing about Wayne Gretzky."

Kariya hadn't been able to showcase that speed as much as he would have liked in recent seasons. He missed parts of 1996–97 and 1997–98 and the last two big international competitions—including the 1998 Olympics in Japan (from where his father's side of the family descends)—because of a succession of injuries. A concussion kept him out of the 1998 Olympics and the end of that season, but he came back well.

Entering 1998-99, Kariya vowed to be aggressive and not stand for opponents taking cheap shots at his head. He played all 82 games that season and was his usual sparkling self, finishing third in the league in points with 101 (teammate Selanne was second with 107). This past season, Kariya missed eight games but still finished fourth in league scoring with 86 points (Selanne mustered 85). With health on his side, Kariya will continue to go warp speed ahead.

ICE TALK

"KARIYA IS SO GOOD BECAUSE HE CAN CARRY THE PUCK AT TOP SPEED."

SCOTTY BOWMAN

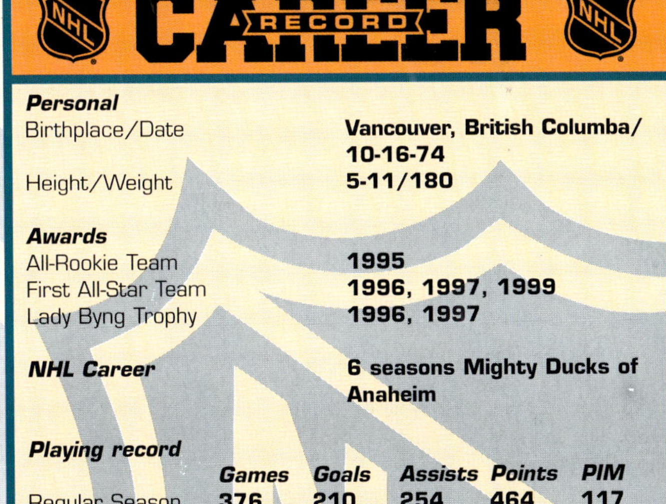

CAREER RECORD

Personal

Birthplace/Date	**Vancouver, British Columba/ 10-16-74**
Height/Weight	**5-11/180**

Awards

All-Rookie Team	**1995**
First All-Star Team	**1996, 1997, 1999**
Lady Byng Trophy	**1996, 1997**

NHL Career — **6 seasons Mighty Ducks of Anaheim**

Playing record

	Games	Goals	Assists	Points	PIM
Regular Season	376	210	254	464	117
Playoffs	14	8	9	17	4

Flyer Sharp-Shooter

JOHN LECLAIR

Hungry for hockey and tough on ice, this rock-loving powerhouse excels at golf, works for good causes, and is a superb role model.

In his days with the Montreal Canadiens, strapping left winger John LeClair had the nickname of Marmaduke, after the playful but uncoordinated comic-strip canine. "John used to fall down a lot," recalled defenseman Kevin Haller, a teammate of LeClair's both in Montreal and in Philadelphia.

"He didn't have real good balance and he wasn't strong on his skates. Now, he's totally the opposite."

Indeed, LeClair, is solid as a rock in every facet of the game. He sends opposing players scattering like bowling pins with his 6-foot-3, 226-pound frame. He has developed into one of the NHL's finest two-way forwards, while at the same time being one of its top sharpshooters, following up on a 51-goal season in 1995-96 with a 50-goal performance the following season and then, in 1997-98, he became the first American in NHL history to record three straight 50-goal seasons as he netted 51 goals.

"He is a great two-way player," said former teammate Mikael Renberg. "He's strong in our zone, and along the boards. He's also a great role model for our younger players."

Rockin' and scorin'

LeClair, the only player from the U.S. state of Vermont to make the NHL, emerged from obscurity with the Canadiens in the 1992-93 playoffs, in which Montreal surprisingly won the Stanley Cup. LeClair scored an overtime goal in both the third and fourth games of the series, which Montreal won in five games. He became the first player to score consecutive overtime game-winners in the Stanley Cup finals since Don Raleigh of the Rangers in 1950.

But LeClair could do no better than a 19-goal output the following season—matching his total of the previous year. Early in the 1994-95 season, with both LeClair and the Canadiens struggling, he was dealt to the Flyers, along with defenseman Eric Desjardins and forward Gilbert Dionne, for the high-scoring Mark Recchi.

The change in scenery had an immediate effect on LeClair. "It was a situation where I wasn't expected to score in Montreal," said LeClair, attempting to account for the transformation. "Here, they put me with Eric Lindros and Mikael right away, and it was an entirely different philosophy."

LeClair started to rock, which is an appropriate term for someone who is a huge fan of U2 and 1980s rock music, with more than 500 CDs in his collection. A tireless worker, LeClair improved his skating, refined his already booming shot, and used his imposing frame to create havoc around the net.

"My shot is hard, but a lot of times it's not how hard you shoot it, it's how quick you get it away," explained LeClair. "I think that's one of the things I've really worked on."

Hungry Flyer

Even as a youngster, growing up in St. Albans, Vermont, which is only a one-hour drive from Montreal, LeClair would spend hour after hour whacking a tennis ball against a shed. That's when he wasn't racing to be the first person in the bathroom each morning, since there were seven in the family.

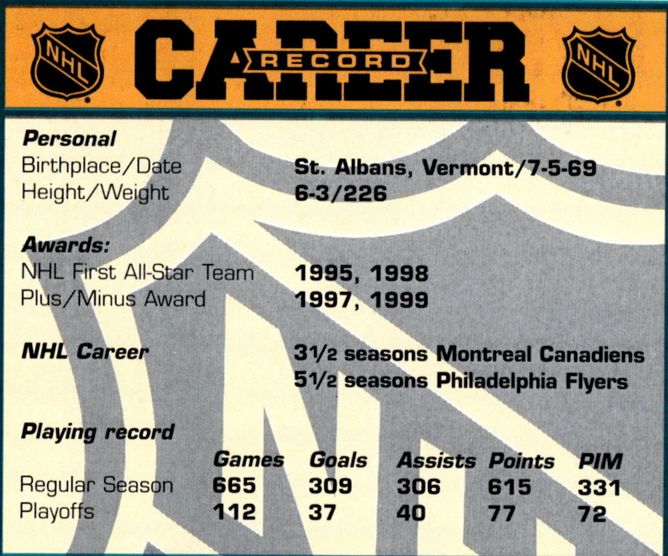

CAREER RECORD

Personal

Birthplace/Date	**St. Albans, Vermont/7-5-69**
Height/Weight	**6-3/226**

Awards:

NHL First All-Star Team	**1995, 1998**
Plus/Minus Award	**1997, 1999**

NHL Career

3 1/2 seasons Montreal Canadiens
5 1/2 seasons Philadelphia Flyers

Playing record

	Games	Goals	Assists	Points	PIM
Regular Season	665	309	306	615	331
Playoffs	112	37	40	77	72

Whether it is golf, a sport at which he also excels—according to Lindros, LeClair has Babe Ruthian drives off a golf tee—or the many charitable causes in which he is involved, LeClair has a hunger to succeed. That passion is evident even at Flyers practices.

"John is the hungriest guy on the ice, even in practice," said former Flyers goaltender Ron Hextall.

The Wonder from Vermont made it three 50-plus seasons on the trot when he notched up 51 goals in the 1997-98 season. Since then, he's had back-to-back 40-goal seasons.

New York's Prime Mover

The Rangers rely heavily upon their captain and he takes care of business at both ends of the rink.

BRIAN LEETCH

A compact package combining quick acceleration and excellent straightahead speed, playmaking brilliance, a hard accurate shot and sound defensive ability, Brian Leetch is a Renaissance player—a defenseman who can do it all.

It was Leetch, lifting his game to new heights of virtuosity, who led the New York Rangers to a Stanley Cup championship in 1994, the club's first in 54 years. He led all playoff scorers with 34 points, including 11 goals. He scored five times in the seven-game final series against the Vancouver Canucks and fully earned the Conn Smythe Trophy as the most valuable performer in the post-season.

Texas hockey

He was the first American-born player—born in Texas, but raised in Connecticut—to capture the Conn Smythe.

He joined the Rangers in 1988-89, after a year with the U.S. National team, and an Olympic appearance as captain of the U.S. team. The international experience, coupled with one year with the Boston College Eagles, had fine-tuned his explosive raw talent—Leetch was named rookie-of-the-year in his first NHL season.

His numbers dropped off the next season, scoring 11 times and adding 45 assists, before being knocked out of action by a fractured left ankle, the first of many disruptive injuries.

But in 1990-91, Leetch re-asserted his claim to being a franchise defenseman by scoring 16 goals and adding 72 assists for 88 points, breaking Hall of Famer Brad Park's team record for most points (82) in a season by a defenseman.

In 1991-92, Leetch totaled 102 points, including 22 goals and won the James Norris Memorial Trophy as the best defenseman in the league. He won the award again in 1996-97.

But some of Leetch's best work came in 1996 with Team USA, which upset Canada to win the inaugural World Cup of Hockey.

Leetch has been a Ranger cornerstone since joining the team as a 20-year-old in 1988.

Undeterred by injury

Injuries hit Leetch in 1992-93, when he missed 34 games with a neck and shoulder problem. Then he slipped on some ice on a Manhattan street, fracturing his right ankle, and he missed the final 13 games of that season.

Since the 1993-94 season, however,Leetch had missed six games—all in 1997-98, a down year for him and the Rangers too—until a broken right arm sidelined him for 11 weeks in 1999-2000. His reliability has been a huge asset for the Rangers. New York demands a lot of its sports heroes and Leetch has grown into the role of captain since the departure of Mark Messier in 1997.

Leetch was strong in the 1994-95 playoffs, generating 14 points (6 goals) in 10 games as the Rangers failed to advance beyond the second round. He was also one of the main reasons that Wayne Gretzky signed with the Rangers as a free agent in 1996.

"As much as I've done offensively, I know that to win championships, you need defense," said Gretzky, who retired in 1999 without a title in the Big Apple, or even a playoff appearance his last two seasons.

"The Rangers have great defense. Playing with Brian Leetch was obviously part of the attraction. He reminds me of Paul Coffey."

Leetch's claim to greatness couldnt possibly be stamped with more authenticity than that.

ICE TALK

"I WOULD BEG ANYONE TO ARGUE THAT BRIAN'S NOT THE BEST TWO-WAY DEFENSEMAN IN THE NHL TODAY."

RANGERS TEAMMATE ADAM GRAVES

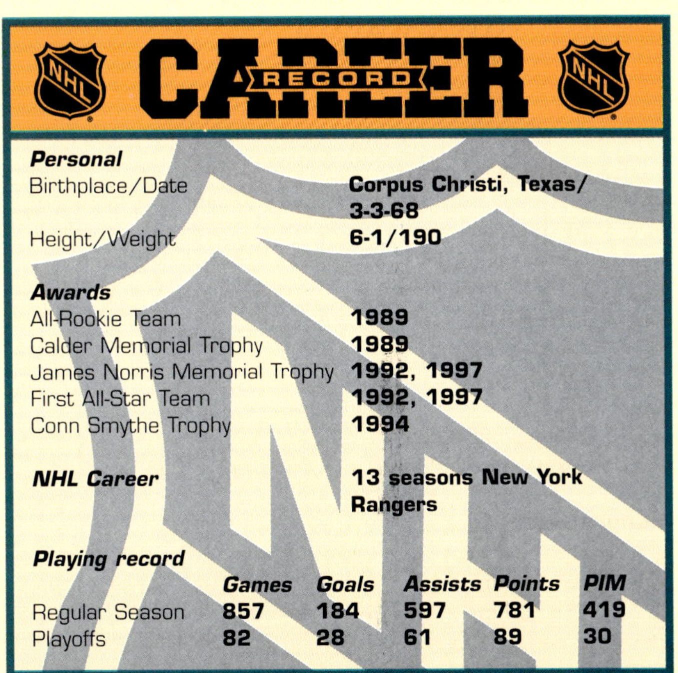

CAREER RECORD

Personal

Birthplace/Date	**Corpus Christi, Texas/ 3-3-68**
Height/Weight	**6-1/190**

Awards

All-Rookie Team	**1989**
Calder Memorial Trophy	**1989**
James Norris Memorial Trophy	**1992, 1997**
First All-Star Team	**1992, 1997**
Conn Smythe Trophy	**1994**

NHL Career — **13 seasons New York Rangers**

Playing record

	Games	Goals	Assists	Points	PIM
Regular Season	857	184	597	781	419
Playoffs	82	28	61	89	30

Power Source
ERIC LINDROS

He combines the finesse of Gretzky, the size of Lemieux and the presence of Messier.

An astonishing blend of fearsome physical strength, speed, skill, rink savvy and unquenchable competitive desire, 6-foot-4, 236-pound center Eric Lindros moved with ridiculous ease up the hockey ladder—junior to international competition to the NHL.

ICE TALK

"His sole focus is getting his team to the Stanley Cup."

Former teammate Craig MacTavish

Before he had played an NHL game he had served notice that he was going to be a force. While still junior age, Lindros helped Canada win the gold medal at the Canada Cup. During that tournament, he knocked rugged Ulf Samuelsson out of action with a devastating check that appeared easy for him.

Lindros is the most imposing star player in the league—he can make an impact with his size, strength, speed, rink savvy and his considerable skill.

The Legion of Doom

Injuries reduced his effectiveness in his first two seasons—yet he still scored 85 goals and chipped in 87 assists in 126 games. Much of that production came while playing on a line with Mark Recchi and Brent Fedyk. The line, called the Crazy Eights, was an instant hit in Philadelphia, where fans quickly warmed to Lindros. But he really hit his NHL stride in 1995 when Flyers coach Terry Murray grouped him with big wingers John LeClair and Mikael Renberg.

As talented as any trio in the league and certainly the best combination of skill and sheer physical power, the line was christened The Legion of Doom. Lindros totaled 70 points, including 29 goals, in 46 games in 1994-95, tying Pittsburgh's Jaromir Jagr for the points lead, but losing the scoring title, on the final day of the shortened season, because Jagr scored three more goals.

Lindros and the Legion led the Flyers to the club's first division title since 1987 and first playoff berth since 1989. The Flyers lost in the conference final to the New Jersey Devils, the eventual Stanley Cup champions. The strong performance by Lindros earned him the Hart Trophy as the most valuable player in the NHL.

The whole package

Few have come into the NHL with a greater upside potential than Lindros, whose leadership abilities were quickly recognized by the Flyers, who named him captain at age 21. In 1995-96, both Lindros and LeClair took serious runs at 50-goal seasons—Lindros finished with 47, LeClair with 51. The Flyers challenged the Penguins and the New York Rangers for first place overall in the Eastern Conference all season long.

Lindros has grown comfortable with the dominant role foreseen for him when the Quebec Nordiques drafted him first overall in 1991. He refused to report to the Nordiques, forcing a trade to the Flyers, who drained their organizational depth chart to land Lindros, sending eight players and $15 million to the Nordiques.

The 1997-98 season was not his best. A concussion kept Lindros out of action for a while, but it was especially poignant for him, because his younger brother's career was curtailed by such an injury.

He had a strong 1998-99, netting 93 points despite missing 11 games, but the nightmare returned this past season. He suffered more concussions, bickered with management over how his injuries were handled, was stripped of his captaincy, and finally made his playoff debut in game 6 of the Conference final, only to go down in a heap with his third concussion of the season (and fifth in two years) courtesy of a clean hit by New Jersey's Scott Stevens.

The off-season brought uncertainty for the center. A restricted free agent, his acrimonious relationship with Flyers GM Bobby Clarke made it doubtful he would return to Philly. But Lindros' main concern was recovering from his concussions to see when, or maybe if, he could return to the ice to resume his role as the league's irresistible force.

CAREER RECORD

Personal

Birthplace/Date: **London, Ontario/2-28-73**
Height/Weight: **6-4/236**

Awards

All-Rookie Team: **1993**
First All-Star Team: **1995**
Lester B. Pearson Award: **1995**
Hart Trophy: **1995**

NHL Career: **8 seasons Philadelphia Flyers**

Playing record

	Games	Goals	Assists	Points	PIM
Regular Season	486	290	369	659	946
Playoffs	50	24	33	57	118

Mr. Intensity

MARK MESSIER

This six-time winner of the Stanley Cup is a legend who just wants to keep winning

Speed defines some hockey players, strength others, still others personify skill. Mark Messier displays ample amounts of all three qualities, but to understand his essence, you start with the glare.

When Messier gets that look, his teammates get into formation behind him and opponents blanch just a little. The glare could translate into a game-breaking goal, a skilful passing play, a bone-rattling body check or even a well-timed, lethal elbow to an opponent's jaw.

Messier is the ultimate hockey player: big, fast, strong, skillful and junkyard-dog mean.

The Edmonton native is above all an incomparable on-ice leader, the capstone player on any team he has played for. He was a central player on five Edmonton Oilers teams that won the Stanley Cup, a leader on three Canadian teams that won the Canada Cup and indisputably the central force that carried the Rangers to the Stanley Cup in 1994, their first championship in 54 years.

Some consider him the fiercest, most inspirational leader in all of North American pro sports. He certainly has the portfolio.

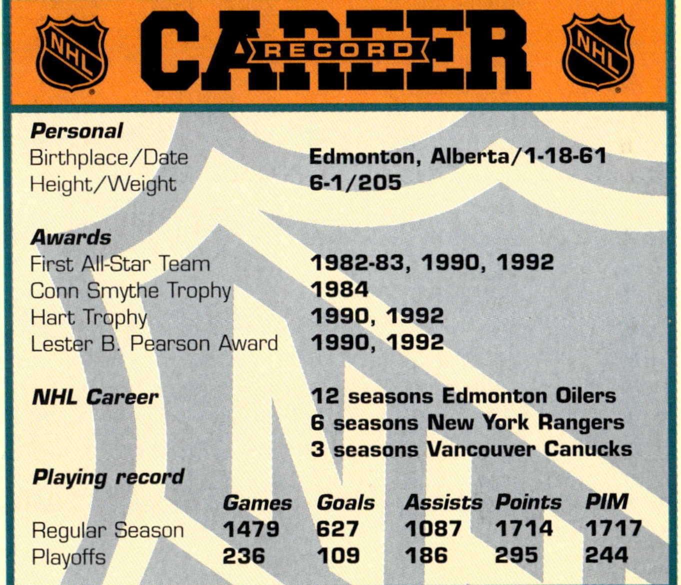

CAREER RECORD

Personal

Birthplace/Date	**Edmonton, Alberta/1-18-61**
Height/Weight	**6-1/205**

Awards

First All-Star Team	**1982-83, 1990, 1992**
Conn Smythe Trophy	**1984**
Hart Trophy	**1990, 1992**
Lester B. Pearson Award	**1990, 1992**

NHL Career

12 seasons Edmonton Oilers
6 seasons New York Rangers
3 seasons Vancouver Canucks

Playing record

	Games	Goals	Assists	Points	PIM
Regular Season	1479	627	1087	1714	1717
Playoffs	236	109	186	295	244

Trail of a giant

He has won two Hart Trophies as the league's most valuable player, one Conn Smythe Trophy as the best individual performer in the playoffs and two Lester B. Pearson Awards as the most outstanding player in the league, as voted on by his peers.

His individual performance chart reveals impressive statistics: one 50-goal season; six seasons of 100 points or more; more than 100 playoff goals and almost 300 post-season points; a record 14 playoff shorthanded goals. But the true measure of Messier seems to be how teams he plays for perform. In 1990-91, Edmonton was 29-20-4 (won-lost-tied) with Messier in the lineup, just 8-17-2 without him. In the 1991 Canada Cup, Team Canada coach Mike Keenan extended an eligibility deadline to make room on the team for Messier. Canada won the tournament that year.

In 1984, even with the Wayne Gretzky Oilers, it was Messier who won the Conn Smythe Trophy as the most valuable player in the Stanley Cup playoffs as Edmonton won its first Cup in franchise history.

Messier is known as one of the most inspirational leaders in hockey, a man who never suffers a lapse in determination and demands the most from his teammates.

No rash promise

The most celebrated illustration of Messier's leadership abilities came before Game 6 of the 1994 Stanley Cup semifinals against the New Jersey Devils.

The Devils held a 3-2 series lead, but Messier told a TV audience he guaranteed a victory by the Rangers in Game 6. He backed it up by scoring the hat trick as the Rangers won the game 4-2, sending the series to a seventh game in Madison Square which the Rangers won in double overtime, the third of three games decided in a second overtime period.

Not since New York Jets quarterback Joe Namath guaranteed a Super Bowl victory over the Baltimore Colts in 1969 had a New York sporting hero been so brash, then backed up his boast. Messier's guarantee had profound resonance for New York hockey fans.

In 1997, free-agent Messier left the Big Apple for Vancouver, where he experienced the other side of the NHL. The Canucks had the worst record in the Western Conference his first two years there, and they were tied for ninth (one spot out of the playoffs) this past season. Messier went on the open market again in the summer of 2000, giving teams the rare chance to bid on one of the league's all-time leaders and winners.

Stars Scorer

MIKE MODANO

Modano has become a complete player in recent seasons, adding a defensive conscience to his array of offensive gifts.

As a kid growing up in Livonia, Michigan, Mike Modano would spend plenty of hours in the family basement honing his hockey skills. Often, he would beg his mother to serve as a goaltender and hold up the top part of a garbage can, which Mike used as a target to develop pinpoint precision in his shooting.

The hours certainly weren't wasted. After a brilliant junior career, the then-Minnesota North Stars made the 6-foot-3, 200-pound center the No. 1 pick overall in the 1988 draft.

Excluding the 1994-95 strike season and an injury-hit 1997-98 campaign, Modano has led the team—which moved to Dallas prior to the 1993 season and became the Stars—in every season since 1991-92,when he collected 77 points. His biggest goal-scoring season, however, came in 1993-94 when he became the first center in the history of the franchise to score 50 goals.

"I started to improve on my ability to go to the net that season," recalled Modano. "That obviously wasn't a part of my game the first few years, but the more you do it, the more you get used to it."

Michigan Mike's career reached its zenith with a Stanley Cup win in 1999.

Sharpshooting leader

On the ice, Modano has blossomed into one of the NHL's swiftest skaters and most feared sharp-shooters. He's also changed his game from that of pure offense to one of two-way dominance. He has bought into Dallas coach Ken Hitchcock's disciplined style, and now he make just as big an impact in his own zone as his does in the opponent's end.

The Stars have become a powerhouse the last few years, capped by their first-ever Stanley Cup in 1999. Modano has proven his toughness in the postseason.

Modano badly injured his wrist in the 1999 Stanley Cup Finals, and was expected to miss some games. But he fought through the pain and didn't miss a game, while giving his usual stellar performance.

He assisted on all five of the Stars' goals in the last three games of the Finals vs. Buffalo, including the series winner in triple overtime of Game 6.

The former pretty boy has become a complete player—complete with a Stanley Cup ring.

Matinee idol

Modano was under a great deal of pressure to produce in the early years. The North Stars had missed the playoffs for two straight seasons prior to drafting Modano, who at the time was only the second American-born player to be selected No. 1. One year after that draft, Modano was a bona fide member of the North Stars, amassing 75 points as a rookie, including 20 points in the Stanley Cup playoffs, as the upstart North Stars went all the way to the final.

Still, Modano was a long ways from refinement. The concern for Bob Gainey, who at the time had the dual role of coach and general manager, was Modano's play in the offensive zone when he didn't have the puck. Gradually, Modano learned to let other players work the puck to him, rather than vacate a good offensive position because of his own impatience and frustration.

Modano's star continued to rise when the North Stars relocated in Dallas. More than a hockey star, he became a matinée idol, especially when his handsome features found their way into some of the top women's magazines, and Giorgio Armani used him as a runway model.

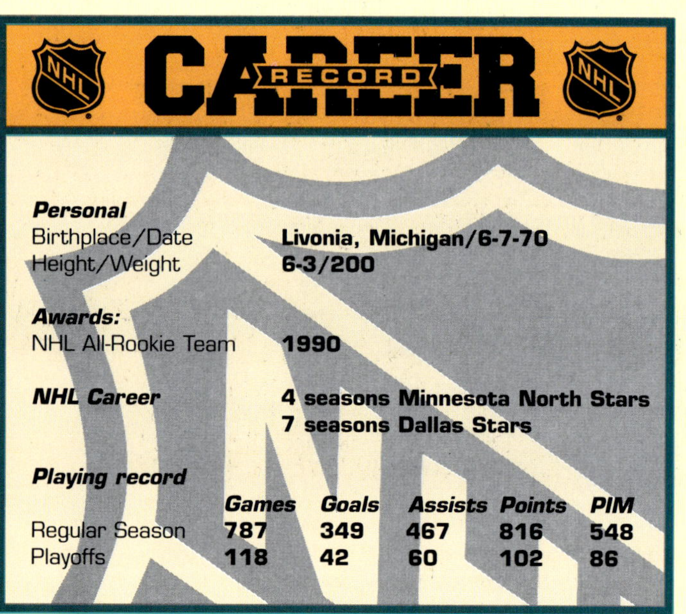

CAREER RECORD

Personal

Birthplace/Date **Livonia, Michigan/6-7-70**
Height/Weight **6-3/200**

Awards:

NHL All-Rookie Team **1990**

NHL Career **4 seasons Minnesota North Stars**
7 seasons Dallas Stars

Playing record

	Games	Goals	Assists	Points	PIM
Regular Season	787	349	467	816	548
Playoffs	118	42	60	102	86

The Blues defenseman has progressed from simple banger to franchise MVP.

Heavy-hitting blueliner
CHRIS PRONGER

There isn't a more dominating physical presence in the NHL these days than Chris Pronger. The 6'6" defenseman clears the slot the way St. Louis baseball slugger Mark McGwire smacks a fastball—with brute force.

But Pronger is no longer just the banger he was when he arrived in the NHL as teenager in 1993. He has evolved into what many consider the best all-around blueliner in the game. He can mix it up physically, has one of the best outlet passes in the game, boasts a long reach which makes it nearly impossible to get around him, and has offensive skills to rival those of just about any other backliner in the league. Most of all, though, he is a workhorse who can average 30 minutes per game and play the 30th minute just as effectively as the first.

Early impact

Pronger made an immediate impact in the NHL. He was drafted second overall in the 1993 Entry Draft by Hartford and he played 81 of a possible 84 games for the Whalers as a rookie in 1993-94, notching five goals and 25 assists to be voted the team's most valuable defenseman. The Ottawa Senators would undoubtedly love to redo that 1993 draft. They picked speedy forward Alexandre Daigle with the top overall pick and gave him a huge contract, but he never lived up to expectations and has traveled around the league.

In 1995, Pronger was half of a big trade which sent star forward Brendan Shanahan to Hartford and Pronger to St. Louis.

Chris Pronger won both the Hart and Norris Trophies in 2000.

At the time it was a swap of a proven commodity (Shanahan) for potential (Pronger). Five years later, both are among the NHL's elite, a rarity in a one-for-one deal.

Pronger became a cornerstone in St. Louis, but he didn't have the pressure in his early years of carrying the load. Future Hall of Famers such as Brett Hull, Grant Fuhr and Al MacInnis and, briefly, current Hall of Famer Wayne Gretzky, were the headliners. But the Blues eventually became Pronger's team. In 1997, he was named captain, the franchise's youngest-ever.

Joining the elite

With Pronger's selection to the 1998 Canadian Olympic team, he had arrived as a premier player. He led the league in plus-minus that season (plus-47) and he's only gotten better since. He and MacInnis combine to form the most lethal one-two defensive punch in the league. The Blues allowed the fewest goals in 1999-2000 on the way to the Presidents' Trophy for most points in the regular season.

Pronger's many individual accomplishments included leading the league in minutes per game (30:14), finishing second among defensemen in scoring (14 goals, 48 assists, 62 points), and another plus-minus title (plus-52). He was a finalist for the Hart Trophy (MVP as voted by media), Pearson Award (MVP as voted by players) and Norris Trophy (best defenseman).

His coach, Joel Quenneville, said: "I'm obviously biased, but I didn't see another player who, game in and game out, shift by shift, controlled the game like Chris did. There were no slumps, no lulls."

Pronger also kept his penalty minutes below 100 for the first time in a full season. Although it's by design that he has toned down his feistiness, he still plays with a chip on shoulder. That's not surprising for a guy whose nickname growing up was "Chaos," which his dad says fit him perfectly because he was hell on wheels. These days, he's hell on skates.

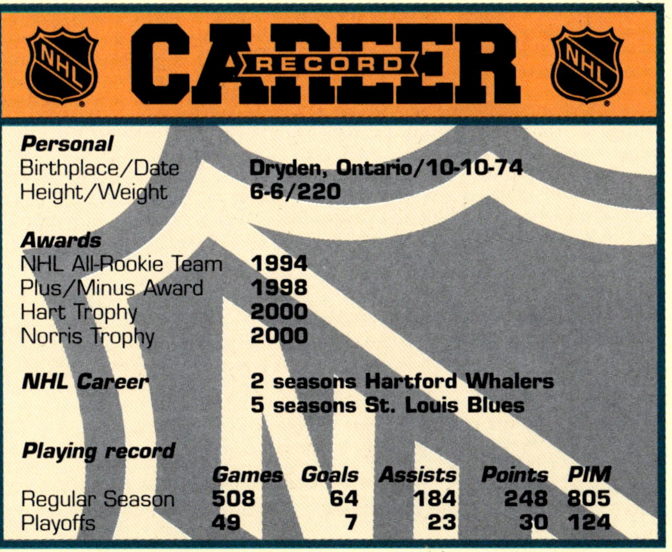

CAREER RECORD

Personal

Birthplace/Date	**Dryden, Ontario/10-10-74**
Height/Weight	**6-6/220**

Awards

NHL All-Rookie Team	**1994**
Plus/Minus Award	**1998**
Hart Trophy	**2000**
Norris Trophy	**2000**

NHL Career **2 seasons Hartford Whalers**
5 seasons St. Louis Blues

Playing record

	Games	Goals	Assists	Points	PIM
Regular Season	508	64	184	248	805
Playoffs	49	7	23	30	124

The Rangers' Good Guy

MIKE RICHTER

An instrumental force in his team's ambitions, this goalie's goaltender keeps his cool and always gives his best.

Take it from one of his goaltending brethren: New York Rangers netminder Mike Richter is one of the best around when it comes to winning a big game or series. "There are not many goalies who can win games by themselves, but Mike is capable of doing it," remarked Martin Brodeur, the New Jersey Devils No. 1 backstop. "He did it in the World Cup, and he did it against us."

In the first instance, Brodeur was referring to Richter's stellar play in the fall of 1996, which spearheaded the United States squad to a 2-1 triumph over Canada in the best-of-three series at the first-ever World Cup hockey tournament. The second allusion was to Richter's performance against the Devils in the 1997 Eastern Conference semifinal, in which Richter stopped 178 of 182 shots, recorded two shutouts and led the Rangers to a five-game upset of the Devils in the best-of-seven series.

Richter wasn't able to lead an injury-decimated Rangers lineup past the Philadelphia Flyers in the Eastern Conference final, but that didn't detract from the accomplishments of the nimble netminder who grew up a Flyers' fan in Flourtown, Pennsylvania. The Rangers would likely not have got as far as they did without a vintage Richter, who compiled a 2.68 regular-season goals-against average.

Notorious success

Before the elimination by the Flyers, Richter revived memories of 1994, when he was an instrumental force in the Rangers ending a 54-year Stanley Cup drought. Richter started all 23 of the Rangers playoff games that year, leading the NHL with 16 wins, posting a 2.07 goals-against average and recording four shutouts, which tied a league record for shutouts in post-season play.

Perhaps Richter's finest moment in that year's playoffs was his 31-save effort in the Rangers' seventh-game double-overtime triumph over New Jersey to win the Eastern Conference finals.

Richter's notoriety earned him guest spots—along with teammates Mark Messier and Brian Leetch—on the David Letterman Show following the Stanley Cup win. Articulate and comfortable as a communicator, Richter, a past winner of the Rangers 'Good Guy Award' for cooperation with the media, was in his element on the popular U.S. late-night television program.

Two years later, Richter was in the spotlight again, when he won the Most Valuable Player Award at the World Cup. With the U.S. team trailing Canada 1-0 in the best-of-three series, Richter made 35 saves in Game 2 as the Americans tied the series and, in Game 3, he kept the U.S. in the game—the team was outshot 22-9 through two periods—enabling it to go on to a 5-2 win in the decisive third game.

Cool courage

When he's not throwing his body in front of pucks, Richter is deeply involved in social causes. He has won awards for 'Excellence and Humanitarian Concern', and an 'Award of Courage' for his work with hospitals. He has also served as honorary hockey chairman of the Children's Health Fund.

Placid and cool under the constant pressures of trying to stifle some of the game's finest sharpshooters, Richter is equally collected in his approach to his craft. "You have to realize you are probably as good or as bad as the team in front of you," he once explained. "But one of the attractions of being a goaltender is that you are the guy on the spot. There's pressure on everybody, but that's a lot easier to bear than not having the opportunity to deliver under pressure."

Mike Richter has backstopped both the New York Rangers and Team USA to championship glory.

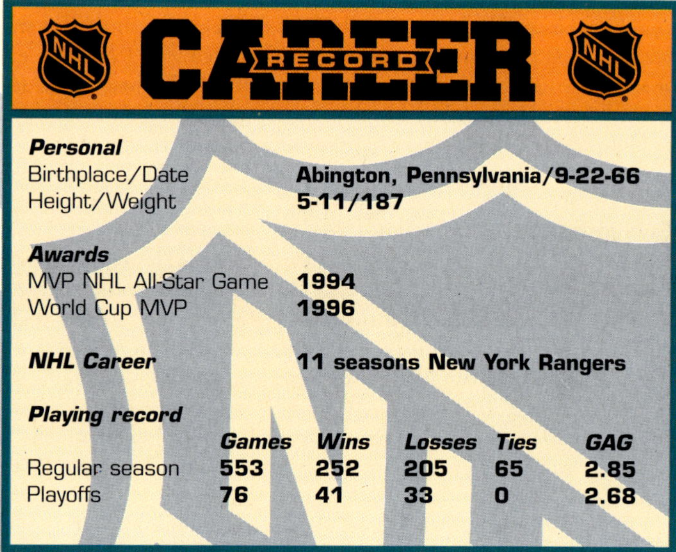

CAREER RECORD

Personal

Birthplace/Date	**Abington, Pennsylvania/9-22-66**
Height/Weight	**5-11/187**

Awards

MVP NHL All-Star Game	**1994**
World Cup MVP	**1996**

NHL Career **11 seasons New York Rangers**

Playing record

	Games	Wins	Losses	Ties	GAG
Regular season	553	252	205	65	2.85
Playoffs	76	41	33	0	2.68

Mile-High Goaltender PATRICK ROY

Miraculous and often unbeatable, the man who made the butterfly style famous shines on

During games, the rookie goaltender talked to his goalposts, and before each game started, he skated 40 feet in front of his net, turned and stared intently at his workplace, skated hard right at the crease, veered away at the last second, then settled into his work station for another night of brilliance.

Even among goaltenders, who are known for their eccentricity, Patrick Roy was a classic from his first NHL season in 1986.

Roy was magnificent during the playoffs as the Canadiens, with a rookie-laden club, won the Stanley Cup, surprising the hockey world, and he won the Conn Smythe Trophy, winning 15 and losing just five playoff games and posting a goals-against average of 1.92. He had staked his claim to the title of the best goalie in the NHL.

The next three seasons, he won the William Jennings Trophy, for the goalie whose team allows the fewest goals against. Three times (1989-90, 1992) Roy also won the Vezina Trophy, awarded to the league's best goalie, as voted on by the general managers.

Roy refined his goaltending technique the hard way. As a junior goalie, playing for the sad sack Granby Bisons of the Quebec Major Junior Hockey League, it was not uncommon for Roy to face 60- or 70-shot barrages.

Stellar start

When he arrived in the NHL as a regular, Roy was only 20, and had played one single, solitary game in minor pro hockey, but he was seasoned, which he quickly proved. Roy has been at his best in pressure situations. His stellar play led the Canadiens to three Stanley Cup finals (1986, 1989, 1993), and two championships.

Both those years, he won the Conn Smythe Trophy as the most valuable player in the playoffs. His performance in the 1993 Stanley Cup playoffs, when the Canadiens won ten of 11 overtime games, was just this side of miraculous. It's not for nothing the Forum came to be known as St. Patrick's Cathedral during his glory years there.

Patrick Roy is known for his postseason successes. He has been playoff MVP twice and in 1999 became the first goalie to win 100 career playoff games.

In 1994, Roy was stricken with appendicitis after two games of the opening-round series against the Boston Bruins and had to be hospitalized. Antibiotics forestalled the need for surgery and Roy rose from his hospital bed to record two straight victories over the Bruins, one a 2-1 overtime thriller at the old Boston Garden in which he made 60 saves.

At his best, Roy is technically flawless, using a butterfly style in which he goes to his knees and splays his leg pads to cover the lower portion of the net, protecting the upper portion with his body and his cat-quick left hand.

Superstar shock

Roy was Montreal's franchise player so it was stunning on December 2, 1995 when the goaltender, embarrassed by an 11-1 pounding he had absorbed from the Detroit Red Wings, told club president Ronald Corey—on national TV—that he had played his last game with the Montreal Canadiens. Three days later, Roy was traded to Colorado. Never mind. Roy would make his new home his shrine. In his first season with the Avalanche, he backstopped Colorado to the Stanley Cup. In 1996-97, he was brilliant again, but the Avalanche were eliminated in the semifinals to eventual Stanley Cup champion Detroit Red Wings.

Roy has continued to show excellent form. The past two seasons he helped Colorado get to the conference finals, where the Avs lost to Dallas in a pair of thrilling seven-game series. Roy added to his postseason lore by becoming the first goalie to win 100 career playoff games. St. Patrick keeps producing miracles.

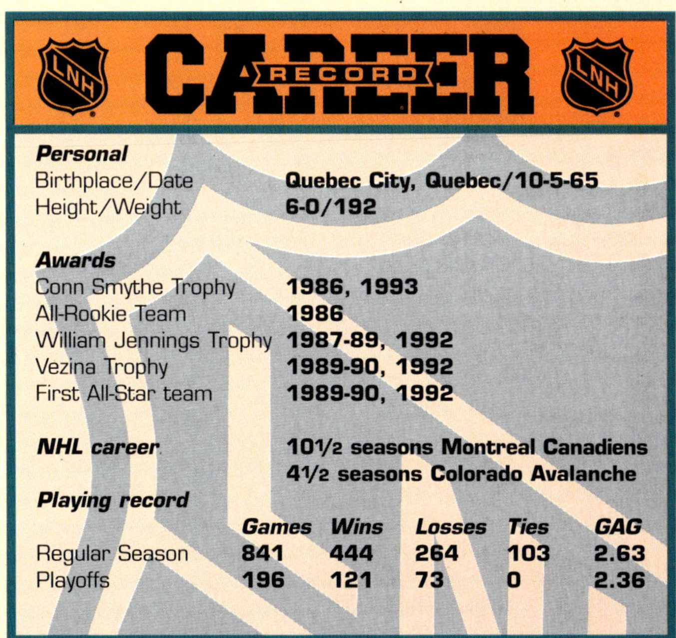

CAREER RECORD

Personal	
Birthplace/Date	**Quebec City, Quebec/10-5-65**
Height/Weight	**6-0/192**
Awards	
Conn Smythe Trophy	**1986, 1993**
All-Rookie Team	**1986**
William Jennings Trophy	**1987-89, 1992**
Vezina Trophy	**1989-90, 1992**
First All-Star team	**1989-90, 1992**
NHL career	**10½ seasons Montreal Canadiens** **4½ seasons Colorado Avalanche**

Playing record

	Games	Wins	Losses	Ties	GAG
Regular Season	841	444	264	103	2.63
Playoffs	196	121	73	0	2.36

Colorado's Sharpshooter

A deadly, stealth-like force on the ice, this sniper has perhaps the most lethal wrister in the game.

JOE SAKIC

He's not big, in fact, he's almost small by National Hockey League standards, but Joe Sakic is water-bug elusive, a slick, clever passer, an accurate shooter and perhaps the most unassuming superstar in hockey.

Sakic was a first-round draft pick by the then-Quebec Nordiques in 1987. He was taken 15th overall after a monster season (60 goals, 133 points) with the Swift Current Broncos of the Western Hockey League.

When he joined the once-mighty Nordiques, for the 1988-89 season, they had just finished last in the Adams Division and were about to embark on the darkest period in franchise history. They would finish last overall in the NHL the next three years in a row. Sakic's NHL apprenticeship did not come easy.

Nordique blues

Sakic was fortunate enough to have Nordiques' star center Peter Stastny around for most of his first two seasons as a role model. Sakic, it turned out, didn't need that much guidance.

He scored 23 goals and added 39 assists for 62 points in his first season, then recorded the first of four 100-plus point seasons the very next year, when he led the Nordiques with 39 goals and 63 assists.

When the Nordiques traded Stastny, their first real superstar, to the New Jersey Devils in 1990, the torch had been passed to the smallish, shifty Sakic. The Nordiques would soon surround Sakic with some of the best young talent in the game. As the club improved, adding players like Owen Nolan, Mats Sundin, Curtis Leschyshyn, Stephane Fiset, Valeri Kamensky etc, expectations also began to soar.

In 1992-93, the Nordiques made the playoffs for the first time in five years and drew provincial rival Montreal Canadiens as their first-round opponent. The talent-rich Nordiques won the first two games.

But Montreal goalie Patrick Roy stiffened and the Canadiens stunned the Nordiques, winning the next four games in a row. The critics howled, many of them at Sakic, but the quiet-spoken Sakic took the loss as a learning experience. In the lockout-shortened 1994-95 season, Sakic's 19 goals and 43 assists put him fourth in league scoring and the Nordiques finished first overall in the Eastern Conference, but lost to the Rangers in the opening round of the Stanley Cup playoffs.

Colorado dawn

In Colorado's first season in Denver, Sakic collected 120 points, finishing third in the regular-season scoring race. Then he guided the Avalanche to the Stanley Cup, winning the Conn Smythe Trophy as the most valuable player in the playoffs.

In the 1997-98 season, things didn't go so well as Sakic picked up an injury while playing for Team Canada in the Nagano Olympics. A collision with teammate Rob Blake during the quarter-final win against Kazakhstan left Sakic with a sprained knee that sidelined him for several weeks. But Sakic, whom many consider to have the best wrist shot in the league, was back in form in 1998–99. He tallied 96 points, the fifth-best total in the league.

He missed a quarter of the past season with assorted injuries but still managed 81 points, tied for eighth in the league. Normally a clutch postseason scorer, Sakic had a subpar spring in 2000, but, at age 31, the restricted free agent is at the top of the hockey mountain.

What Sakic lacks in size he makes up for in smarts, quickness and heart. He is a quiet leader for the Avalanche.

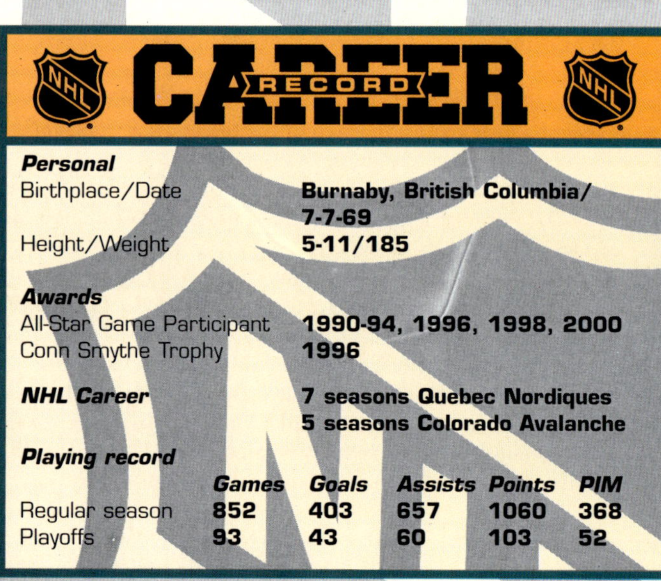

CAREER RECORD

Personal

Birthplace/Date	**Burnaby, British Columbia/ 7-7-69**
Height/Weight	**5-11/185**

Awards

All-Star Game Participant	**1990-94, 1996, 1998, 2000**
Conn Smythe Trophy	**1996**

NHL Career — **7 seasons Quebec Nordiques**, **5 seasons Colorado Avalanche**

Playing record

	Games	*Goals*	*Assists*	*Points*	*PIM*
Regular season	852	403	657	1060	368
Playoffs	93	43	60	103	52

TEEMU SELANNE

The Finnish Flash is a potent combination of blazing speed and scoring smarts.

When you blend world-class skill and offensive creativity with eye-popping speed, you really discombobulate a defense. That description fits Teemu Selanne perfectly.

The Finnish Flash blazed through the National Hockey League in his first season with the Winnipeg Jets, scoring 76 goals and adding 56 assists. His goal total shattered the NHL's rookie record.

Fully-grown rookie

The 6-foot, 200-pound Finnish speedster zoomed into the NHL in 1992. To say he adjusted from Jokerit in the Finnish Elite League with ease is to understate the magnitude of his achievement.

Selanne recorded his first three-goal hat trick in his fifth NHL game. In late February that season, Selanne scored four goals in a defeat of Minnesota, and produced a string of scoring streaks that left Jets fans dizzy: a 17-game streak that produced 20 goals and 14 assists, nine games (14 goals), eight games (nine goals and 11 assists) and five games (11 goals). In the Jets' final six games, Selanne blasted 13 goals and added two assists.

In his first NHL playoff game, against the Vancouver Canucks, he not only scored a goal, he recorded another three-goal hat trick.

His Calder Memorial Trophy award as the top rookie in the league was expected. Astonishing was his arrival as a fully formed superstar, competing with both rookies *and* the best players.

His 76 goals tied for the league lead with Alexander Mogilny and he was selected as the right winger on the first All-Star team.

Kid start

Selanne was a mature player upon arrival in North America because he had not hurried his development in his native Finland.

He grew up in the minor hockey system in Helsinki, playing for KalPa-Espoo from the age of five. By nine, he was competing against players two years his senior, and at 16 he joined Jokerit, one of the most successful of the teams in the Finnish Elite League for five seasons before he made the jump to the NHL.

"It is good to play there and get better and then come (to the NHL) later, when you are ready," he has said. "I had dreams to play in the World Championship and the Olympic Games before I came here and when I came here, I had done all that. I left with a clear conscience."

It is clear Anaheim plans to construct a championship team around Selanne and Paul Kariya, who give Anaheim one of the most highly skilled duos in all of hockey.

Kariya was sidelined for much of the 1997-98 season, but Selanne recorded 52 goals and was the MVP of the All-Star game. The hat-trick he scored in that game was the first by a European in all All-Star game. In 1998-99, they ranked second and third, respectively, in league scoring—Selanne with 107 points and Kariya with 101; last year, they were fourth (Kariya with 86 points) and fifth (Selanne, 85) in the scoring race.

When those two get revved up, it's lights out for their opponents.

CAREER RECORD

Personal

Birthplace/date	**Helsinki, Finland/7-3-70**
Height/Weight	**6-0/200**

Awards

Calder Memorial Trophy	**1993**
"Rocket" Richard Trophy	**1999**
All-Rookie Team	**1993**
First All-Star Team	**1993, 1997**

NHL Career — **3½ seasons Winnipeg Jets; 4½ seasons Mighty Ducks of Anaheim**

Playing record

	Games	Goals	Assists	Points	PIM
Regular Season	564	346	383	729	197
Playoffs	21	13	7	20	8

ICE TALK

"When I was younger, the NHL was just a dream because I did not know how much of a sacrifice it took to make it to this level. But when I was 18 or 19, I started having more success and then my goal was to play in the NHL."

Teemu Selanne

Selanne scored 47 goals in 1998–99 to capture the inaugural Maurice Richard Trophy, given to the league's top goal scorer.

Detroit's Fighting Forward

BRENDAN SHANAHAN

Wicked one-timers and bodychecks are equal parts of his arsenal.

The Detroit Red Wings were so eager to welcome rugged left winger Brendan Shanahan into the fold that the team delayed a morning practice so that Shanahan, who was on a flight from Hartford following his trade from the Whalers in October 1996, could join them.

There were definitely great expectations for Shanahan—and with good reason. While Detroit was the fourth stop for the quintessential power forward, Shanahan had established a reputation as one of the NHL's premier players. Selected No. 2 overall by New Jersey in the 1987 entry draft, Shanahan scored 81 goals in his last three seasons with the Devils prior to being dealt to St. Louis, where he topped 50 goals in two of his four seasons, and then it was on to Hartford, where he had 78 points in 74 games in 1995-96.

Disgruntled in Hartford, Shanahan pressed for a trade because the club wasn't a contender, and the cash-strapped franchise really couldn't afford to keep him. Enter the Red Wings, a team that had both the money and contending status, and needed a productive, strapping forward to put it over the top.

Fighting start

The October 9 trade saw Shanahan and defenseman Brian Glynn head to Detroit for Keith Primeau, Paul Coffey, and a 1997 first-round draft pick. "I don't look at this as the end of something," Shanahan said when he learned of the trade. "I look at it as the beginning. The Red Wings' game is to win the Stanley Cup, and that's my game, too."

They were prophetic words indeed. Shanahan fit into the Red Wings lineup like a glove, blending strong physical play—he got into his first fight four minutes into his first game with Detroit—along with a knack around the net to score 46 goals and collect 87 points in 79 regular-season games. He also racked up 131 minutes in penalties.

Shanahan contributed nine goals and eight assists in 20 post-season games, helping the Red Wings end a 42-year Stanley Cup drought. It was mission accomplished, both for Shanahan and the Red Wings, who were still smarting from a four-game sweep by the New Jersey Devils in the Stanley Cup final two years earlier.

Missing link

Shanahan said watching the Devils, his former team, win the Cup, only increased his yearning to join a contender. "I saw friends and fans I know celebrate that Cup win, and it hit pretty close to home," said Shanahan, who had left New Jersey when St. Louis signed him as a free agent in July, 1991. The Devils were awarded defenseman Scott Stevens as compensation for signing Shanahan. "I really thought I was going to get a Cup win in St. Louis," added Shanahan. But in July, 1995, he was on the move again—to Hartford for defenseman Chris Pronger. To some, the Blues made the trade for economic reasons. Shanahan believes it was because Blues coach Mike Keenan "wanted to bring in his own guys."

In his only full season with the Whalers, Shanahan was named the team captain, a testimony to his leadership abilities. When he arrived in Detroit, he was immediately made an assistant captain to captain Steve Yzerman.

In 1998, the Wings repeated their Cup championship. The past two seasons have ended in second-round playoff losses to archrival Colorado. Shanahan still is a big key to helping the Wings remain among the elite.

He had a monster regular season in 1999-2000, finishing sixth in the league with 41 goals, and he signed a four-year, $26 million contract just before season's end. At age 31 he is in his hockey prime. It should be Shanny time for a while to come.

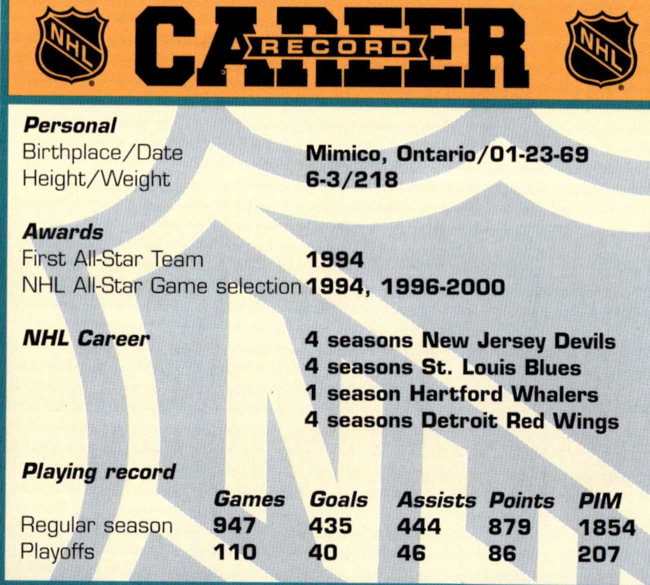

CAREER RECORD

Personal

Birthplace/Date	**Mimico, Ontario/01-23-69**
Height/Weight	**6-3/218**

Awards

First All-Star Team	**1994**
NHL All-Star Game selection	**1994, 1996-2000**

NHL Career	**4 seasons New Jersey Devils**
	4 seasons St. Louis Blues
	1 season Hartford Whalers
	4 seasons Detroit Red Wings

Playing record

	Games	Goals	Assists	Points	PIM
Regular season	947	435	444	879	1854
Playoffs	110	40	46	86	207

Power forward Brendan Shanahan provides grit, drive, leadership and offense for the Red Wings.

The Maple Leafs' Leader

MATS SUNDIN

With his seemingly effortless offensive prowess, Sundin is the engine that drives the Leafs.

Mats Sundin had franchise player written all over him when he was drafted first overall in the 1989 Entry Draft. As things have unfolded, Sundin has filled that office for not one franchise, but two.

Big, strong, a swift, powerful skater with a hard, accurate shot and an impressive bag of creative offensive tricks, Sundin certainly has the requisite tools to be the key player wherever he earns his pay cheque.

For four years, Sundin was one of the building blocks around whom the Quebec Nordiques were going to surge from the ashes to contend for a Stanley Cup.

But Sundin only had one shot at Stanley Cup playoff action with Quebec (now the Colorado Avalanche). That was in 1992-93, the year Sundin scored 47 goals and totalled 114 points in all, tops on the talent-rich Nordiques, whose lineup boasted Joe Sakic and Valeri Kamensky.

Tall hustler

The Nordiques won the first two games of their only playoff series that spring against the Montreal Canadiens, but that was it. The Canadiens would ride the goaltending brilliance of Patrick Roy to the Stanley Cup championship that season, while the Nordiques would take a year to recover from the shock. The following season, they missed the playoffs altogether.

For many, a lasting image of that Stanley Cup opening-round failure is that of then-Nordiques head coach Pierre Page yelling in Sundin's ear on national TV as the seconds ticked down on the final loss of the series.

Some fans, too, can be critical of Sundin, whose sublime offensive achievements often appear too effortless.

"Sometimes it doesn't look like bigger guys hustle as much as the little guy who has to take maybe three strides while the bigger guy takes one," Sundin says. "I'm known to have been criticized sometimes, when people say that I'm kind of cruising around or pacing myself. I'm 6-foot-4 1/2, almost 6-foot-5, and I know that when I'm on the ice, I'm always working hard."

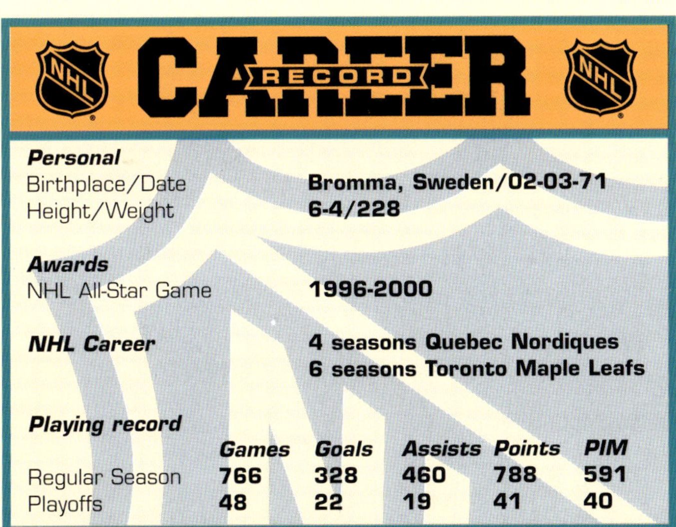

CAREER RECORD

Personal

Birthplace/Date	**Bromma, Sweden/02-03-71**
Height/Weight	**6-4/228**

Awards

NHL All-Star Game	**1996-2000**

NHL Career	**4 seasons Quebec Nordiques** **6 seasons Toronto Maple Leafs**

Playing record

	Games	*Goals*	*Assists*	*Points*	*PIM*
Regular Season	**766**	**328**	**460**	**788**	**591**
Playoffs	**48**	**22**	**19**	**41**	**40**

Sundin has led the Maple Leafs in scoring all six seasons he has played there: the first Leaf to achieve such a level of consistency since Darryl Sittler.

Toronto hope

Sundin was traded to the Toronto Maple Leafs in a blockbuster trade that sent popular Maple Leafs winger Wendel Clark to Quebec. If there was pressure in replacing the fan idol Clark, it has not been evident. Sundin has led the Maple Leafs in scoring all six seasons he has played there — the first Leaf to achieve such a level of consistency since Darryl Sittler. Toronto finally has found a supporting cast to take some of the pressure off the captain.

The Leafs experienced a major rebirth in 1998-99, earning a fourth seed in the postseason after missing the playoffs two straight seasons. The Leafs advanced to the Eastern Conference finals. Leading the charge was Sundin, who tied for 11th in the regular season with 83 points, then had an impressive playoff run with 16 points (including two game-winning goals) in 17 games. The Leafs were strong again last season, and they should be a serious contender as long as lucky No. 13 is leading the way.

The Tough Coyote

KEITH TKACHUK

The prototype power forward can crash and bang or shoot and score with equal effectiveness

Captain Courageous: If the Phoenix Coyotes are going to live up to their considerable potential, it will be due to the leadership and talent of players like Keith Tkachuk.

To long-suffering fans in hockey-crazed Winnipeg, Keith Tkachuk was nothing less than the saviour when he arrived there as a 19-year-old following the 1992 Winter Olympics in Albertville, France.

It did not take him long to demonstrate he belonged in The Show. In his first complete season—1992-93—Tkachuk scored 28 goals and racked up 201 minutes in penalties. The following season, Tkachuk was named captain of the Jets at the tender age of 21, the youngest captain in franchise history. Being captain of the Jets was no trivial responsibility, and Tkachuk has the grey hair to prove it.

"Try being captain of the Winnipeg Jets at age 21 and see what it does to your hair," Tkachuk once said.

Making the grade

When he joined Winnipeg, it was in the middle of one of its periodic rebuilding campaigns but still underachieving, despite the likes of Teemu Selanne and Alexei Zhamnov in the lineup. To make matters worse, the franchise in remote Manitoba was in rocky financial shape. Tkachuk, through no fault of his own, put them deeper in a hole because Winnipeg matched a five-year, $17-million offer sheet he had signed with the Chicago Blackhawks after he became a restricted free agent. Tkachuk quickly became target of the fans' frustration.

Despite the pressure, Tkachuk lived up to the trust shown him when he was named captain by scoring 41 goals and adding 40 assists and staking a solid claim to being one of the best young power forwards in hockey. But it was in 1995-96 and 1996-97 that Tkachuk really blossomed. He scored 50 goals in 1995-96 and 52 in 1996-97, the franchise's first in its new home in Phoenix as the Coyotes, not the Jets.

Smile for the hitman

The 1996-97 preseason was when Tkachuk established himself on the international hockey stage by helping lead Team USA to the gold medal in the inaugural World Cup of Hockey in September.

He scored five goals in seven games and managed to find an outlet for his renowned toughness, too, breaking the nose of Claude Lemieux in a fight.

"There were a lot of toothless smiles around the league," said former Coyotes teammate Jim McKenzie.

Tkachuk's style always has involved blending physical toughness with offensive skill, and he managed it again during the 1997-98 season as he racked up 40 goals in 69 games.

He managed 36 goals in just 68 games the following season, and last season the big winger was hounded by a chronic ankle sprain which limited him to 50 regular season games. In the playoffs, he even shot up the ankle with pain killers to try to play through the injury, but the Coyotes were eliminated in five games of the first round. In fact, postseason success is all that's left for Tkachuk to conquer. This two-time Olympian (1992 and 1998) has never played more than seven playoff games in a season. He's won a World Cup—now he's hungry for a Stanley Cup.

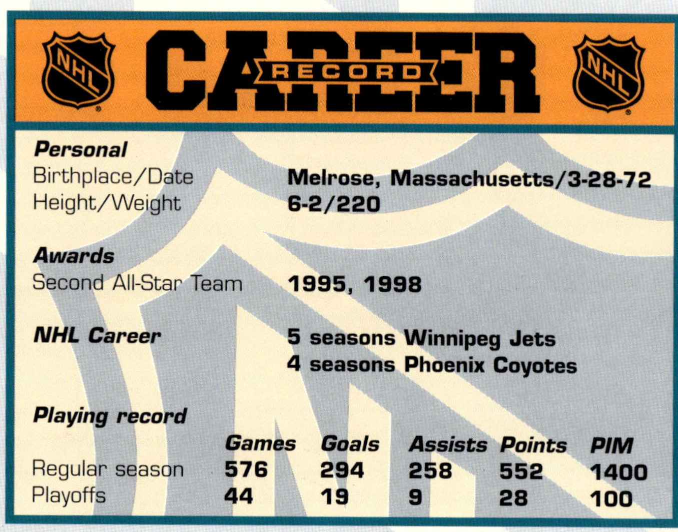

CAREER RECORD

Personal

Birthplace/Date: **Melrose, Massachusetts/3-28-72**

Height/Weight: **6-2/220**

Awards

Second All-Star Team: **1995, 1998**

NHL Career

5 seasons Winnipeg Jets

4 seasons Phoenix Coyotes

Playing record

	Games	Goals	Assists	Points	PIM
Regular season	576	294	258	552	1400
Playoffs	44	19	9	28	100

The Motor City Marvel

STEVE YZERMAN

The Red Wings inspirational captain is hockey's most potent two-way threat.

With Ray Bourque having departed the Boston Bruins, no player in the NHL is as closely associated with his team as Steve Yzerman is with the Detroit Red Wings. Fans in Detroit have taken to calling their city Hockeytown, USA, and Stevie Y is clearly the mayor.

Yzerman came to the Motor City in 1983 as a fresh-faced 18-year-old whom the Wings had selected with the fourth overall pick that summer. He brought an arsenal of offensive skills and made an immediate impact, scoring 39 goals as a rookie and finishing second to Buffalo goalie Tom Barrasso in voting for the Calder Trophy.

Back in his early days with the team, the Red Wings were derisively called the Dead Things. They had missed the playoffs 15 of the 17 seasons prior to Yzerman's debut. Although Detroit earned a playoff berth in each of his first two pro seasons—making a quick, first-round exit both times—by year three the Wings finished last in the league, 14 points behind the next-worst team.

The Captain

There was only one way for the team to go—up. And it would be a long and often frustrating climb for the Wings' franchise player. But Yzerman and the team would eventually reach the NHL summit. The ascent began when Jacques Demers came in as coach in 1986-87. He installed a young Yzerman as captain, and No. 19 has worn the "C" on his sweater ever since, making him the longest-serving captain in NHL history.

Starting in 1987-88, Yzerman posted five straight 100-point seasons. The Wings made it to the conference final in 1987 and 1988, losing both times to eventual Stanley Cup champion Edmonton. In 1988-89, Yzerman notched an incredible 65 goals and 90 assists to earn the coveted Lester B. Pearson Award—league MVP as voted by the players. His 155 points that year is the highest total ever for a player not named Wayne Gretzky or Mario Lemieux.

In the early and mid 1990s, the Wings were consistently one of the best regular-season teams, but Detroit couldn't break through in the playoffs, suffering first-round ousters in 1993 and 1994 despite 100-point seasons, and being swept in the Finals in 1995 by New Jersey. Yzerman was a target of trade rumors during this time, and there were whispers about whether Detroit would be able to win with him.

Two-way star

Any doubts were laid to waste in 1997 and 1998, when the Wings won back-to-back Stanley Cups. It was a different Yzerman who led the way. He had evolved from flashy goal scorer into the ultimate two-way star. He could still dazzle with his offense, but he was perhaps even more committed to strong defensive play.

"He does the little things that inspire other players—block shots, dishes out hits, goes into the corner for the puck," said teammate Darren McCarty. "He's what you expect in a leader."

In the Motor City, he's known simply as "The Captain." In fact, Yzerman is the longest-serving captain in NHL history.

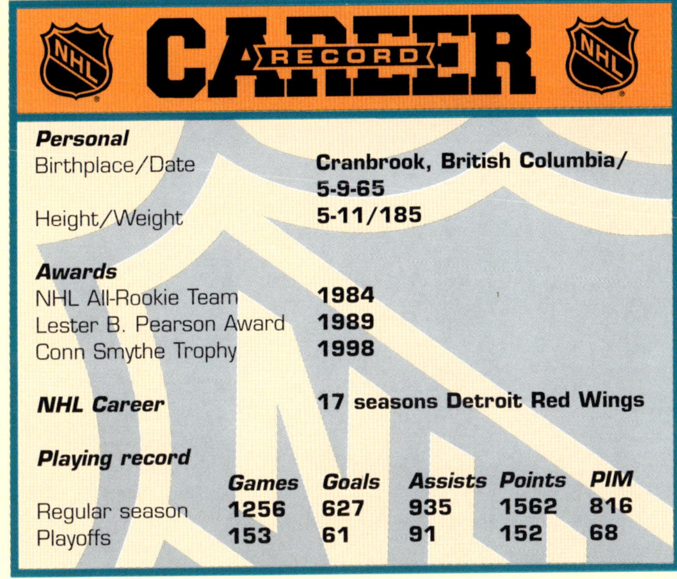

CAREER RECORD

Personal					
Birthplace/Date	**Cranbrook, British Columbia/ 5-9-65**				
Height/Weight	**5-11/185**				
Awards					
NHL All-Rookie Team	**1984**				
Lester B. Pearson Award	**1989**				
Conn Smythe Trophy	**1998**				
NHL Career	**17 seasons Detroit Red Wings**				
Playing record					
	Games	**Goals**	**Assists**	**Points**	**PIM**
Regular season	**1256**	**627**	**935**	**1562**	**816**
Playoffs	**153**	**61**	**91**	**152**	**68**

These days, Yzerman never has to pick up a check in Detroit. He is as popular a sports hero as that town has ever had. And he's still producing—he is tied with Mark Messier for sixth on the all-time goals list with 627 and he was a finalist for the 2000 Selke Award as top defensive forward. Expect another term from Stevie Y as mayor of Hockeytown.

MAROONS
ALEX SMITH
CANADIENS
of
WORLDS
1924

THE STANLEY CUP

THE ULTIMATE GOAL

It's known as the National Hockey League's second season and it may well be the most exciting post-season tournament in professional sports. The Stanley Cup playoffs stretch from mid-April to mid-June as 16 of the NHL's 30 teams compete for the Stanley Cup, one of the most cherished pieces of sporting silverware in the world. The champion must win four best-of-seven series—16 games out of a possible 28 in total, all played after the 82-game regular season concludes in mid-April.

This annual North American Rite of Spring has unfolded, in various formats, since 1893, one year after Lord Stanley, the Earl of Preston and Governor-General of Canada, donated the challenge cup to symbolize the hockey championship of Canada.

Lord Stanley returned to England without ever seeing a championship game or personally presenting the trophy that bears his name. He wasn't around when the Montreal Amateur Athletic Association hockey club became the first winner of the trophy. He certainly could not have foreseen that his trophy would become the property of the National Hockey League, which did not exist until 1917 and did not assume control of the Stanley Cup competition until the 1926-27 season.

Still, the rich and colorful history attached to the silver cup that Lord Stanley purchased for 10 guineas ($48.67 Cdn) more than lives up to the spirit of the annual hockey competition he envisoned more than 100 years ago.

The institution of the trophy kicked off a parade of legendary performances. In 1904, One-Eyed Frank McGee scored a record five goals in an 11-2 victory for the Ottawa Silver Seven over the Toronto Marlboros. The following year, McGee scored 14 goals for the Silver Seven, who demolished the Dawson City Nuggets 23-2. The Nuggets had journeyed to Ottawa via dogsled, boat and train to challenge for Lord Stanley's Cup.

Alberta Magic: Few would have guessed that Wayne Gretzky's fourth Stanley Cup in Edmonton would be his last in an Oiler uniform.

A special time

The quality of competition has tightened considerably since those early days, and transportation is decidedly less rustic, also. But the mystique of the best four-out-of-seven game final series still holds powerful appeal for hockey fans.

The Stanley Cup final can pit speed and finesse against size and toughness, slick offense versus stingy defense, age against youth and, sometimes, brother against brother. The first time that happened was March 16, 1923 when the Denneny brothers, Cy and Corb, and the Boucher siblings, George and Frank, faced off against each other. Cy and George were members of the Ottawa Senators, Corb and Frank played for the Vancouver Maroons. Ottawa won that game 1-0 and went on to capture the Stanley Cup.

In a playoff game between the Montreal Canadiens and the Quebec Nordiques in the 1980s, Montreal's Mark Hunter missed a golden opportunity to pot an overtime winner at one end, then watched, crestfallen as older brother Dale put the game away for the Nordiques (now the Colorado Avalanche) at the other end.

The Stanley Cup tournament is a special event, when there's no time for injuries to heal, so the great ones simply play through the pain, no matter how excruciating. Hall of Fame defenseman Jacques Laperriere once played the finals with a broken wrist, and goaltender John Davidson gritted his teeth and played with a wonky knee in the 1979 finals. Montreal left winger Bob Gainey once completed a playoff series against the New York Islanders with not one but two shoulder separations. And in 1964, Toronto Maple Leafs defenseman Bob Baun scored an overtime winner with a broken ankle in Game 6, then played Game 7 without missing a shift. He then spent two months on crutches recuperating. No doubt, the Stanley Cup ring helped soothe his pain.

The Stanley Cup is about unlikely heroes, like Montreal goalie Ken Dryden being called up from the minors to backstop Montreal to a first-round upset over the heavily favored Boston Bruins in 1971, then going on to win the Conn Smythe Trophy, not to mention the Stanley Cup, both before winning the Calder Trophy as rookie-of-the-year the following season.

It's a showcase for the game's greatest stars, like Maurice (Rocket) Richard, who once scored five goals in a playoff game in 1944. Richard's record of six career playoff overtime goals has stood up for more than 40 years.

A fitting showcase

In the past decade, the first round of the playoff tournament has captivated hockey fans, providing some stunning upsets, like the expansion San Jose Sharks knocking out the Detroit Red Wings in seven games in 1994. The Sharks rolled right to the Western Conference semifinal, extending the Toronto Maple Leafs to seven games before losing.

In 1993, the New York Islanders surprised the Washington Capitals in the opening round, then stunned the two-time defending champion Pittsburgh Penguins in the division final, a series victory that helped pave the way for Montreal's surprising Stanley Cup triumph. The Canadiens had fallen behind 2-0 to the talent-rich Quebec Nordiques before winning four straight games to eliminate their provincial rivals from the tournament.

There are those who criticize the Stanley Cup playoffs as far too long, who suggest, not without justification, that hockey is simply not meant to be played in June, taxing the ice-making machinery, the fans' attention span and the players' fitness level.

Few would dare to suggest, however, that the two-month-long tournament is not a fitting showcase for professional hockey. Boring is something the Stanley Cup playoffs most certainly are not.

Lord Stanley never knew what he missed; nor had he any idea how rich a sporting tradition he initiated all those years ago.

Cup of Honor: Lanny McDonald (left), the Calgary Flames' bearded veteran, capped off a 16-year NHL career with a Stanley Cup triumph in 1989.

1993 Stanley Cup Finals

Overtime Powerplay

Goaltender Patrick Roy—St. Patrick to his Montreal fans—backstopped the Canadiens to ten straight overtime victories and a surprise Cup.

RESULTS

	Game	Site	Winner	Score	GWG
June 1	Game 1	Montreal	Los Angeles	4-1	Luc Robitaille
June 3	Game 2	Montreal	Montreal	3-2 (OT)	Eric Desjardins
June 5	Game 3	Los Angeles	Montreal	4-3 (OT)	John LeClair
June 7	Game 4	Los Angeles	Montreal	3-2 (OT)	John LeClair
June 9	Game 5	Montreal	Montreal	4-1	Kirk Muller

Captain Kirk: Montreal's surprise Stanley Cup in 1993 was due in significant part to the gritty play of Kirk Muller.

Patrick Roy's legend reached its zenith this year as his goaltending keyed ten straight overtime victories by Montreal en route to their 24th Stanley Cup victory. The Canadiens had upset favored Quebec, swept the Buffalo Sabres and beaten the New York Islanders to reach the final series.

Los Angeles, led by Wayne Gretzky, had advanced past the Calgary Flames, Vancouver Canucks and the Toronto Maple Leafs.

In Game 1 of the Stanley Cup final, Luc Robitaille's two goals powered the Kings to a 4-1 victory. In Los Angeles, this was supposed to be the year Gretzky led the Kings to a championship.

All was going well for them, Roy or no Roy, when catastrophe struck. Canadiens captain Guy Carbonneau had noticed that Kings defenseman Marty McSorley used a stick blade whose curvature exceeded the legal one inch limit.

With just 1:45 remaining in the third period and the Kings leading 2-1, referee Kerry Fraser measured the stick. As 18,000 fans and a vast TV audience watched, the blade was shown to be clearly over the limit. McSorley was banished to the penalty box for two minutes.

During the ensuing power play, Montreal defenseman Eric Desjardins beat Kings goalie Kelly Hrudey to tie the game, sending it into overtime.

Just 51 seconds later, Desjardins scored again, lifting Montreal to a 3-2 victory. The series was tied 1-1.

Confidence restored

It gave Montreal new life.

When the series moved to LA, the Canadiens twice extended the Kings to overtime.

Twice in a row, power forward John LeClair scored the gamewinner.

The Canadiens returned to the Forum leading the series 3-1. The demoralized Kings were frustrated by Roy, whose nearly flawless play infused his teammates with confidence.

In Game 5, McSorley, seeking to make amends for his stick gaffe, scored a rare goal to lift the Kings into a 1-1 tie. It wasn't enough.

Kirk Muller, with the Stanley Cup-winning goal, made it 2-1 before the second period was over and Stephan Lebeau padded Montreal's lead with a power-play goal at 11:31 of the period. Paul DiPietro's third-period goal was merely insurance.

The Canadiens clinched the Cup with an emphatic victory in which the Kings managed just 19 shots—only five in the final period— at Roy.

Roy won the Conn Smythe Trophy as the most valuable player in the playoffs, the second time he won the award.

1994 Stanley Cup Finals

We Won, We Won

The long-suffering Rangers silenced their many critics by winning their first Stanley Cup championship in fifty-four years.

The biggest game in New York's first Stanley Cup triumph in 54 years probably came not in the exciting, final against Vancouver, but in the seven-game semifinal against New Jersey.

It was before Game 6, with the Devils holding a 3-2 series lead, that Rangers captain Mark Messier guaranteed a New York victory to push the series to a seventh game. Then he backed up his prediction with three goals as the Rangers won 4-2 to send the series to a seventh game.

Team for a win

In the final, Vancouver grabbed a 1-0 lead, winning 3-2, but the Rangers methodically rolled to a 3-1 series lead.

Rangers' general manager Neil Smith had carefully constructed a championship team, blending talented draft selections like goalie Mike Richter, Brian Leetch, Alexei Kovalev and Sergei Nemchinov with veterans acquired through trades.

Messier was the centerpiece acquisition, but the cast of players included ex-Oilers like Glenn Anderson, Jeff Beukeboom, Adam Graves, Kevin Lowe, Craig MacTavish and Esa Tikkanen, and role players such as Stephane Matteau, Brian Noonan and Jay Wells.

The Vancouver Canucks, meanwhile, had built their team around Russian speedster Pavel Bure and Trevor Linden, their on-ice leader, who would have to go head-to-head with Messier.

An end to waiting

In Game 5, the Canucks spoiled the party at Madison Square Garden by stunning the Rangers 6-3 as Geoff Courtnall and Bure each scored twice. That meant both teams—and the Cup iself—had to make another trip to Vancouver, where the Canucks tied the series, by posting a 4-1 victory.

The final score in Game 7 was 3-2 for the Rangers, but New York was in command of the game, without question.

Leetch and Graves provided a 2-0 first-period lead, and after Linden's short-handed goal sliced the lead to one goal early in the second, Messier responded with a power-play score in the 14th minute that restored the New York lead to two goals.

Linden's power-play goal at 4:50 of the third period gave the Canucks renewed hope, but the Rangers were able to hold them off to bring the Cup back to their fans for the first time since 1940. The victory touched off days of celebrations and tributes to the Rangers.

Defenseman Leetch won the Conn Smythe Trophy, becoming the first American-born player to do so. He led all playoff scorers with 34 points, including 11 goals.

Broadway Championship: Head coach Mike Keenan piloted the Rangers to the Stanley Cup in 1994, 54 years after their previous championship in 1940.

RESULTS

	Game	Site	Winner	Score	GWG
May 31	Game 1	New York	Vancouver	3-2 (OT)	Greg Adams
June 2	Game 2	New York	NY Rangers	3-1	Glenn Anderson
June 4	Game 3	Vancouver	NY Rangers	5-1	Glenn Anderson
June 7	Game 4	Vancouver	NY Rangers	4-2	Alexei Kovalev
June 9	Game 5	New York	Vancouver	6-3	David Babych
June 11	Game 6	Vancouver	Vancouver	4-1	Geoff Courtnall
June 14	Game 7	NY Rangers	NY Rangers	3-2	Mark Messier

1995 Stanley Cup Finals

Devils' Trap

Once described as a "Mickey Mouse" franchise by Wayne Gretzky, the Devils received their due with a stunning upset over Detroit.

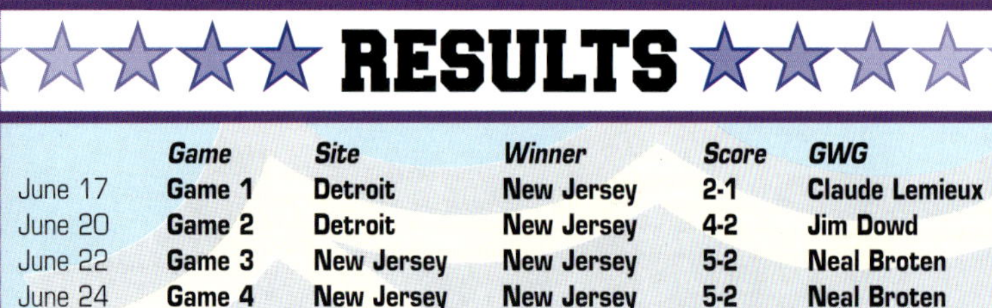

RESULTS

	Game	Site	Winner	Score	GWG
June 17	Game 1	Detroit	New Jersey	2-1	Claude Lemieux
June 20	Game 2	Detroit	New Jersey	4-2	Jim Dowd
June 22	Game 3	New Jersey	New Jersey	5-2	Neal Broten
June 24	Game 4	New Jersey	New Jersey	5-2	Neal Broten

The Cup Goes to the Devils: Claude Lemieux, who helped the Montreal Canadiens win a Stanley Cup in 1986, led the Devils' scorers as New Jersey won their first Stanley Cup.

The New Jersey Devils sprung a speed trap on Detroit in 1995 and stopped the flashy Red Wings dead in their tracks in a too-brief Stanley Cup final series. The trap—known as the neutral-zone trap and designed to choke off an opponent's attack in the neutral zone and create turnovers—couldn't have been a surprise to the Red Wings. New Jersey head coach Jacques Lemaire had the Devils using the delayed forechecking system throughout the lockout-shortened 1994-95 season.

The Devils had no easy route to the final. They had withstood the Philadelphia Flyers, who had dismissed the New York Rangers.

The Red Wings, the top team in the league during the 48-game regular season, had cruised to the final, losing just two games in three series along the way.

But the Devils rode the flawless goaltending of Martin Brodeur, the crashing, banging ensemble work of their forwards and the physical play of defensemen like Scott Stevens and Ken Daneyko to the Stanley Cup. And they made it look easy.

No chance

In three of the four series games, the Devils held the potent Red Wings—the likes of Fedorov, Yzerman, Kozlov and Sheppard—to fewer than 20 shots. The Wings managed just seven scores in the four games against New Jersey.

In Game 1, Claude Lemieux scored the gamewinner in the third period. It was his 12th goal of the playoffs and he would score 13 to lead all playoff snipers before the series was over.

In Game 2, the Devils broke open a 2-1 game with three straight third-period goals for a 2-0 lead.

In Game 3, the Devils raced to a 5-0 lead. Fedorov and Yzerman just managed to score power-play goals within the game's final three minutes.

Game 4 was similarly one-sided, as the Devils held the Red Wings to just 16 shots in winning 5-2 again to capture the first Stanley Cup in franchise history.

Red Wings head coach Scotty Bowman termed the defeat "humiliating."

Lemieux won the Conn Smythe Trophy for his steady playoff scoring, and longtime Devils veterans like John MacLean, Bruce Driver, and Ken Daneyko won their first Stanley Cup after years of struggling in mediocrity.

The Devils gained bragging rights in the all-important New York City media market. Long the forgotten franchise, third in the public imagination behind the Rangers and Islanders, it was the Devils' turn to bask in some Stanley Cup glory.

1996 Stanley Cup Finals

Avalanche on a Roll

Upstart third-year expansion team Florida Panthers were on a playoff roll to victory until Colorado Avalanche swept their hopes away.

The Colorado Avalanche and the Florida Panthers were surprise Stanley Cup finalists in the playoff year that will forever be known as the Year of the Rat. Fans at the Miami Arena brought a new ritual to Stanley Cup play—tossing toy plastic rats onto the ice after a Panthers goal. Rats rained down on the Boston Bruins, Philadelphia Flyers, and Pittsburgh Penguins as each was eliminated.

With nightly miracles by John Vanbiesbrouck in goal, a sound, aggressive defensive system, and total commitment to hard work, the Panthers got on an effective playoff roll—first-year head coach Doug MacLean had them believing they could defeat anyone.

But in the final they confronted a team with far more talent, size, speed, and skill than they could contain.

In Game 1, Tom Fitzgerald gave the Panthers a 1-0 first-period lead, but the Avalanche's superior firepower showed up in the second period. Scott Young, Mike Ricci and Uwe Krupp scored consecutive goals in a span of two minutes 49 seconds as momentum shifted irrevocably to Colorado.

Outgunned

The outmanned Panthers were swept aside in Game 2 as Colorado took a 2-0 series lead with a 8-1 win. Swedish forward Peter Forsberg was the scoring star with three goals.

Goaltender Patrick Roy was the key to Colorado's Game 3 victory, a 3-2 squeaker in Miami which saw the toy rats make their first series appearance. Avalanche winger Claude Lemieux, back from a two-game suspension, converted a pass from Valeri Kamensky at 2:44 of the opening period.

Then, at 9:14, Florida's Ray Sheppard prompted the first rat shower, scoring on the power play to tie the game, and Rob Niedermayer scored a 2-1 lead just over two minutes later.

But the Avalanche soon dominated, with Mike Keane scoring at 1:38 and Sakic beating Vanbiesbrouck for the gamewinner on a breakaway at 3:00. A brilliant Roy held off the Panthers until game's end.

Game 4 was a festival of saves by both Roy and Vanbiesbrouck—turning away 119 shots between them over 104 minutes and 31 seconds.

Colorado defenseman Uwe Krupp ended the third-longest game in Stanley Cup history when his slap shot from the right point at 4:31 of the third overtime period handed the Avalanche their first Stanley Cup—and the only rain of rats for the opposing team at the Miami Arena.

The rats symbolized a fairy tale Stanley Cup run for the Panthers. Colorado's performance was embodied by their team captain, Joe Sakic, who led all playoff scorers with 18 goals,16 assists and 34 points, to earn the Conn Smythe Trophy.

Rush for the Cup: Colorado's Valeri Kamensky couldn't solve Panthers' netminder John Vanbiesbrouck on this rush, but in the end it was Patrick Roy of the Avalanche who won the goalies' duel as the Avalanche swept Florida 4-0 to claim their first Stanley Cup.

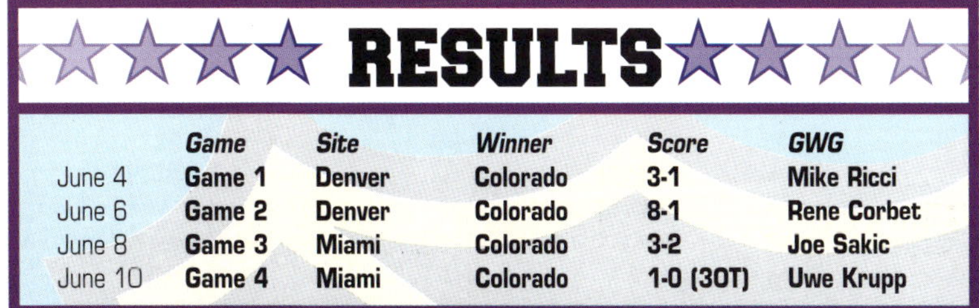

RESULTS

	Game	Site	Winner	Score	GWG
June 4	Game 1	Denver	Colorado	3-1	Mike Ricci
June 6	Game 2	Denver	Colorado	8-1	Rene Corbet
June 8	Game 3	Miami	Colorado	3-2	Joe Sakic
June 10	Game 4	Miami	Colorado	1-0 (3OT)	Uwe Krupp

1997 Stanley Cup Finals

Red Wings Soar

A dominating total team effort swept Detroit from 42 years of disappointment to a Stanley Cup victory for Hockeytown, USA.

Detroit put 42 years of Stanley Cup disappointment behind it in June 1997 by sweeping away the listless Philadelphia Flyers to win their first championship since 1955. In that bygone time, the heroes were the legendary Gordie Howe, Terry Sawchuk, (Terrible) Ted Lindsay and Sid Abel.

The 1997 champions were led by Steve Yzerman, their classy captain, goaltender Mike Vernon, who won the Conn Smythe Trophy as the most valuable player in the playoffs, and Sergei Fedorov.

It had been 42 years since the Red Wings and their fans shared a Stanley Cup moment, so the Joe Louis Arena faithful and their heroes savored the thrill of ultimate victory in grand style.

RESULTS

	Game	Site	Winner	Score	GWG
May 31	Game 1	Philadelphia	Detroit	4-2	Sergei Fedorov
June 3	Game 2	Philadelphia	Detroit	4-2	Kirk Maltby
June 5	Game 3	Detroit	Detroit	6-1	Sergei Fedorov
June 7	Game 4	Detroit	Detroit	2-1	Darren McCarty

But, just as the Red Wings had suffered an embarrassing collective collapse in 1995 when the New Jersey Devils swept them in four straight in the Stanley Cup final series, this time their dominance over the Flyers was a total team effort, as well.

As frequently happens in the Stanley Cup playoffs, unlikely heroes emerged and shone brightly for the Red Wings and their incomparable head coach, Scotty Bowman.

Rising to the occasion

In Game 1, the Red Wings grabbed a 2-0 lead on a pair of Flyers defensive lapses. On the first, checking line center Kris Draper stripped Flyers captain Eric Lindros of the puck and sped away on a two-on-nothing break with Kirk Maltby during a Flyers power play. The pair of speedy Wings exchanged passes before Maltby finished off the rush by lifting a shot over a spread-eagled Ron Hextall to give the Wings an early lead.

On the second goal Philadelphia defenseman Kjell Samuelsson made an ill-conceived pass that Joey Kocur intercepted just inside the Flyers' blue line. He then danced in, with Yzerman along as a decoy. Hextall guessed that the modestly talented Kocur would pass to the future Hall of Famer Yzerman. Instead, Kocur held the puck and flicked a shot high over Hextall, and it was 2-0.

Detroit's fourth goal of the game, scored on a routine shot from just inside the blue line by Steve Yzerman, had the biggest impact on the series, though. That goal apparently convinced Philadelphia head coach Terry Murray to switch to backup goalie Garth Snow for the second game of the series.

Snow didn't last long. He, too, was victimized on a pair of long-range shots as Detroit won Game 2.

Hextall was back in goal for Game 3, when Detroit's offensive gears meshed smoothly, and the Red Wings whacked the Flyers 6-1. The next day, Flyers coach Murray suggested his players were "choking" in an apparent attempt to motivate his over-matched team.

The Flyers, who held the lead in the series for just two minutes, certainly brought more intensity to Game 4 of the series, but to little avail.

The coup de grace was applied by unlikely scoring hero Darren McCarty, who scored the Cup-winning goal on a sublime rush on which he feinted magically past Flyers defenseman Janne Niinimaa, then swept the puck past a sliding Hextall on the backhand.

This prompted a dance of ecstasy by McCarty, a foreshadowing of a night-long party by the long-suffering Detroit fans.

Finally, the Stanley Cup had come back to stay, for a while at least, in the city that bills itself as Hockeytown, USA.

1998 Stanley Cup Finals

THE WONDER WINGS

The Detroit Red Wings repeated their Cup success of 1997 and confirmed their status as one of the teams of the decade.

This time, the wait between Stanley Cups was much shorter for the Detroit Red Wings. When the team won the Cup in 1997, they ended a 42-year drought. When the Red Wings won the Cup again in 1998, they became just the second team of the decade to win back-to-back championships, joining the 1991/1992 Pittsburgh Penguins as members of the exclusive club.

The Wings were a team of destiny. Any complacency that might have settled in after their first Cup victory was wiped away six days later when star defenseman Vladimir Konstantinov and team masseur Sergei Mnatsakanov were seriously injured in a limo accident.

The Wings dedicated the season to their comrades and duly swept the Washington Capitals in the Stanley Cup Finals. It was the fourth straight Finals to end in a sweep, with Detroit having started the trend by losing to the New Jersey Devils in four games in 1995.

Brilliant Bowman

Detroit's win gave coach Scotty Bowman eight Stanley Cup rings as a coach, which tied him for the most ever with his mentor and idol Toe Blake, the great Montreal Canadiens' bench boss. Bowman got his eighth Cup thanks to a complete team effort.

The Wings boasted throughout the playoffs that they could roll four lines at any team and that held true. Evidence came in Game 1, when Grind Line winger Joe Kocur started off the scoring with his fourth goal of the playoffs. Star defenseman Nick Lidstrom added a second goal in the first period and that would be all the scoring Detroit would need in the 2-1 win at home. Wings goalie Chris Osgood faced the pressure of stepping in for the 1997 Conn Smythe Trophy winner Mike Vernon, who moved on to San Jose after the Wings' 1997 triumph. Although he let in three long goals in the first three rounds of the playoffs, he started the Finals magnificently, making 16 saves.

In Game 2, the Capitals seemed to be in control of the game in the third period. Washington led 3-1 after two periods, but even when Steve Yzerman cut the gap to 3-2 on a short-handed goal, the Caps responded 28 seconds later to stretch the lead to 4-2. Washington forward Esa Tikkanen, seemed ready to ice the game when he faked Osgood and had an open net to shoot at late in the third with the Caps ahead 4-3. But he missed the shot, and the Wings' Doug Brown scored shortly thereafter and the game headed to overtime. In the extra session, Grind Line center Kris Draper became the hero with his first goal of the playoffs.

Game 3 was played on the anniversary of the limo crash, and Detroit came out flying, outshooting the Caps 13-1 in the first period. But they only managed one goal, and Washington stayed in the game thanks to outstanding goaltending by Olaf Kolzig.

RESULTS

	Game	Site	Winner	Score	GWG
June 9	Game 1	Detroit	Detroit	2-1	Nicklas Lidstrom
June 11	Game 2	Detroit	Detroit	5-4	Kris Draper
June 13	Game 3	Washington	Detroit	2-1	Sergei Fedorov
June 16	Game 4	Washington	Detroit	4-1	Martin Lapointe

Brian Bellows tied the game in the third, but Detroit's Sergei Fedorov made a spectacular one-on-one rush to net the game-winner with five minutes to play.

Game 4 seemed more a formality than anything. Detroit got the first two goals and never looked back. Doug Brown scored twice. Konstantinov was on hand, and he made his way down to the ice in his wheelchair for the postgame celebration. The first person Yzerman handed the Stanley Cup to was an easy choice – Konstantinov. Destiny had become reality.

Detroit Red Wings Captain Steve Yzerman drinks from the Stanley Cup of success as he celebrates a second straight Cup victory for his team, this time a four-game sweep of the Washington Capitals.

1999 Stanley Cup Finals

Dallas Reach the Stars

Controversy reigned as the Dallas Stars claimed their first Stanley Cup, thanks to a triple-overtime goal from Brett Hull, a 1998 free-agent signing

After four straight years of sweeps in the Stanley Cup Finals, everyone who loves NHL hockey was hoping for a tight series between the Dallas Stars and Buffalo Sabres. And that's exactly what the Stars and Sabres provided.

What no one wanted was controversy. Unfortunately, that's exactly what Dallas winger Brett Hull's left skate provided.

In triple-overtime of Game 6 in Buffalo, with Dallas leading the series three games to two, Hull whacked home his own rebound to give the Stars the win and their first-ever Stanley Cup championship. Replays, however, showed that Hull's left skate was in the crease prior to the puck on the winning score.

The Stars players streamed onto the ice to celebrate while Buffalo coach Lindy Ruff fumed. He felt he never got the review of the play his team deserved, and felt that had the play been reviewed, the goal would have been disallowed. But Bryan Lewis, NHL director of officiating, insisted during a heated news conference that the goal was reviewed. "Having looked at it, the determination by those of us upstairs in the goal judge's location, including myself, was in fact that Hull played the puck," he explained. "Hull had possession and control of the puck, the rebound off the goalie does not change anything. It is his puck then to shoot and score, albeit a foot may or may not be in the crease prior to it."

The Stars shine

That goal ended the second-longest game in Finals history (just 22 seconds shy of the record) and capped a brilliant season for Dallas. With their smothering defensive style, the Stars won their second straight Presidents' Trophy for compiling the most points during the regular season. They continued to apply the brakes in the Finals, holding Buffalo to a mere nine goals in six games. Ed Belfour, who many said couldn't win the big one, was brilliant throughout, outdueling his former Chicago Blackhawks backup Dominik Hasek, a two-time league MVP.

It was the lowest-scoring six-game Finals ever. It was also extremely tight. The two teams were within one goal of each other for all but six minutes of the 400-plus minutes of the series. Joe Nieuwendyk earned the Conn Smythe Award as playoff MVP by leading the league with 11 postseason goals, including both of Dallas' tallies in Game 3 of the Finals, which the Stars won 2-1. In that game, Dallas held Buffalo to a Finals-record-low 12 shots.

It was the third time in the 1990s a team from Dallas beat a Buffalo team in a major championship. The Dallas Cowboys scored two Super Bowl wins over the Buffalo Bills.

The big-name players kept making big plays for the Stars.

RESULTS

	Game	Site	Winner	Score	GWG
June 8	Game 1	Dallas	Buffalo	3-2 (OT)	Jason Woolley
June 10	Game 2	Dallas	Dallas	4-2	Brett Hull
June 12	Game 3	Buffalo	Dallas	2-1	Joe Nieuwendyk
June 15	Game 4	Buffalo	Buffalo	2-1	Dixon Ward
June 17	Game 5	Dallas	Dallas	2-0	Darryl Sydor
June 19	Game 6	Buffalo	Dallas	2-1 (3OT)	Brett Hull

Center Mike Modano assisted on all five of the Stars' goals in Games 4-6, despite an extremely painful wrist injury. Hull provided the final heroics, despite serious injuries of his own.

Said Dallas coach Ken Hitchcock after Game 6: "I think the story on Brett Hull when the dust settles is going to be an incredible story. He has a grade III full-blown (torn) MCL. He has a torn groin. He came back and played on one leg and no groins the last three shifts. He limped around the ice. The goal he scored, if you watch the shift, he limped into the corner, he limped in front of the net."

Sabre rattling: The area in front of Dominik Hasek's net is very crowded as the Stars go looking for a goal in Game 6. Brett Hull's controversial triple-overtime score gave Dallas the Cup.

2000 Stanley Cup Finals

Devils outshine Stars

New Jersey had been considered unfashionable Stanley Cup champions in 1995, but there was no doubt about their style in winning in 2000.

So much for the "Wizard of Oz" theory that there's no place like home. In the 2000 Stanley Cup Finals, the road was the place to be as the defending champion Dallas Stars and the 1995 Cup-winners New Jersey Devils combined to lose at home five times.

While the series went only six games, there was over seven games worth of hockey played. The two proud clubs made it a marathon in the final two contests. Down three games to on, the Stars be-Deviled New Jersey with a Mike Modano goal in the third overtime session. That was the first and only goal scored in more than 106 minutes of play.

Game 6 had a similar plot line. Dallas still faced elimination, and there was a lot of tight defense and many spectacular saves by the Stars' Ed Belfour and the Devils' Martin Brodeur. Patrik Elias threw a backhand pass into the slot and Jason Arnott buried the shot 8:20 into the second overtime, giving the Devils a 2–1 win and their second Stanley Cup.

Bone crusher

The Conn Smythe Trophy for playoff MVP usually goes to a prolific scorer or an impenetrable goaltender. In 2000, the award went to a punishing, physical player who set the tone for his team's style of play. Devils defenseman Scott Stevens passed out crunching bodycheck after crunching bodycheck throughout the playoffs. The captain even collected an assist on the Cup-winning goal.

It was the first Stanley Cup as a head coach for Larry Robinson – a six-time champion as a player – and it was unexpected. He started the season as Robbie Ftorek's assistant, and took over the division-leading but disgruntled Devils when Ftorek was let go with just eight games left in the season. Robinson guided New Jersey to an improbable comeback in the Eastern Conference finals, where it trailed Philadelphia three games to one.

The Finals started easy for New Jersey—a 7-3 to the Devils in Game 1—but it got very difficult after that. Game 2 was close throughout, and Brett Hull scored with less than five minutes to play to give Dallas a 2-1 victory. Game 3 went 2-1 in the Devils' favor, and game four was tight until New Jersey scored on three consecutive shots in the third period to win 3-1. Then it was on to the overtime classics.

The final game had to be stopped three times in the first period for injuries. Stars defenseman Darryl Sydor hurt his left ankle spinning away from a check and he did not return. Teammate Joe Nieuwendyk, the 1999 Conn Smythe winner, was dumped on a faceoff by Arnott and lay on the ice dazed for a few moments, though he did not miss a shift. Devils forward Petr Sykora was crunched by Derian Hatcher after skating the puck over the Dallas blue line. Sykora went to hospital for observation, but he was OK. Czech linemate Elias wore Sykora's jersey during postgame celebrations and the team planned to take the Cup to the hospital.

The two stars of the series were Belfour and Brodeur, who seemed impossible to beat. But Arnott got to live out the fantasy of the overtime goal to win the Cup.

"It feels great," said Arnott, who was extra thankful because his teammates killed off his cross checking penalty, the only power-play in the two overtimes. "It's a dream come true. Every player dreams about this. The last couple of years, we had something to prove."

RESULTS

	Game	Site	Winner	Score	GWG
May 30	Game 1	New Jersey	New Jersey	7-3	Scott Stevens
June 1	Game 2	New Jersey	Dallas	2-1	Brett Hull
June 3	Game 3	Dallas	New Jersey	2-1	Petr Sykora
June 5	Game 4	Dallas	New Jersey	3-1	John Madden
June 8	Game 5	New Jersey	Dallas	1-0 (3OT)	Mike Modano
June 10	Game 6	Dallas	New Jersey	2-1 (2OT)	Jason Arnott

Jason Arnott's (25) Stanley Cup-winning goal came 8.20 into the second overtime period of Game 6. The Finals showcased outstanding goaltending from New Jersey's Martin Brodeur and Dallas' Eddie Belfour.

Stanley Cup Results 1927-2000 (NHL assumed control of the Cup in 1927)

Year	W/L	Winner	Coach	Runner-up	Coach
2000	4-2	New Jersey	Larry Robinson	Dallas	Ken Hitchcock
1999	4-2	Dallas	Ken Hitchcock	Buffalo	Lindy Ruff
1998	4-0	Detroit	Scott Bowman	Washington	Ron Wilson
1997	4-0	Detroit	Scott Bowman	Philadelphia	Terry Murray
1996	4-0	Colorado	Marc Crawford	Florida	Doug MacLean
1995	4-0	New Jersey	Jacques Lemaire	Detroit	Scott Bowman
1994	4-3	NY Rangers	Mike Keenan	Vancouver	Pat Quinn
1993	4-1	Montreal	Jacques Demers	Los Angeles	Barry Melrose
1992	4-0	Pittsburgh	Scott Bowman	Chicago	Mike Keenan
1991	4-2	Pittsburgh	Bob Johnson	Minnesota	Bob Gainey
1990	4-1	Edmonton	John Muckler	Boston	Mike Milbury
1989	4-2	Calgary	Terry Crisp	Montreal	Pat Burns
1988	4-0	Edmonton	Glen Sather	Boston	Terry O'Reilly
1987	4-3	Edmonton	Glen Sather	Philadelphia	Mike Keenan
1986	4-1	Montreal	Jean Perron	Calgary	Bob Johnson
1985	4-1	Edmonton	Glen Sather	Philadelphia	Mike Keenan
1984	4-1	Edmonton	Glen Sather	NY Islanders	Al Arbour
1983	4-0	NY Islanders	Al Arbour	Edmonton	Glen Sather
1982	4-0	NY Islanders	Al Arbour	Vancouver	Roger Neilson
1981	4-1	NY Islanders	Al Arbour	Minnesota	Glen Sonmor
1980	4-2	NY Islanders	Al Arbour	Philadelphia	Pat Quinn
1979	4-1	Montreal	Scott Bowman	NY Rangers	Fred Shero
1978	4-2	Montreal	Scott Bowman	Boston	Don Cherry
1977	4-0	Montreal	Scott Bowman	Boston	Don Cherry
1976	4-0	Montreal	Scott Bowman	Philadelphia	Fred Shero
1975	4-2	Philadelphia	Fred Shero	Buffalo	Floyd Smith
1974	4-2	Philadelphia	Fred Shero	Boston	Bep Guidolin
1973	4-2	Montreal	Scott Bowman	Chicago	Billy Reay
1972	4-2	Boston	Tom Johnson	NY Rangers	Emile Francis
1971	4-3	Montreal	Al MacNeil	Chicago	Billy Reay
1970	4-0	Boston	Harry Sinden	St. Louis	Scott Bowman
1969	4-0	Montreal	Claude Ruel	St. Louis	Scott Bowman
1968	4-0	Montreal	Toe Blake	St. Louis	Scott Bowman
1967	4-2	Toronto	Punch Imlach	Montreal	Toe Blake
1966	4-2	Montreal	Toe Blake	Detroit	Sid Abel
1965	4-3	Montreal	Toe Blake	Chicago	Billy Reay
1964	4-3	Toronto	Punch Imlach	Detroit	Sid Abel
1963	4-1	Toronto	Punch Imlach	Detroit	Sid Abel
1962	4-2	Toronto	Punch Imlach	Chicago	Rudy Pilous
1961	4-2	Chicago	Rudy Pilous	Detroit	Sid Abel
1960	4-0	Montreal	Toe Blake	Toronto	Punch Imlach
1959	4-1	Montreal	Toe Blake	Toronto	Punch Imlach
1958	4-2	Montreal	Toe Blake	Boston	Milt Schmidt
1957	4-1	Montreal	Toe Blake	Boston	Milt Schmidt
1956	4-1	Montreal	Toe Blake	Detroit	Jimmy Skinner
1955	4-3	Detroit	Jimmy Skinner	Montreal	Dick Irvin
1954	4-3	Detroit	Tommy Ivan	Montreal	Dick Irvin
1953	4-1	Montreal	Dick Irvin	Boston	Lynn Patrick
1952	4-0	Detroit	Tommy Ivan	Montreal	Dick Irvin
1951	4-1	Toronto	Joe Primeau	Montreal	Dick Irvin
1950	4-3	Detroit	Tommy Ivan	NY Rangers	Lynn Patrick
1949	4-0	Toronto	Hap Day	Detroit	Tommy Ivan
1948	4-0	Toronto	Hap Day	Detroit	Tommy Ivan
1947	4-2	Toronto	Hap Day	Montreal	Dick Irvin
1946	4-1	Montreal	Dick Irvin	Boston	Dit Clapper
1945	4-3	Toronto	Hap Day	Detroit	Jack Adams
1944	4-0	Montreal	Dick Irvin	Chicago	Paul Thompson
1943	4-0	Detroit	Jack Adams	Boston	Art Ross
1942	4-3	Toronto	Hap Day	Detroit	Jack Adams
1941	4-0	Boston	Cooney Weiland	Detroit	Ebbie Goodfellow
1940	4-2	NY Rangers	Frank Boucher	Toronto	Dick Irvin
1939	4-1	Boston	Art Ross	Toronto	Dick Irvin
1938	3-1	Chicago	Bill Stewart	Toronto	Dick Irvin
1937	3-2	Detroit	Jack Adams	NY Rangers	Lester Patrick
1936	3-1	Detroit	Jack Adams	Toronto	Dick Irvin
1935	3-0	Mtl. Maroons	Tommy Gorman	Toronto	Dick Irvin
1934	3-1	Chicago	Tommy Gorman	Detroit	Herbie Lewis
1933	3-1	NY Rangers	Lester Patrick	Toronto	Dick Irvin
1932	3-0	Toronto	Dick Irvin	NY Rangers	Lester Patrick
1931	3-2	Montreal	Cecil Hart	Chicago	Dick Irvin
1930	2-0	Montreal	Cecil Hart	Boston	Art Ross
1929	2-0	Boston	Cy Denneny	NY Rangers	Lester Patrick
1928	3-2	NY Rangers	Lester Patrick	Mtl. Maroons	Eddie Gerard
1927	2-0-2	Ottawa	Dave Gill	Boston	Art Ross

THE ALL-STAR GAME

It's ironic that the NHL All-Star Game, sometimes labeled a non-contact version of hockey, came into being because of an unfortunate incident that ended a player's career. The first, unofficial All-Star game was a benefit for Ace Bailey, who had been gravely injured in a regular-season game between the Toronto Maple Leafs and the Boston Bruins on December 12, 1933.

Bruins' star Eddie Shore had been knocked down while carrying the puck up the ice. Enraged, he charged Bailey, who had not been the culprit, and upended him viciously. Bailey's head struck the ice, knocking him unconscious. Bailey never played again.

On February 14, 1934, the Maple Leafs played a team of NHL All-Stars at Maple Leaf Gardens in a benefit for Bailey. More than $23,000 Cdn. was raised for Bailey, but the format did not exactly capture the imagination of the league's governors.

Two more unofficial All-Star games were staged, both owing to personal tragedy. In November 1937, a game was organized after the death following complications from a broken leg of Montreal Canadiens star Howie Morenz.

And in 1939, a similar game was held to benefit the widow of Babe Siebert, who had drowned that summer.

It's official

The first official All-Star Game was held in 1947, with the reigning Stanley Cup champions, the Toronto Maple Leafs, playing an All-Star team. The Stars won 4-3, establishing the format that would remain for most of the next two decades.

The Dream Game notion was that the true test of just how good the Stanley Cup champions were was to pit the best players from around the league against them. There was one obvious flaw with this set-up. The All-Star team selections often were dominated, understandably, by members of the Stanley Cup champions.

In 1958-59, for example, the Montreal Canadiens placed four players on the first All-Star team and two on the second team. Inevitably, the All-Star team that faced the champions took the ice minus several of its best players.

The league experimented with a different format for two years in the early 1950s, pitting the first All-Star team against the Second Team, but otherwise did not deviate from the Stars against the Stanley Cup champions until 1969.

This was the first All-Star Game following the first major expansion in NHL history, a project that doubled the size of the league from six to 12 teams.

From 1969 through 1971, the All-Star Game pitted the stars from the so-called Original Six against the stars from the six expansion clubs. That period featured the first All-Star Game held in an expansion city when St. Louis played host to the game in 1970.

The established stars of the East won that game 4-1, but the expansion stars surprised the Original Six when they won the 1971 game in Boston 2-1.

In 1972, the first of a series of realignments shifted the established Chicago Blackhawks into the West Division, and further expansion would continue to alter the makeup of the division.

By 1975, the league had grown to 18 teams, organized into two nine-team conferences: the Prince of Wales Conference; and the Clarence Campbell Conference, named after the longtime president of the NHL.

The Wales did All-Star battle with the Campbells until 1994, when the NHL realigned its conferences and divisions geographically, replacing the Campbell with the Western Conference, and the Wales with the Eastern. The Central and Pacific Divisions comprise the Western Conference, while the Atlantic and Northeast Divisions make up the Eastern.

New trends

The league also had new uniforms designed, in teal and violet colors, and placed new emphasis on the skills competition, a fan-friendly feature the NHL had borrowed from a highly successful skills format used in the National Basketball Association.

The game itself remains an exhibition, a non-contact shootout which showcases plenty of offensive flash but involves little or no bodychecking and little commitment to defense. The goaltenders often have to perform at their best, and just as often they are buried in an avalanche of shots.

Injuries are rare in the All-Star Game, since no one is dishing out any bodychecks. Penalties are rare, too. The 1992 and 1994 games were penalty-free, while the 1993 game involved a single infraction, a minor penalty handed out to defenseman Dave Manson.

The marketing-savvy NHL front office sees the All-Star Game as a chance to market its stars and win new fans. Not content with resting on its laurels, the league altered the All-Star Game's format the past three seasons, eager to continue the growth of the game through reinvention and fresh ideas.

To add some sense of rivalry to the exhibition, the NHL has pitted a team of North American stars from Canada and the United States against a World team of players from the rest of the globe, replacing the previous Eastern Conference Vs Western Conference match-up.

The format has proved a success with fans and has provided the game with some added spice as the two sets of players compete for bragging rights. It was the North America All-Stars who won those rights in both 1998 and 1999 but in 2000 the World All-Stars exacted revenge in Toronto's Air Canada Centre.

The NHL, it seems, has got the rivalry it wanted.

All-Star Game Results 1947-2000

Year	Venue	Score	Coaches
2000	Toronto	World 9, North America 4	Scotty Bowman; Pat Quinn
1999	Tampa Bay	North America 8, World 6	Ken Hitchcock; Lindy Ruff
1998	Vancouver	North America 8, World 7	Scott Bowman; Ken Hitchcock
1997	San Jose	Eastern 11, Western 7	Doug MacLean; Marc Crawford
1996	Boston	Eastern 5, Western 4	Doug MacLean; Scott Bowman
1994	New York	Eastern 9, Western 8	Jacques Demers; Barry Melrose
1993	Montreal	Wales 16, Campbell 6	Scott Bowman; Mike Keenan
1992	Philadelphia	Campbell 10, Wales 6	Bob Gainey; Scott Bowman
1991	Chicago	Campbell 11, Wales 5	John Muckler; Mike Milbury
1990	Pittsburgh	Wales 12, Campbell 7	Pat Burns; Terry Crisp
1989	Edmonton	Campbell 9, Wales 5	Glen Sather; Terry O'Reilly
1988	St. Louis	Wales 6, Campbell 5(OT)	Mike Keenan; Glen Sather
1986	Hartford	Wales 4, Campbell 3(OT)	Mike Keenan; Glen Sather
1985	Calgary	Wales 6, Campbell 4	Al Arbour; Glen Sather
1984	New Jersey	Wales 7, Campbell 6	Al Arbour; Glen Sather
1983	NY Islanders	Campbell 9, Wales 3	Roger Neilson; Al Arbour
1982	Washington	Wales 4, Campbell 2	Al Arbour; Glen Sonmor
1981	Los Angeles	Campbell 4, Wales 1	Pat Quinn; Scott Bowman
1980	Detroit	Wales 6, Campbell 3	Scott Bowman; Al Arbour
1978	Buffalo	Wales 3, Campbell 2 (OT)	Scott Bowman; Fred Shero
1977	Vancouver	Wales 4, Campbell 3	Scott Bowman; Fred Shero
1976	Philadelphia	Wales 7, Campbell 5	Floyd Smith; Fred Shero
1975	Montreal	Wales 7, Campbell 1	Bep Guidolin; Fred Shero
1974	Chicago	West 6, East 4	Billy Reay; Scott Bowman
1973	New York	East 5, West 4	Tom Johnson; Billy Reay
1972	Minnesota	East 3, West 2	Al McNeill; Billy Reay
1971	Boston	West 2, East 1	Scott Bowman; Harry Sinden
1970	St. Louis	East 4, West 1	Claude Ruel; Scott Bowman
1969	Montreal	East 3, West 3	Toe Blake; Scott Bowman
1968	Toronto	Toronto 4, All-Stars 3	Punch Imlach; Toe Blake
1967	Montreal	Montreal 3, All-Stars 0	Toe Blake; Sid Abel
1965	Montreal	All-Stars 5, Montreal 2	Billy Reay; Toe Blake
1964	Toronto	All-Stars 3, Toronto 2	Sid Abel; Punch Imlach
1963	Toronto	All-Stars 3, Toronto3	Sid Abel; Punch Imlach
1962	Toronto	Toronto 4, All-Stars1	Punch Imlach; Rudy Pilous
1961	Chicago	All-Stars 3, Chicago 1	Sid Abel; Rudy Pilous
1960	Montreal	All-Stars 2, Montreal 1	Punch Imlach; Toe Blake
1959	Montreal	Montreal 6, All-Stars 1	Toe Blake; Punch Imlach
1958	Montreal	Montreal 6, All-Stars 3	Toe Blake; Milt Schmidt
1957	Montreal	All-Stars 5, Montreal 3	Milt Schmidt; Toe Blake
1956	Montreal	All-Stars 1, Montreal 1	Jim Skinner; Toe Blake
1955	Detroit	Detroit 3, All-Stars 1	Jim Skinner; Dick Irvin
1954	Detroit	All-Stars 2, Detroit 2	King Clancy; Jim Skinner
1953	Montreal	All-Stars 3, Montreal 1	Lynn Patrick; Dick Irvin
1952	Detroit	1st Team 1, 2nd Team 1	Tommy Ivan; Dick Irvin
1951	Toronto	1st Team 2, 2nd Team 2	Joe Primeau; Hap Day
1950	Detroit	Detroit 7, All-Stars 1	Tommy Ivan; Lynn Patrick
1949	Toronto	All-Stars 3, Toronto 1	Tommy Ivan; Hap Day
1948	Chicago	All-Stars 3, Toronto 1	Tommy Ivan; Hap Day
1947	Toronto	All-Stars 4, Toronto 3	Dirk Irvin; Hap Day

All-Star Hockey Mosts

Most Games Played
23 Gordie Howe, from 1948 through 1980.

Most Goals
13 Wayne Gretzky, in 17 appearances.

Most Points, One Game
6 Mario Lemieux, Wales, 1988 (3 goals, 3 assists)

Most Goals In One Game
4 Wayne Gretzky, Campbell, 1983
Mario Lemieux, Wales, 1990
Vincent Damphousse, Campbell, 1991
Mike Gartner, Wales, 1993

Most Goals, Both Teams, One Game
22 Wales 16, Campbell 6, 1993 at Montreal

1996 All-Star Game

FoxTraxing in Boston

Eastern 5 - Western 4

The 1995 All-Star Game was one of the casualties of the lockout-shortened 1994-95 season. The 1996 All-Star was held in Boston, but not at historic Boston Garden, which had officially closed before the season began.

Literally inches away from the funky, intimate Garden, the Bruins owners had built the FleetCenter, a state-of-the-art, 17,565-seat amphitheater.

The center of attention during the game, at least for fans watching on Fox, was a high-tech puck the network had designed to enhance viewers' ability to follow the disk in the heat of the action.

The FoxTrax puck, fashioned with infrared-emitting diodes, gave off a pale blue haze as it slid about the ice in its debut.

When a player teed up a shot at 120-kilometres-an-hour or faster, the puck became a red rocket as it zoomed netward, with a comet-like tail, describing its flight path for the viewers.

The puck was a public relations smash as the NHL and Fox generated plenty of media attention.

Hockey purists in Canada sniffed at the innovation, but Fox, attempting to boost interest in the sport across the United States, was encouraged by the fancy puck.

Local hero

The game, meanwhile, provided the perfect ending for Bruins fans, and gave them a chance to salute one of the game's greatest stars, Boston captain and wheelhorse defenseman Ray Bourque, who was playing in his 14th All-Star Game.

The early thunder in the game belonged to goaltender Martin Brodeur, who pitched a shutout in the first period, stopping 12 shots from the best of the West. The Buffalo Sabres goaltender, Dominik Hasek, faced 13 shots for the Eastern team in the third period, giving up just one goal.

It was a relatively low-scoring affair, as these things go, but the final one was a masterpiece.

That one came at 19:23 of the final period, when Bourque beat Toronto Maple Leafs goalie Felix Potvin to hand the victory to the Eastern team, take the MVP award and bask in the heat of an enormous ovation from the Boston fans.

Hometown Hero: Boston Bruins defenseman Ray

1997 All-Star Game

Knowing the Way in San Jose

Eastern 11 - Western 7

This was the All-Star game in which the local hero called his shot before firing in the final goal in his three-goal hat-trick and still couldn't win the All-Star game most valuable player award.

It was the All-Star game in which the guy who did win the MVP also scored a hat-trick but was booed by the understandably partisan crowd at the San Jose Arena, home of the Sharks.

"They booed me and they'll probably boo me next time I come here," said Montreal Canadiens winger Mark Recchi, whose three-goal performance helped the East All-Stars outscore the West. "I thought (the media) would give it to the home-town boy." That would have been Owen Nolan, the Sharks' power forward who also scored three goals, including one at 17:57 of the third period on Buffalo Sabres goaltender Dominik Hasek.

That one was special. Nolan pointed to an opening, then promptly threaded the needle with a shot that cleanly beat The Dominator. The goal didn't win the game for the West, but the spectacle brought the house down. The media members were apparently unmoved.

For openers, Nolan had scored his first two goals, which came late in the second period, just eight seconds apart—an All-Star Game record. No big deal, the media ruled, awarding the MVP to Recchi, the latest in a lengthy line of Montreal Canadiens snipers.

"There are a lot of great all-stars who have played for the Canadiens," Recchi said. "I'm told I remind some of (Hall of Famer) Yvan Cournoyer, which is quite an honor."

Due honors

The 47th All-Star game also was an occasion to pay homage to some of the greatest players ever to play in the NHL, including the Magnificent One, Mario Lemieux.

Out of respect for Lemieux, East coach Doug MacLean sent Lemieux out for the game's final shift along with Wayne Gretzky and Mark Messier, with Raymond Bourque and Paul Coffey on defense.

"That was impressive," West goaltender Andy Moog said, ignoring the fact that he was beaten for six goals in the second period. "As I watched them, I thought, Gretz has 18 years, Mark 17, Bourque 18, Coffey 18 and Mario about 13 or 14. It was a nice tribute to the elder statesmen."

As with most NHL All-Star games, this was another chance for the snipers to shine and goalies to cringe. Even Patrick Roy, who can lay a strong claim to being the best goalie in the business, was beaten for four goals on 15 shots. He handled the blitzkrieg with his customary aplomb.

"You accept the risk when you accept the invitation," Roy said. "I enjoy everything about this weekend—except the game."

But the 17,422 fans who jammed the Arena enjoyed the game just fine, thanks.

Eric Lindros and the Eastern Conference prevailed over the Western Conference in a goal-scoring spectacular in the 1997 NHL All-Star game.

1998 All-Star Game

New Look Proves a Winner

North America All-Stars 8 - World All-Stars 7

In honor of the NHL's international season, the league changed the format for the 1998 All-Star Game at Vancouver's GM Place. Rather than pit the usual Eastern Conference vs. Western Conference, the format was changed to allow a little nationalistic pride. Or, to be more accurate, continental pride.

It was the North American All-Stars vs. the World All-Stars. The World All-Stars was made up of the best players from Europe, while the North American squad featured a blend of talent from Canada and the United States. The World coach, Ken Hitchcock, added some flair when he put together national lines – the Russians, the Swedes, the Finns, the Czechs. The coach was fascinated by the way his players interacted with each other, like a mini United Nations.

Dynamic duo

But the combination that had everyone talking afterward was that of Wayne Gretzky and Mark Messier. The longtime buddies in Edmonton's glory years, who were reunited for one season with the Rangers in 1996–97, recaptured some of their old magic. Gretzky fed his old buddy for the winning goal in an 8–7 win for the North American team. Caught flatfooted on the play was another prominent figure from the Oilers' dynasty days – Jari Kurri, playing as a member of the Finland line on the World team. "People make so much of the fact that Mark and I are 37," said Gretzky, who with two assists became the career points leader in all-star competition. "But we really love to play. After Mark scored, you could see how excited we were on the ice."

"Gretzky still fools me," Kurri said, laughing. "I told him in the faceoff, 'I backcheck all those years for you (in Edmonton) and that's how you treat me? In my last all-star game? You made me look bad, awful bad.' "

The MVP of the game was Mighty Ducks of Anaheim star Teemu Selanne. He got a hat trick for the losing team, becoming the first European to record three goals in an All-Star Game. Selanne's two early goals along with one by Jaromir Jagr gave the World team a 3-0 lead just four minutes into the game, but the North American team rallied to tie the game at three by the first intermission. "I like the format," said Selanne, who won a truck as the game's MVP. "It was really nice to (play) with the other Europeans. Now North American players respect us more and more."

Slovakian Zigmund Palffy in action for the World All-Stars during their unique clash with the North American All-Stars.

Gretzky does it one last time

North America All-Stars 8 - World All-Stars 6

No one knew it at the time, but the 1999 All-Star Game in Tampa Bay was a swan song for the player many consider to be the greatest in NHL history. And Wayne Gretzky went out in style, winning his third All-Star Game MVP award in what proved to be his final NHL season before retiring.

The NHL kept with the successful 1998 All-Star Game format—pitting a North America team of Canadian and American stars against a World team composed of the top players from the rest of the globe. The North America squad won, 8-6, an almost identical score to its 8-7 triumph in 1998.

Gretzky recorded a goal and two assists for the winning side to claim the Dodge Durango given to the game's MVP. "It was a wonderful weekend," said The Great One after the game. North America jumped to a 4–1 lead in the first period on goals by Mike Modano, Luc Robitaille, Paul Kariya and Mark Recchi. Both teams scored three goals in the second period. The World team outscored the North American squad in the third period, 2–1, but it wasn't enough to overcome its big, early deficit.

No need for Hitchcock to go psycho

Nobody was more relieved with the North American victory than the team's coach, Ken Hitchcock, head man of the Dallas Stars. Heading into the game he was 0–11 as a coach in All-Star Games, including 0–2 in the NHL. Ending the streak was special, but the coach could resist praising the MVP after the game.

"It's not just his game. It's the professionalism that he exhibits," said Hitchcock of Gretzky. "Just little things—there were some special people who came in the dressing room and he made sure every player was there. He pulled guys out of the changing rooms to make sure that people like Vladimir Konstantinov (a former player seriously injured in a limo accident in 1997) and the young kids were greeted by everyone. He just loves the game."

Neither team was shy about shooting either, and once again the six All-Star goalies saw plenty of rubber. The successful North America team fired 49 shots, and the World team countered with 36.

Nobody knew it at the time, but MVP Wayne Gretzky was playing in his 18th and final All-Star Game before his retirement in April 1999.

2000 All-Star Game

Russians Rock in Toronto

World All-Stars 9 - North America All-Stars 4

It was World domination in the new millennium. Fans at Toronto's Air Canada Centre were treated to a close-fought game until it was blown open in the final period as the World team scored four unanswered goals.

The NHL changed the format for the All-Star Game in 1998 from Eastern Conference vs. Western Conference to North America (players from the United States and Canada) vs. the World (non-North American players). And in the first two years of the new alignment, the World team won the SuperSkills competition (fastest skater, puck control relay, hardest shot, etc.) on All-Star Game eve but lost the game itself.

Not so in the year 2000. Powered by Florida Panthers star and native Russian Pavel Bure, the World team not only won the SuperSkills for the third straight year, it also blew out the North America squad in the All-Star Game, 9-4. The score was no fluke either, as the World squad outshot the North Americans, 48-32.

Brothers in arms

Bure netted a hat trick and added an assist to take MVP honors in the 50th edition of the annual classic. And he wasn't the only Bure to figure prominently in the scoring. His younger brother Valeri, a Calgary Flames forward playing in his first All-Star Game, assisted on both of his big brother's second-period goals.

"It was great," said Pavel. "It couldn't get any better. When I heard Bure scored from Bure, that was unbelievable."

The World team also got a pair of goals from St. Louis Blues sniper Pavol Demitra, the second of which ignited a 4-0 third period which buried the North America squad. The North Americans had gained some life by scoring a pair of goals (Chicago's Tony Amonte and Florida's Ray Whitney) to close the second period, bringing the score from 5-2 to 5-4. But the North Americans couldn't carry that momentum into the third.

Just like the first All-Star Game in 1947, the 50th event took place in Toronto, but this time in the year-old Air Canada Centre rather than historic Maple Leaf Gardens. Wayne Gretzky, who grew up in nearby Brantford and retired after the 1999 season, got a huge ovation when he dropped the ceremonial opening face-off.

Pavel Bure, left, shone brightest in the 2000 NHL All-Star Game at Toronto, netting a hat-trick and providing an assist too.

The Hockey Hall of Fame

The building that houses the state-of-the-art Hockey Hall of Fame in Toronto is a former Bank of Montreal that was built in the previous century. It's appropriate that the National Hockey League showcases its rich history in a vintage 1885 building. After all, the first recorded advertisement for a hockey game comes from the same era, having been placed in the *Montreal Gazette* in 1875.

The game that came to be known as hockey had been played for decades across Canada by that time, in a variety of forms, with a variety of names. Its 'invention' was a product of rural isolation and the need for some activity to enliven the months-long winter.

Unlike baseball, though, hockey has no Abner Doubleday, no personage who can be said, however inaccurately, to have invented the game, no bucolic equivalent of Cooperstown to cherish as the cradle of the game.

Numerous hockey historians make cases for the game originating in, variously, Kingston, Ontario, or Montreal, or a certain rural pond in Nova Scotia. Which claim is the most legitimate? Flip a coin.

But if there is no one mythology surrounding the location of the Hockey Hall of Fame it doesn't seem to matter. The ultra-modern facility is fraught with lore, rich in tradition, bursting with memories.

Hall of Honor: The great rotunda in the imposing Hockey Hall of Fame in Toronto is a fitting setting for the array of plaques honoring all the greats of the NHL game.

Golden memories

The Hall fills 51,000 square feet of space at BCE Place in downtown Toronto, a modern skyscraper that incorporates the century-old former bank building into its sprawling complex.

The displays include a surprisingly life-like re-creation of the fabled Montreal Canadiens dressing room in the old Forum, a large collection of the many strikingly artistic protective masks worn by the league's goaltenders over the years, and interactive displays that enable visitors, for example, to try their hand at play-by-play description of some of the game's golden moments.

The centerpiece of the building, which opened on 18 June 1993, is the Great Hall, a magnificent dome-ceilinged room that proudly showcases the plaques honoring the members as well as the NHL's glittering family of trophies.

The most famous trophy in the collection, of course, is the Stanley Cup, donated by Lord Stanley in 1893, the oldest trophy continuously competed for by professional athletes in North America.

The plaques honor the Hall of Fame's 316 members: 216 players, 86 builders (coaches, general managers, owners) and 14 referees and linesmen.

There are also 62 members from the media—broadcasters and print reporters—whose work helped raise awareness about, and helped foster the mythology of the game.

Honor for a league

The Hall of Fame was first established in 1943, its early members first honored in 1945. But a permanent location to house the legacy of the game wasn't found until 26 August 1961, when the collection was set up in a building on the grounds of the Canadian National Exhibition on Toronto's lakeshore.

The current location updates the museum for the new millennium. Which is not surprising for the Hall of Fame of a league that has expanded five-fold since the Original Six era ended in 1967.

Fallen Eagleson

Alan Eagleson, once one of the most powerful men in pro hockey, became the first person to resign from the Hockey Hall of Fame. He did so in March 1998 under heavy pressure. There were strong indications that if he did not resign he would be removed from the Hall's roster after former hockey stars such as Bobby Orr, Brad Park and Ted Lindsay threatened to quit the Hall had Eagleson been allowed to stay.

Eagleson was elected to the builders' category of the Hall of Fame in 1989 for his role in the formation of the NHL Players' Association and international hockey tournaments like the 1972 Canada-Soviet Union 'Summit Series'. His misdeeds included stealing Canada Cup tournament rinkboard advertising money between 1984 and 1991. He was also found guilty of fraud involving player pensions, player career-ending disability insurance money and overcharging players as head of their union. "I do not wish the board of directors to be forced to consider a review of my status and membership in the Hall of Fame under the circumstances of threatened renunciation of membership by a number of players," the disgraced Eagleson wrote in his resignation letter.

Inspirational Leader: Bobby Clarke overcame limited natural ability and diabetes through sheer hard work and dedication to become the key player on the Philadelphia Flyers in the 1970s.

Jean Beliveau: center. A native of Victoriaville, Quebec, Beliveau became a star center with the Quebec Aces of the Quebec Senior League. Le Colisée in Quebec, where the Aces played their games, was nicknamed the House that Beliveau Built, but it wasn't his hockey home for long. In 1952, Beliveau joined the Montreal Canadiens, who held his pro rights. He remained with them for his entire 18-year NHL career, and led the Canadiens to ten Stanley Cup victories. He was the first winner of the Conn Smythe Trophy as the most valuable player in the playoffs and twice won the Hart Trophy. He retired after leading the Canadiens to the Stanley Cup in 1970-71, having played 1125 NHL games and scored 507 goals.

Hector (Toe) Blake: left winger, coach. Blake played 578 NHL games, scoring 235 goals and adding 292 assists. The left wing beside center Elmer Lach and right winger Maurice Richard on the legendary Punch Line, Blake was nicknamed the Old Lamplighter for his scoring prowess. Many regard him as the best coach in the history of the NHL. For 13 seasons he coached the Canadiens, who won eight Stanley Cups under his regime, including five straight from 1956-60. He retired after coaching his eighth Cup victory in 1968.

Mike Bossy: right winger. As a junior star, Bossy was considered a soft player, a one-dimensional scorer whose offensive skills would be muted in the NHL, whose defensive skills would be a liability. The Montreal Canadiens, among other teams, passed on Bossy in the Entry Draft and lived to regret it. Bossy became the best right winger in the NHL in the 1980s, scoring 573 goals in just 752 regular-season games. For nine straight years, he scored 50 or more goals. He was the sniper on the Trio Grande—a line with Bryan Trottier at center and Clark Gillies at left wing. Bossy added 85 goals in 129 playoff games as he helped the New York Islanders win four straight Stanley Cup championships from 1980-83. Chronic back trouble forced him into retirement in 1987.

Johnny Bower: goaltender. Scar-faced Bower didn't make it to the NHL for good until he was 34. He played 11 seasons for the Toronto Maple Leafs, helping them win four Stanley Cups, including the fabled upset in 1967 when an aging Toronto team beat the favored Montreal Canadiens. Bower and Terry Sawchuck shared the goaltending duties that season, as well as the Vezina Trophy as the best netminding duo in the league. He retired after the 1969-70 season, the only one in which he wore a protective mask.

Scotty Bowman: coach, general manager. He apprenticed in the Montreal Canadiens system under Sam Pollock before becoming the coach of the expansion St. Louis Blues, whom he led to three straight Stanley Cup finals. Repatriated to the Canadiens as head coach in 1971, Bowman led them to five Stanley Cup victories. He worked for the Sabres from 1979 to 1987 but didn't return to the Stanley Cup final until 1992, with the Penguins, replacing the late Bob Johnson as head coach. Now the head coach of the Detroit Red Wings, Bowman is the most successful coach in NHL history with well over 800 victories.

Clarence Campbell: NHL president, 1947-78. Campbell was a Rhodes Scholar and won the Order of the British Empire after working as a prosecutor with the Canadian War Crimes Commission in Germany. He is remembered mostly as the man who suspended Maurice (Rocket) Richard after he slugged linesman Cliff Thompson in March 1955. Campbell's presence at the Forum on March 16, 1955 touched off a riot by outraged Montreal fans. But Campbell withstood that storm. In 1968, when he oversaw the expansion of the NHL from six to 12 teams. When he retired in 1978, the league had grown to 18 teams.

Gerry Cheevers: goaltender. Starting goalie for the Boston Bruins in the Bobby Orr-Phil Esposito era. Known as a great money goaltender, Cheevers was at his best in the playoffs. He helped Boston win the Stanley Cup in 1970 and 1972.

Straight On: Al Arbour coached one of the best teams in the history of the NHL during the New York Islanders' run of four straight Stanley Cups in the 1980s.

Bobby Clarke: center, coach, general manager. In 1968-69, Clarke piled up 137 points with the Flin Flon Bombers of the Western Hockey League, but many teams were leery of his diabetic condition and he was taken 17th overall in the NHL entry draft. He proved the skeptics wrong, playing 15 NHL seasons for the Philadelphia Flyers, winning the Hart Trophy three times and leading the Flyers to two straight Stanley Cups in the early 1970s. He was the first player on a post-1967 expansion team to score 100 or more points in a season. His grit, determination and leadership were central to the Flyers becoming the first expansion club ever to win the Stanley Cup.

Yvan Cournoyer: right winger. Cournoyer's speed earned him the nickname 'The Roadrunner,' but he was anything but birdlike. His speed came from thickly muscled legs that teammate Ken Dryden once compared to "two enormous roasts spilling over his knees." When he joined the Montreal Canadiens in 1963-64, Cournoyer was used as a power-play specialist. He developed into one of the most explosive forwards in the game, scoring 428 goals in 16 seasons, and helping Montreal win ten Stanley Cups. He was the Canadiens captain for their four-straight Stanley Cup run in the 1970s.

Marcel Dionne: center. Dionne was chosen second overall behind Guy Lafleur in the 1970 entry draft and played most of his career in brilliant obscurity. After racking up 366 points in four seasons with Detroit, Dionne was traded to the Los Angeles Kings, where he quietly piled up points for years, centering the Triple Crown Line with wingers Charlie Simmer and Dave Taylor. He won a scoring championship with the Kings and ended his 18-year career with 731 goals and 1,040 assists, but no Stanley Cup victories.

Ken Dryden: goaltender. Dryden, 23-year-old law student and a 6-foot-4, 210-pound giant, backstopped the Montreal Canadiens to a surprise Stanley Cup victory in 1970-71 after playing just six regular-season games with the club. He was awarded the Conn Smythe Trophy as the most valuable player in the playoffs, and followed that up by winning the Calder Trophy (rookie-of-the-year) the next season. Dryden played eight seasons for the Canadiens, helping them win six Stanley Cups, while winning the Vezina Trophy five times. He retired after the 1978-79 season, after helping the Canadiens win a fourth straight Cup. On March 2, 1971, he made hockey history when he faced brother Dave Dryden of the Buffalo Sabres. The pair were the first goaltending brothers ever to face each other in goal.

Phil Esposito: center, coach, general manager. Esposito was a competent, but unremarkable center for the Chicago Blackhawks when he was traded, with Ken Hodge and Fred Stanfield, to the Boston Bruins in 1967 for Hubert (Pit) Martin, Jack Norris and Gilles Marotte. Esposito blossomed as a Bruin, becoming the first player to score more than 100 points in a season. He won five scoring titles in eight-and-a-half seasons in Boston, where he and Bobby Orr led the Bruins to two Stanley Cups. He won two Hart Trophies and scored 55 goals or more in five straight seasons. He played 18 seasons in all, scoring 717 goals and adding 873 assists. He retired in 1981, finishing his career as a New York Ranger.

The Roadrunner: Montreal Canadiens sniper Yvan Cournoyer used blazing speed to zoom past opponents and score big goals.

Bill Gadsby: defenseman. Gadsby played standout defense for Chicago, New York Rangers and the Detroit Red Wings for 20 seasons over three decades, stretching from 1946-47 to 1965-66. Gadsby was fortunate to have a career at all. When he was 12, he and his mother were returning from England when the ship they were traveling on was torpedoed and sunk. He was rescued after spending five hours in the frigid Atlantic. In 1952, he overcame a bout of polio so severe doctors told him he would never play again. He played—well enough to be named an All-Star seven times. Strangely, he never won a Stanley Cup.

Bernard (Boom-Boom) Geoffrion: left wing. Geoffrion earned his nickname by becoming the first to consistently use the slap shot as an offensive weapon in the 1950s. He won the Calder Trophy in 1952 and led the NHL in scoring in 1955. He was the second player, after teammate Maurice Richard, to score 50 goals in a season and helped Montreal win five Stanley Cups. He frequently played the point (defense) on the power play to take advantage of his booming shot. He also coached, briefly, for the New York Rangers, Atlanta Flames and Montreal Canadiens.

Wayne Gretzky: center. The man known as The Great One certainly lived up to his nickname. In a 20-year NHL career starting with the Edmonton Oilers in 1979 and ending with the New York Rangers in 1999, Gretzky dominated the game. He held or shared 61 league records at retirement and won four Stanley Cups (all with the Oilers). The blockbuster trade that sent him to the Los Angeles Kings in 1988 made hockey hip in Southern California. Since that trade, Sun Belt states like Texas, Florida, North Carolina and Arizona have become part of the NHL family. In a comprehensive poll by the *Hockey News*, Gretzky was named the game's greatest ever player.

Doug Harvey: defenseman. Many consider Harvey, who played 20 NHL seasons from 1947-48 to 1968-69, the best defenseman in the history of the game. He won the Norris Trophy as the league's best defenseman seven times and helped the Montreal Canadiens win six Stanley Cups. He was the point man on the great Montreal power-play unit that included Jean Beliveau, Maurice (Rocket) Richard, Dickie Moore and Bernard (Boom-Boom) Geoffrion. The power-play unit was so effective that the NHL altered its rules so that a penalized player could leave the penalty box before his two minutes was up if the opposing team scored a goal. It was said of Harvey that he was so skilled he could control the tempo of a game, speeding its pace or slowing it down to suit the situation.

Gordie Howe: right winger. Howe, a physically powerful, awesomely talented but shy and humble farm boy from Floral, Saskatchewan, fully earned the nickname Mr. Hockey. Howe played 26 seasons, 34 pro seasons in all, covering five decades from 1946-47 to 1979-80. He played 1767 NHL games, scored 801 goals, added 1049 assists. At one time, he held NHL records for most games played, most goals, assists, and points in both regular season and playoffs. He became the first NHLer over the age of 50 to score a goal and the first to play on a line with his sons, Mark and Marty.

GLENN HALL: goaltender. The man who became known as Mr. Goalie didn't earn the title for nothing. Hall played 18 seasons—ten with Chicago—and was named an All-Star 11 times. He led the NHL in shutouts for six seasons, played in 115 Stanley Cup playoff games and set a league record for most consecutive games by a goalie—502, stretching from 1955 to November 7, 1962. He finished his remarkable career sharing goaltending duties with fellow Hall of Famer Jacques Plante in St. Louis, where he backstopped the Blues to three straight Stanley Cup final appearances.

BOBBY HULL: left winger. Blond-haired and dimple-cheeked handsome and built like an Adonis, Hull also had blazing speed (29.7 mph top speed) and a frighteningly hard slap shot that once was clocked at 118.3 mph. Hull quickly became known as The Golden Jet in the NHL. He scored 610 goals in a 16-year NHL career during which he became the first player ever to record more than one 50-goal season (he had five). He won the Art Ross Trophy as the league's top scorer three times, the Lady Byng Trophy once, the Hart twice. He led the Blackhawks to the Stanley Cup in 1961, the first of his 50-goal seasons. He was the first big-name superstar to jump to the World Hockey Association when he signed a $1 million Cdn. contract with the Winnipeg Jets.

GEORGE (PUNCH) IMLACH: coach, general manager, Toronto Maple Leafs, Buffalo Sabres. Imlach was a bundle of superstitions and hockey acumen who piloted the Maple Leafs to four Stanley Cups in the 1960s. In 1970-71 he gave the expansion Buffalo Sabres instant credibility when he became their first coach and general manager. Imlach was instantly recognized by his trademark lucky fedoras. His superstition prevented him from changing suits when his team was on a winning streak.

GUY LAFLEUR: right winger. Lafleur, lightning-fast, creative and possessed of a wicked slap shot, was the NHL's dominant scorer of the 1970s. He was the first to score 50 goals or more in six consecutive seasons and six straight 100-point seasons. He also was the youngest player in history to score 400 goals and attain 1,000 points. He helped the Canadiens win five Stanley Cups, including four straight during his heyday from 1976-79.

Old World Flash: Swedish defenseman Borje Salming brought an elegant skating stride and a large basket of skills to the Toronto Maple Leafs in the early 1970s. He was the first true European superstar in the NHL.

MARIO LEMIEUX: center. Super Mario was one of the most gifted players the game has ever seen, but his magnificent playing career was cut short by chronic back problems and a battle with Hodgkin's disease (a form of cancer). When he retired in 1997, he earned the rare honor of having the three-year waiting period waived, so that he could immediately be inducted into the Hockey Hall of Fame. Lemieux was the first player taken in the 1984 draft, by the struggling Pittsburgh Penguins. He helped renew local interest in the Penguins with his stellar play, but it took a while for a talented team to be built around him. Led by Lemieux, Pittsburgh won back-to-back titles in 1991 and '92. A tall player who possessed uncanny skill for his size, Lemieux finished his career with six Art Ross Trophies as league scoring champ and a .823 goals-per-game average, best in NHL history.

FRANK MAHOVLICH: left winger. The man better known to hockey fans as The Big M possessed a booming slap shot and perhaps the smoothest, most powerful skating stride the game has ever seen. He scored 48 goals as a 23-year-old with Toronto in 1961 and helped the Maple Leafs win four Stanley Cups in the 1960s. Traded to Detroit in 1968, Mahovlich played on a line with Gordie Howe and Alex Delvecchio. Detroit traded him to Montreal in 1971 and The Big M set a playoff scoring record with 27 points and 14 goals to lead the Canadiens to the Stanley Cup. He also helped the Canadiens win the Cup in 1973.

LANNY MCDONALD: right winger. McDonald scored 500 goals and added 506 assists in his 16-year career with Toronto, Colorado and Calgary. McDonald teamed up with Sittler as a potent one-two punch with the Maple Leafs until club owner Harold Ballard traded him to Colorado, largely out of spite. McDonald concluded a distinguished career in style, scoring a goal in Calgary's Cup-winning game against the Montreal Canadiens in 1989, the only Cup victory of his career.

STAN MIKITA: center. Born in Czechoslovakia, Mikita entered the NHL as a feisty, clever centerman, but he underwent a transformation into a gentlemanly player winning the Art Ross, Hart and Lady Byng trophies in 1967 and 1968, the first player ever to win all three in a single season. He is credited with introducing the curved stick blade to the NHL, by accident, it turns out. An angry Mikita tried to snap his stick blade by closing the door to the team bench on it. The stick bent, but did not break, and Mikita discovered it enhanced his shooting immensely.

FRANK NIGHBOR: center, defenseman. They called Nighbor the Pembroke Peach and he is credited with perfecting the poke check. He played 13 seasons in the NHL, from 1917-18 to 1929-30. He won five Stanley Cups, one with the Vancouver Millionaires in 1915, four more with the Ottawa Senators. In 1923, he became the first winner of the Hart Trophy as the NHL's most valuable player. In 1925, he was the first recipient of the Lady Byng Trophy, awarded to the league's most sportsmanlike player.

BOBBY ORR: defenseman. Played junior hockey for the Oshawa Generals and joined the Boston Bruins, at age 18, in 1966-67. Orr, one of the fastest skaters in the NHL in his time, revolutionized the defense position. With his quick acceleration, excellent straightahead speed and lateral mobility, Orr played defense like a point guard in basketball. More often than not, it was Orr who led the Bruins' offensive attacks, dishing a pass off to a teammate, or going end to end to take a shot on goal. He scored 296 goals in his 13 NHL seasons and was the first defenseman to score more than 40 goals and record more than 100 points in a season. He was the first defenseman to win the Conn Smythe Trophy. He also won the Norris Trophy eight times, the Hart three times and twice won the league scoring championship. He led the Bruins to two Stanley Cups. His career was foreshortened by a series of knee injuries.

BRAD PARK: defenseman. Contemporary of Orr and Potvin. Park played 17 years in the NHL, never for a team that missed the playoffs; but never for a team that won the Stanley Cup. He was named a first-team All-Star five times and became the second defenseman in NHL history to record 500 assists—after Orr. He scored 213 goals and added 683 assists in his career, which, like Orr's, was plagued by knee injuries. Early in his career, Park revived the seemingly lost art of the open-ice body check. Often cast in the shadow of first Orr, then Denis Potvin, Park was a superb two-way defenseman.

GILBERT PERREAULT: center. Won two Memorial Cups while a member of the Montreal Junior Canadiens. Perreault was the first draft pick of the Buffalo Sabres, for whom he played his entire 17-year career. Perreault centered the dangerous French Connection line with wingers Rene Robert and Richard Martin, amassing 1,336 points (512 goals) in his brilliant career. A virtuoso performer, Perreault was a strong, fast, slightly bow-legged skater, whose head and shoulder fakes and quicksilver stickhandling mystified opponents. The Sabres built a credible NHL franchise in Buffalo around Perreault, who retired after the 1987-88 season.

JACQUES PLANTE: goaltender. Plante redefined his position. He was the first to roam away from the goal crease to handle loose pucks in the corners and along the end boards. After he suffered a nasty facial cut in a game in 1959, Plante donned a protective mask of his own design and, over the protests of his coach, Toe Blake, wore one from then on. Plante played 19 years in the NHL, with Montreal, New York, Toronto, St. Louis and Boston, but his years in Montreal were his finest. He won seven Vezina Trophies, six Stanley Cups and one Hart Trophy during his career.

DENIS POTVIN: defenseman. After a brilliant five-year junior career with the Ottawa 67s that Potvin began as a 14-year-old, the defenseman joined the New York Islanders as their indisputable franchise player. He led the Islanders to four straight Stanley Cups in the early 1980s. Potvin, a rugged, highly skilled player, chafed at comparisons with Orr. When his 15-year career was over, Potvin had recorded more goals (310), assists (742) and points (1,052) than any defenseman in NHL history.

Big Bird: Larry Robinson was one of the famous Big Three defenseman in Montreal, with Guy Lapointe and Serge Savard in the 1970s.

MAURICE RICHARD: right winger. The Rocket, as he was known, was a passionate presence on the ice who often saved his most brilliant performances for the most dramatic of circumstances. Among the 82 playoff goals he scored, 18 were game-winners, six of those in sudden-death overtime. He was the first player to score 50 goals in 50 games in a single season and the first to score 500 in his career. He scored 544 goals during his career, won eight Stanley Cups and won the Hart Trophy. Ironically, the man many consider the league's best-ever pure scorer, never won the Art Ross Trophy as the NHL's leading scorer.

TERRY SAWCHUK: goaltender. Many consider Sawchuk to be the best goalie who ever played in the NHL. He posted an NHL-record 103 shutouts during his 21-year career, which saw him play for Detroit, Toronto, Boston, Los Angeles and New York Rangers. In 1952, Sawchuk carried the Red Wings to a Stanley Cup, posting four shutouts in Detroit's eight straight victories, and allowing just five goals overall. Sawchuk won the Vezina Trophy three times, including one award he shared with Johnny Bower for Toronto in 1967.

DARRYL SITTLER: center. Sittler was the heart and soul of some exciting Toronto Maple Leafs teams in the 1970s. He is remembered, as much as anything, for one brilliant night when he scored six goals and added four assists in an 11-4 Maple Leafs victory over the Boston Bruins in 1976. The same year, he scored five goals in a playoff game against the Flyers. He was the first member of the Maple Leafs to score 100 points in a season. He finished his career with 484 goals.

VLADISLAV TRETIAK: goaltender. In a perfect world, Tretiak, the brilliant goaltender for the Soviet Red Army and Soviet national teams, might have played for the Montreal Canadiens, who held his NHL rights. As a 20-year-old, Tretiak established himself as an excellent goaltender in the eight-game Canada-Soviet Summit Series in 1972. Viktor Tikhonov, the legendary Soviet coach, pulled Tretiak after the first period in the famous Miracle on Ice loss to the U.S. team at the Winter Olympics in 1980 in Lake Placid. Tikhonov would admit later this was his biggest regret as a coach.

Hockey Hall of Fame Membership Roster

(Players Only)

Sid Abel: center, Detroit Red Wings (1938-43 and 1945-52), Chicago Blackhawks (1952-54). Inducted 1969.

Jack Adams: forward, Toronto Arenas (1917-19), Toronto St. Pats (1922-26), Ottawa Senators (1926-27). Inducted 1959.

Syl Apps: center, Toronto Maple Leafs (1936-43 and 1945-48). Inducted 1961.

George Armstrong: center, Toronto Maple Leafs (1949-71). Inducted 1975.

Irvine (Ace) Bailey: forward, Toronto Maple Leafs (1926-34). Inducted 1975.

Dan Bain: forward, Winnipeg Victorias (1895-1902). Inducted 1945.

Hobey Baker: forward, Princeton University (1910-1914). Inducted 1945.

Bill Barber: forward, Philadelphia Flyers (1972-84). Inducted 1990.

Marty Barry: forward, NY Americans (1927-28), Boston Bruins (1929-35), Detroit Red Wings (1935-39), Montreal Canadiens (1939-40). Inducted 1965.

Andy Bathgate: right winger, NY Rangers (1952-64), Toronto Maple Leafs (1964-65), Detroit Red Wings (1965-67), Pittsburgh Penguins (1967-68 and 1970-71). Inducted 1978.

Bobby Bauer: right winger, Boston Bruins (1936-42, 1945-47 and 1951-52). Inducted 1996.

Jean Beliveau: center, Montreal Canadiens (1950-51 and 1952-71). Inducted 1972.

Clint Benedict: goaltender, Ottawa Senators (1912-24), Montreal Maroons (1924-30). Inducted 1965.

Doug Bentley: forward, Chicago Blackhawks (1939-44 and 1945-52), NY Rangers (1953-54). Inducted 1964.

Max Bentley: forward, Chicago Blackhawks (1940-43 and 1945-47), Toronto Maple Leafs (1947-53), NY Rangers (1953-54). Inducted 1966.

Hector (Toe) Blake: left winger, Montreal Maroons (1934-35), Montreal Canadiens (1935-48). Inducted 1966.

Leo Boivin: defenseman, Toronto Maple Leafs (1951-54), Boston Bruins (1954-66), Detroit Red Wings (1966-67), Pittsburgh Penguins (1967-69), Minnesota North Stars (1969-70). Inducted 1986.

Dickie Boon: defenseman, Montreal AAAs (1899-03), Montreal Wanderers (1904-06). Inducted 1952.

Mike Bossy: right winger, New York Islanders (1977-87). Inducted 1991.

Emile (Butch) Bouchard: defenseman, Montreal Canadiens (1941-1956). Inducted 1966.

Frank Boucher: forward, Ottawa Senators (1921-22), NY Rangers (1926-38 and 1943-44). Inducted 1958.

George Boucher: defenseman, Ottawa Senators (1915-1929), Montreal Maroons (1928-31), Chicago Blackhawks (1931-32). Inducted 1960.

Johnny Bower: goaltender, NY Rangers (1953-55 and 1956-57), Toronto Maple Leafs (1958-70). Inducted 1976.

Russell (Dubbie) Bowie: forward, Montreal Victorias (1898-1908). Inducted 1945.

Frank Brimsek: goaltender, Boston Bruins (1938-43 and 1945-49), Chicago Blackhawks (1949-50). Inducted 1966.

Harry (Punch) Broadbent: forward, Ottawa Senators (1912-15 and 1918-24 and 1927-28), Montreal Maroons (1924-27), NY Americans (1928-29). Inducted 1962.

Walter (Turk) Broda: goaltender, Toronto Maple Leafs (1936-43 and 1945-52). Inducted 1967.

John Bucyk: left winger, Detroit Red Wings (1955-57), Boston Bruins (1957-78). Inducted 1981.

Billy Burch: forward, Hamilton Tigers (1922-25), NY Americans (1925-32), Boston Bruins (1932-33), Chicago Blackhawks (1933). Inducted 1974.

Harry Cameron: defenseman, Toronto Blue Shirts (1912-16), Toronto 228th Battalion (1916-17), Montreal Wanderers (1917), Toronto Arenas (1917-19), Ottawa Senators (1919), Toronto St. Pats (1919-20 and 1921-23), Montreal Canadiens (1920). Inducted 1962.

Gerry Cheevers: goaltender, Toronto Maple Leafs (1961-62), Boston Bruins (1965-72 and 1975-80). Inducted 1985.

Francis (King) Clancy: defenseman, Ottawa Senators (1921-30), Toronto Maple Leafs (1930-37). Inducted 1958.

Aubrey (Dit) Clapper: right winger/defenseman, Boston Bruins (1927-47). Inducted 1947.

Bobby Clarke: center, Philadelphia Flyers (1969-84). Inducted 1987.

Sprague Cleghorn: defenseman, Montreal Wanderers (1911-17), Ottawa Senators (1918-21), Toronto St. Pats (1921), Montreal Canadiens (1921-25), Boston Bruins (1925-28). Inducted 1958.

Neil Colville: center/defenseman, NY Rangers (1935-42 and 1944-49). Inducted 1967.

Charlie Conacher: forward, Toronto Maple Leafs (1929-38), Detroit Red Wings (1938-39), NY Americans (1939-41). Inducted 1961.

Lionel Conacher: defenseman, Pittsburgh Pirates (1925-38), NY Americans (1926-30), Montreal Maroons (1930-33 and 1934-37,) Chicago Black Hawks (1933-34). Inducted 1994.

Roy Conacher: left winger, Boston Bruins (1938-42 and 1945-46), Detroit Red Wings (1946-47), Chicago Black Hawks (1947-52). Inducted 1998.

Alex Connell: goaltender, Ottawa Senators (1924-31 and 1932-33), Detroit Falcons (1931-32), NY Americans (1933-34), Montreal Maroons (1934-35 and 1936-37). Inducted 1958.

Bill Cook: forward, NY Rangers (1926-37). Inducted 1952.

Fred (Bun) Cook: forward, NY Rangers (1926-36), Boston Bruins (1936-37). Inducted 1995.

Art Coulter: defenseman, Chicago Blackhawks (1931-36), NY Rangers (1936-42). Inducted 1974.

Yvan Cournoyer: right winger, Montreal Canadiens (1963-79). Inducted 1982.

Bill Cowley: forward, St. Louis Eagles (1934-35), Boston Bruins (1935-47). Inducted 1968.

Rusty Crawford: forward, Quebec Bulldogs (1912-17), Ottawa Senators (1917-18), Toronto Arenas (1918-19). Inducted 1962.

Jack Darragh: forward, Ottawa Senators (1910-1924). Inducted 1962.

Allan (Scotty) Davidson: forward, Toronto Blueshirts (1912-14). Inducted 1950.

Clarence (Hap) Day: defenseman, Toronto St. Pats (1924-26), Toronto Maple Leafs (1926-37), NY Americans (1937-38). Inducted 1961.

Alex Delvecchio: center, Detroit Red Wings (1950-74). Inducted 1977.

Cy Denneny: forward, Toronto Shamrocks (1914-15), Toronto Blueshirts (1915-16), Ottawa Senators (1916-28), Boston Bruins (1928-29). Inducted 1959.

Marcel Dionne: center, Detroit Red Wings (1971-75), LA Kings (1975-87), NY Rangers (1987-89). Inducted 1992.

Gordie Drillon: forward, Toronto Maple Leafs (1936-42), Montreal Canadiens (1942-43). Inducted 1975.

Graham Drinkwater: forward, Montreal AAAs (1892-93), Montreal Victorias (1894-99). Inducted 1950.

Ken Dryden: goaltender, Montreal Canadiens (1970-73 and 1974-79). Inducted 1983.

Woody Dumart: forward, Boston Bruins (1935-42 and 1945-54). Inducted 1992.

Tommy Dunderdale: forward, Winnipeg Victorias (1906-08), Toronto Shamrocks (1909-10), Quebec Bulldogs (1910-11), Victoria Aristocrats 1911-15 and 1918-23), Portland Rosebuds (1915-18), Saskatoon/Edmonton (1923-24). Inducted 1974.

Bill Durnan: goaltender, Montreal Canadiens (1943-50). Inducted 1964.

Mervyn (Red) Dutton: defenseman, Montreal Maroons (1926-30), NY Americans (1930-36). Inducted 1958.

Cecil (Babe) Dye: forward, Toronto St. Pats (1919-26), Hamilton Tigers (1920), Chicago Blackhawks (1926-28), NY Americans (1928-29), Toronto Maple Leafs (1930-31). Inducted 1970.

Phil Esposito: center, Chicago Blackhawks (1963-67), Boston Bruins (1967-75), NY Rangers (1975-81). Inducted 1984.

Tony Esposito: goaltender, Montreal Canadiens (1968-69), Chicago Blackhawks (1969-84). Inducted 1988.

Arthur Farrell: forward, Montreal Shamrocks (1896-1901). Inducted 1965.

Fernie Flaman: defenseman, Boston Bruins (1944-50 and 1954-61), Toronto Maple Leafs (1950-54). Inducted 1990.

Frank Foyston: forward, Toronto Blueshirts (1912-15), Seattle Metros (1915-24), Victoria Aristocrats (1924-26), Detroit Cougars (1926-28). Inducted 1958.

Frank Fredrickson: forward, Victoria Aristocrats (1920-26), Boston Bruins (1926-29), Detroit Falcons (1926-27 and 1930-31), Pittsburgh Pirates (1928-30). Inducted 1958.

Bill Gadsby: defenseman, Chicago Blackhawks (1946-54), NY Rangers (1954-61), Detroit Red Wings (1961-66). Inducted 1970.

Bob Gainey: left winger, Montreal Canadiens (1973-89). Inducted 1992.

Chuck Gardiner: goaltender, Chicago Blackhawks (1927-34). Inducted 1945.

Herb Gardiner: defenseman, Montreal Canadiens (1926-29), Chicago Blackhawks (1928-29). Inducted 1958.

Jimmy Gardner: forward, Montreal AAAs (1900-03), Montreal Wanderers (1903-11), New Westminster Royals (1911-13), Montreal Canadiens (1913-15). Inducted 1962.

Bernard (Boom Boom) Geoffrion: right winger, Montreal Canadiens (1951-64), NY Rangers (1966-68). Inducted 1972.

Eddie Gerard: leftwinger/defenseman, Ottawa Victorias (1907-08), Ottawa Senators (1913-23). Inducted 1945.

Eddie Giacomin: goaltender, NY Rangers (1965-75), Detroit Red Wings (1975-78). Inducted 1987.

Rod Gilbert: forward, NY Rangers (1960-78). Inducted 1982.

Billy Gilmour: forward, Ottawa Senators (1902-06 and 1908-09 and 1915-16), Montreal Victorias (1907-08). Inducted 1962.

Frank (Moose) Goheen: defenseman, St. Paul Athletic Club (1914-28). Inducted 1952.

Ebbie Goodfellow: center/defenseman, Detroit Cougars (1929-30), Detroit Falcons (1930-32), Detroit Red Wings (1932-43). Inducted 1963.

Wayne Gretzky: center, Edmonton Oilers (1979-88), LA Kings (1988-96), St. Louis Blues (1996), NY Rangers (1996-99). Inducted 1999.

Michel Goulet: left winger, Quebec Nordiques (1979-90). Chicago Blackhawks (1990-94). Inducted 1998.

Mike Grant: defenseman, Montreal Victorias (1893-1902). Inducted 1950.

Wilf (Shorty) Green: forward, Hamilton Tigers (1923-25), NY Americans (1925-27). Inducted 1962.

Si Griffis: forward/defenseman, Rat Portage Thistles (1902-06), Kenora Thistles (1906-07), Vancouver Millionaires (1911-19). Inducted 1950.

George Hainsworth: goaltender, Montreal Canadiens (1926-33 and 1936-37), Toronto Maple Leafs (1933-36). Inducted 1961.

Glenn Hall: goaltender, Detroit Red Wings (1952-53 and 1954-57), Chicago Blackhawks (1957-67), St. Louis Blues (1967-71). Inducted 1975.

Joe Hall: defenseman, Quebec Bulldogs (1910-17), Montreal Canadiens (1917-19). Inducted 1961.

Doug Harvey: defenseman, Montreal Canadiens (1947-61), NY Rangers (1961-64), Detroit Red Wings (1966-67), St. Louis Blues (1967-69). Inducted 1973.

George Hay: forward, Chicago Blackhawks (1926-27), Detroit Cougars (1927-30), Detroit Falcons (1930-31), Detroit Red Wings (1932-34). Inducted 1958.

Riley Hern: goaltender, Montreal Wanderers (1906-11). Inducted 1962.

Bryan Hextall: forward, NY Rangers (1936-44 and 1945-48). Inducted 1969.

Harry (Hap) Holmes: goaltender, Toronto Blue Shirts (1912-16), Seattle Metros (1915-17 and 1918-24), Toronto Arenas (1917-19), Victoria Aristocrats (1924-26), Detroit Cougars (1926-28). Inducted 1972.

Tom Hooper: forward, Rat Portage Thistles (1901-05), Kenora Thistles (1906-07), Montreal Wanderers (1907-08), Montreal AAAs (1907-08). Inducted 1962.

G. Reginald (Red) Horner: defenseman, Toronto Maple Leafs (1928-40). Inducted 1965.

Tim Horton: defenseman, Toronto Maple Leafs, 1949-70), NY Rangers (1970-71), Pittsburgh Penguins (1971-72), Buffalo Sabres (1972-74). Inducted 1977.

Gordie Howe: right winger, Detroit Red Wings (1946-71), Houston Aeros (1973-77), New England Whalers (1977-79), Hartford Whalers (1979-80). Inducted 1972.

Syd Howe: forward, Ottawa Senators (1929-30 and 1932-34), Philadelphia Quakers (1930-31), Toronto Maple Leafs (1931-32), St. Louis Eagles (1934-35), Detroit Red Wings (1935-46). Inducted 1965.

Harry Howell: defenseman, NY Rangers (1952-69), Oakland Seals (1969-71), LA Kings (1971-73). Inducted 1979.

Robert Marvin (Bobby) Hull: left winger, Chicago Blackhawks (1957-72), Winnipeg Jets (1972-80), Hartford Whalers (1980). Inducted 1983.

Bouse Hutton: goaltender, Ottawa Senators (1898-1904). Inducted 1962.

Harry Hyland: forward, Montreal Shamrocks (1908-09), Montreal Wanderers (1909-11 and 1912-18), New Westminster Royals (1911-12), Ottawa Senators (1918). Inducted 1962.

Dick Irvin: forward, Portland Rosebuds (1916-17), Regina Capitals (1921-25), Portland Capitals (1925-26), Chicago Blackhawks (1926-29). Inducted 1958.

Harvey (Busher) Jackson: forward, Toronto Maple Leafs (1929-39), NY Americans (1939-41), Boston Bruins (1941-44). Inducted 1971.

Ernie Johnson: forward, Montreal Victorias (1903-05), Montreal Wanderers (1905-11), New Westminster Royals (1911-14), Portland Rosebuds (1914-18), Victoria Aristocrats (1918-22). Inducted 1952.

Ivan Wilfrid (Ching) Johnson: defenseman, NY Rangers (1926-37), NY Americans (1937-38). Inducted 1958.

Tom Johnson: defenseman, Montreal Canadiens (1947-48 and 1949-63), Boston Bruins (1963-65). Inducted 1970.

Aurel Joliat: forward, Montreal Canadiens (1922-38). Inducted 1947.

Gordon (Duke) Keats: forward, Toronto Blueshirts (1915-17), Edmonton Eskimos (1921-26), Boston Bruins (1926-27), Detroit Cougars (1927) Chicago Black Hawks (1927-29). Inducted 1958.

Leonard (Red) Kelly: defenseman, center, Detroit Red Wings (1947-60), Toronto Maple Leafs (1960-67). Inducted 1969.

Ted (Teeder) Kennedy: forward, Toronto Maple Leafs (1942-55 and 1956-57). Inducted 1966.

Dave Keon: center, Toronto Maple Leafs (1960-75), Hartford Whalers (1979-82). Inducted 1986.

Elmer Lach: center, Montreal Canadiens (1940-54). Inducted 1966.

Guy Lafleur: right winger, Montreal Canadiens (1971-85), NY Rangers (1988-89), Quebec Nordiques (1989-91). Inducted 1988.

Edouard (Newsy) Lalonde: forward, Montreal Canadiens (1909-11 and 1912-22), NY Americans (1926-27). Inducted 1950.

Jacques Laperriere: defenseman, Montreal Canadiens (1962-74). Inducted 1987.

Edgar Laprade: center, NY Rangers (1945-55). Inducted 1993.

Guy Lapointe: defenseman, Montreal Canadiens (1968-82), St. Louis Blues (1982-83), Boston Bruins (1983-84). Inducted 1993.

Jack Laviolette: defenseman/right winger, Montreal Nationals (1903-04), Michigan Soo Indians (1904-07), Montreal Shamrocks (1907-09), Montreal Canadiens (1909-18). Inducted 1962.

Hugh Lehman: goaltender, New Westminster Royals (1911-14), Vancouver Millionaires (1914-26), Chicago Blackhawks (1926-28). Inducted 1958.

Jacques Lemaire: left winger, center, Montreal Canadiens (1967-79). Inducted 1984.

Mario Lemieux: center, Pittsburgh Penguins (1984-94, 1995-97). Inducted 1997.

Percy LeSueur: goaltender, Ottawa Senators (1905-14), Toronto Shamrocks (1914-15), Toronto Blueshirts (1915-16). Inducted 1961.

Herbie Lewis: forward, Detroit Cougars (1928-30), Detroit Falcons (1930-33), Detroit Red Wings (1933-39). Inducted 1989.

Ted Lindsay: left winger, Detroit Red Wings (1944-57 and 1964-65), Chicago Blackhawks (1957-60). Inducted 1966.

Harry Lumley: goaltender, Detroit Red Wings (1943-50), Chicago Blackhawks (1950-52), Toronto Maple Leafs (1952-56), Boston Bruins (1957-60). Inducted 1980.

Mickey MacKay: forward, Vancouver Millionaires (1914-19 and 1920-24), Vancouver Maroons (1924-26), Chicago Blackhawks (1926-28), Pittsburgh Pirates (1928), Boston Bruins (1928-30). Inducted 1952.

Frank Mahovlich: left winger, Toronto Maple Leafs (1956-68), Detroit Red Wings (1968-71), Montreal Canadiens (1971-74). Inducted 1981.

Joe (Phantom) Malone: forward, Quebec Bulldogs (1908-09, 1910-17 and 1919-20), Waterloo (1909-10), Montreal Canadiens (1917-19, 1920-21 and 1922-24), Hamilton Tigers (1921-22). Inducted 1950.

Sylvio Mantha: defenseman, Montreal Canadiens (1923-36), Boston Bruins (1936-37). Inducted 1960.

Jack Marshall: forward, Winnipeg Victorias (1900-01), Montreal Victorias (1901-03), Montreal Wanderers (1903-05 and 1906-07 and 1909-12 and 1915-17), Montreal Montagnards (1905-06), Montreal Shamrocks (1907-09), Toronto Tecumsehs (1912-13), Toronto Ontarios (1913-14), Toronto Shamrocks (1914-15). Inducted 1965.

Fred Maxwell: forward, Winnipeg Monarchs (1914-16), Winnipeg Falcons (1918-25). Inducted 1962.

Lanny McDonald: right winger, Toronto Maple Leafs (1973-79), Colorado Rockies (1979-81), Calgary Flames (1981-89). Inducted 1992.

Frank McGee: forward, Ottawa Senators (1902-06). Inducted 1945.

Billy McGimsie: forward, Rat Portage Thistles (1902-03 and 1904-06), Kenora Thistles (1906-07). Inducted 1962.

George McNamara: defenseman, Montreal Shamrocks (1907-09), Halifax Crescents (1909-12), Waterloo (1911), Toronto Tecumsehs (1912-13), Ottawa (1913-14), Toronto Shamrocks (1914-15), Toronto Blueshirts (1915-16), 228th Battalion (1916-17). Inducted 1958.

Stan Mikita: center, Chicago Blackhawks (1958-80). Inducted 1983.

Richard (Dickie) Moore: left winger, Montreal Canadiens (1951-63), Toronto Maple Leafs (1964-65), St. Louis Blues (1967-68). Inducted 1974.

Paddy Moran: goaltender, Quebec Bulldogs (1901-09 and 1910-17), Halleybury Comets (1909-10). Inducted 1958.

Howie Morenz: forward, Montreal Canadiens (1923-34 and 1936-37), Chicago Blackhawks (1934-36), NY Rangers (1936). Inducted 1945.

Bill Mosienko: forward, Chicago Blackhawks (1941-55). Inducted 1965.

Frank Nighbor: center, Ottawa Senators (1915-30), Toronto Maple Leafs (1930). Inducted 1947.

Reginald Noble: forward/defenseman, Toronto Arenas (1917-19), Toronto St. Patricks (1919-24), Montreal Maroons (1924-27), Detroit Cougars (1927-30), Detroit Falcons (1930-32), Montreal Maroons (1932-33). Inducted 1962.

Buddy O'Connor: forward, Montreal Canadiens (1941-47), NY Rangers (1947-51). Inducted 1988.

Harry Oliver: forward, Boston Bruins (1926-34), NY Americans (1934-37). Inducted 1967.

Bert Olmstead: left winger, Chicago Blackhawks (1948-50), Montreal Canadiens (1950-58), Toronto Maple Leafs (1958-62). Inducted 1985.

Robert (Bobby) Orr: defenseman, Boston Bruins (1966-76), Chicago Blackhawks (1976-79). Inducted 1979.

Bernard Parent: goaltender, Boston Bruins (1965-67), Philadelphia Flyers (1967-71 and 1973-79), Toronto Maple Leafs (1970-72). Inducted 1984.

Brad Park: defenseman, NY Rangers (1968-75), Boston Bruins (1975-83), Detroit Red Wings (1983-85). Inducted 1988.

Joseph Lynn Patrick: forward, NY Rangers (1934-43 and 1945-46). Inducted 1980.

Lester Patrick: defenseman, Brandon (1903-04), Westmount (1904-05), Montreal Wanderers (1905-07), Edmonton (1907-08), Renfrew Creamery Kings (1909-10), Victoria Aristocrats (1911-16 and 1918-22), Spokane (1916-17), Seattle Metros (1917-18), Victoria Cougars (1925-26), NY Rangers (1926-27). Inducted 1947.

Gilbert Perreault: center, Buffalo Sabres (1970-87). Inducted 1990.

Tom Phillips: forward, Montreal AAAs (1902-03), Toronto Marlboroughs (1903-04), Rat Portage Thistles (1904-06), Kenora Thistles (1906-07), Ottawa Senators (1907-08), Vancouver Millionaires (1911-12). Inducted 1945.

Pierre Pilote: defenseman, Chicago Blackhawks (1955-68), Toronto Maple Leafs (1968-69). Inducted 1975.

Didier Pitre: forward/defenseman, Montreal Nationals (1903-05), Montreal Shamrocks (1907-08), Renfrew Creamery Kings (1908-09), Montreal Canadiens (1909-13 and 1914-23), Vancouver Millionaires (1913-14). Inducted 1962.

Jacques Plante: goaltender, Montreal Canadiens (1952-63), NY Rangers (1963-65), St. Louis Blues (1968-70), Toronto Maple Leafs (1970-73), Boston Bruins (1972-73). Inducted 1978.

Denis Potvin: defenseman, NY Islanders (1973-88). Inducted 1991.

Walter (Babe) Pratt: defenseman, NY Rangers (1935-42), Toronto Maple Leafs (1942-46), Boston Bruins (1946-47). Inducted 1966.

Joe Primeau: center, Toronto Maple Leafs (1927-36). Inducted 1963.

Marcel Pronovost: defenseman, Detroit Red Wings (1949-65), Toronto Maple Leafs (1965-70). Inducted 1978.

Bob Pulford: forward, Toronto Maple Leafs (1956-70), LA Kings (1970-72). Inducted 1991.

Harvey Pulford: defenseman, Ottawa Senators (1893-1908). Inducted 1945.

Bill Quackenbush: defenseman, Detroit Red Wings (1942-49), Boston Bruins (1949-56). Inducted 1976.

Frank Rankin: forward, Stratford (1906-09), Eaton's Athletic Association (1910-12), St. Michaels' (1912-14). Inducted 1961.

Jean Ratelle: center, NY Rangers (1960-75), Boston Bruins (1975-81). Inducted 1985.

Chuck Rayner: goaltender, NY Americans (1940-41), Brooklyn Americans (1941-42), NY Rangers (1945-53). Inducted 1973.

Kenneth Joseph Reardon: defenseman, Montreal Canadiens (1940-42 and 1945-50). Inducted 1966.

Henri Richard: center, Montreal Canadiens (1955-75). Inducted 1979.

Maurice (Rocket) Richard: right winger, Montreal Canadiens (1942-60). Inducted 1961.

George Richardson: forward, 14th Regiment (1906-13), Queens University (1908-09). Inducted 1950.

Gordon Roberts: forward, Ottawa Senators (1909-10), Montreal Wanderers (1910-16), Vancouver Millionaires (1916-17 and 1919-20), Seattle Metropolitans (1917-18). Inducted 1971.

Larry Robinson: defenseman, Montreal Canadiens (1972-89), Los Angeles Kings (1989-92). Inducted 1995.

Art Ross: defenseman, Westmount (1904-05), Brandon (1906-07), Kenora Thistles (1906-07), Montreal Wanderers (1907-09 and 1910-14 and 1916-18), Halleybury Comets (1909-10), Ottawa Senators (1914-16). Inducted 1945.

Blair Russel: forward, Montreal Victorias (1899-1908). Inducted 1965.

Ernie Russell: forward, Montreal AAAs (1904-05), Montreal Wanderers (1905-08 and 1909-14). Inducted 1965.

Jack Ruttan: defenseman, Armstrong's Point (1905-06), Rustler (1906-07), St. Johns College (1907-08), Manitoba Varsity (1909-12), Winnipeg (1912-13). Inducted 1962.

Borje Salming: defenseman, Toronto Maple Leafs (1973-89), Detroit Red Wings, (1989-90). Inducted 1996.

Serge Savard: defenseman, Montreal Canadiens (1966-81), Winnipeg Jets (1981-83). Inducted 1986.

Terry Sawchuk: goaltender, Detroit Red Wings (1949-55 and 1957-64 and 1968-69), Boston Bruins (1955-57), Toronto Maple Leafs (1964-67), LA Kings (1967-68), NY Rangers (1969-70). Inducted 1971.

Fred Scanlan: forward, Montreal Shamrocks (1897-1901), Winnipeg Victorias (1901-03). Inducted 1965.

Milt Schmidt: center, Boston Bruins (1936-42 and 1945-55). Inducted 1961.

Sweeney Schriner: forward, NY Americans (1934-39), Toronto Maple Leafs (1939-43 and 1944-46). Inducted 1962.

Earl Seibert: defenseman, NY Rangers (1931-36), Chicago Blackhawks (1936-45), Detroit Red Wings (1945-46). Inducted 1963.

Oliver Seibert: forward, Berlin Rangers (1900-06). Inducted 1961.

Eddie Shore: defenseman, Boston Bruins (1926-40). Inducted 1947.

Steve Shutt: left winger, Montreal Canadiens (1972-1984), LA Kings (1984-85). Inducted 1993.

Albert Charles (Babe) Siebert: left winger/defenseman, Montreal Maroons (1925-32), NY Rangers (1932-33), Boston Bruins (1933-36), Montreal Canadiens (1936-39). Inducted 1964.

Joe Simpson: defenseman, Edmonton Eskimos (1921-25), NY Americans (1925-31). Inducted 1962.

Darryl Sittler: center, Toronto Maple Leafs (1970-82), Philadelphia Flyers (1982-84), Detroit Red Wings (1984-85). Inducted 1989.

Alf Smith: forward, Ottawa Senators, 1894-97 and 1903-08), Kenora Thistles (1906-07). Inducted 1962.

Billy Smith: goaltender: LA Kings (1971-72), NY Islanders (1972-89). Inducted 1993.

Clint Smith: forward, NY Rangers (1936-43), Chicago Blackhawks (1943-47). Inducted 1991.

Reginald (Hooley) Smith: forward, Ottawa Senators (1924-27), Montreal Maroons (1927-36), Boston Bruins (1936-37), NY Americans (1937-41). Inducted 1972.

Tommy Smith: forward, Ottawa Victorias (1905-06), Ottawa Senators (1906), Brantford Indians (1908-10), Cobalt Silver Kings (1909-10), Galt (1910-11), Moncton (1911-12), Quebec Bulldogs (1912-16 and 1919-20), Ontarios (1914-15), Montreal Canadiens (1916-17). Inducted 1973.

Allan Stanley: defenseman, NY Rangers (1948-54), Chicago Blackhawks (1954-56), Toronto Maple Leafs (1958-68), Philadelphia Flyers (1968-69). Inducted 1981.

Barney Stanley: forward, Vancouver Millionaires (1914-19), Calgary Tigers (1921-22), Regina Capitals (1922-24), Edmonton Eskimos (1924-26). Inducted 1962.

Peter Stastny: center, Quebec Nordiques (1980-90), New Jersey Devils (1990-93), St. Louis Blues (1994-95). Inducted 1998.

Jack Stewart: defenseman, Detroit Red Wings (1938-43 and 1945-50), Chicago Blackhawks (1950-52). Inducted 1964.

Nelson Stewart: forward, Montreal Maroons (1925-32), Boston Bruins (1932-35 and 1936), NY Americans (1935-40). Inducted 1962.

Bruce Stuart: forward, Ottawa Senators (1898-1900, 1901-02 and 1908-11), Quebec Bulldogs (1900-01), Montreal Wanderers (1907-08). Inducted 1961.

William Hodgson (Hod) Stuart: defenseman, Ottawa Senators (1898-1900), Quebec Bulldogs (1900-02), Montreal Wanderers (1906-07). Inducted 1945.

Frederic (Cyclone) Taylor: forward/defenseman, Ottawa Senators (1907-09), Renfrew Cream Kings (1909-11), Vancouver Millionaires (1912-21 and 1922-23). Inducted 1947.

Cecil R. (Tiny) Thompson: goaltender, Boston Bruins (1928-38), Detroit Red Wings (1938-40). Inducted 1959.

Vladislav Tretiak: goaltender, Central Red Army (1969-84), Soviet National Team (1969-84). Inducted 1989.

Harry Trihey: forward, Montreal Shamrocks (1896-1901). Inducted 1950.

Bryan Trottier: center, New York Islanders (1979-90), Pittsburgh Penguins (1990-92 and 1993-94). Inducted 1997.

Norm Ullman: center, Detroit Red Wings (1955-68), Toronto Maple Leafs (1968-75), Edmonton Oilers (1975-77). Inducted 1982.

Georges Vezina: goaltender, Montreal Canadiens (1910-26). Inducted 1945.

Jack Walker: forward, Toronto Blueshirts (1912-15), Seattle Metros (1915-24), Victoria Cougars (1924-26), Detroit Cougars (1926-28). Inducted 1960.

Marty Walsh: forward, Ottawa Senators (1907-12). Inducted 1962.

Harry (Moose) Watson: left winger, St. Andrews (1915), Aura Lee Juniors (1918), Toronto Dentals (1919), Toronto Granites (1920-25), Toronto Sea Fleas (1931). Inducted 1962.

Harry (Whipper) Watson: left winger, Brooklyn Americans (1941-42), Detroit Red Wings (1942-46), Toronto Maple Leafs (1946-54), Chicago Blackhawks (1954-57). Inducted 1994.

Ralph (Cooney) Weiland: forward, Boston Bruins (1928-32 and 1935-39), Ottawa Senators (1932-33), Detroit Red Wings (1933-35). Inducted 1971.

Harry Westwick: forward, Ottawa Senators (1894-98 and 1900-08), Kenora Thistles (1906-07). Inducted 1962.

Fred Whitcroft: forward, Kenora Thistles (1906-08), Edmonton (1908-10), Renfrew Cream Kings (1909-10). Inducted 1962.

Gordon Allan (Phat) Wilson: defenseman, Port Arthur War Veterans (1918-20), Iroquois Falls Eskimos (1921), Port Arthur Bearcats (1923-33). Inducted 1962.

Lorne (Gump) Worsley: goaltender, NY Rangers (1952-63), Montreal Canadiens (1963-70), Minnesota North Stars (1970-74). Inducted 1980.

Roy Worters: goaltender, Pittsburgh Pirates (1925-28), NY Americans (1928-37), Montreal Canadiens (1930). Inducted 1969.

Glossary of Hockey Terms

Art Ross Trophy: Awarded to the player who wins the scoring championship during the regular season.
Assist: A pass that leads to a goal being scored. One or two, or none, may be awarded on any goal.
Backchecking: Skating with an opponent through the neutral and defensive zones to try to break up an attack.
Backhand: A pass or shot, in which the player cradles the puck on the off- or backside of the stick blade and propels it with a shoveling motion..
Back pass: A pass left or slid backwards for a trailing teammate to recover.
Blocker: A protective glove worn on the hand a goaltender uses to hold his stick so that the goalie can deflect pucks away from the net.
Blue lines: The lines, located 29 feet from each side of the center red line, which demarcate the beginning of the offensive zone.
Boarding: Riding or driving an opponent into the boards. A two- or five-minute penalty may be assessed, at the referee's discretion.
Boards: Wooden structures, 48 inches high, topped by plexiglass fencing, that enclose the 200 feet by 85 feet ice surface.
Bodycheck: Using the hips or shoulders to stop the progress of the puck carrier.
Breakaway: The puck carrier skating toward the opposition's net ahead of all the other players.
Butt-Ending: Striking an opponent with the top end of the hockey stick, a dangerously illegal act that brings a five-minute penalty.
Calder Memorial Trophy: Awarded to the goaltender, defenseman or forward judged to be the best first-year, or rookie, player.
Central Scouting Bureau: An NHL agency that compiles statistical and evaluative information on all players eligible for the Entry Draft. The information, which includes a rating system of all players, is distributed to all NHL teams.
Charging: Skating three strides or more and crashing into an opponent. Calls for a two-minute or five-minute penalty at the referee's discretion.
Conn Smythe Trophy: Awarded to the top performer throughout the Stanley Cup playoffs.
Crease: A six-foot semicircular area at the mouth of the goal that opponents may not enter. Only the goaltender may freeze the puck in this space.
Crossbar: A red, horizontal pipe, four feet above the ice and six feet long across the top of the goal cage.
Crosschecking: Hitting an opponent with both hands on the stick and no part of the stick on the ice. Warrants a two-minute penalty.
Defensemen: The two players who form the second line of defense, after the goalie. Defensemen try to strip opponents of the puck in their own zone and either pass to teammates or skate the puck up-ice themselves to start an attack. When retreating from the opponent's zone, defensemen move back toward their zone by skating backwards, facing the oncoming opponents.
Deflection: Placing the blade of the stick in the path of a shot on goal, causing the puck to change direction and deceive the goaltender. A puck may also deflect off a player's skate or pads.
Delay of game: Causing the play to stop by either propelling the puck outside the playing surface or covering it with the hand. Warrants a two-minute penalty.
Delayed penalty: An infraction, signaled by the referee's upraised right hand, but not whistled until the offending team regains possession of the puck. During the delay, the other team can launch a scoring attack, sometimes by replacing their goaltender with a skater. If the team scores during the delay, the penalized player does not sit out his penalty.
Elbowing: Striking an opponent with the elbow. Calls for a two-minute penalty.
Entry Draft: An annual event, at which all 26 NHL teams submit claims on young players who have not signed professional contracts. The talent pool consists of players from the Canadian junior leagues, U.S. high schools and universities and European elite and junior leagues.
Faceoff: A play that initiates all action in a hockey game, in which the referee or a linesman drops the puck onto a spot between the poised stick blades of two opponents. Marks the start of every period, also occurs after every goal and every play stoppage.
Fighting: Players dropping their gloves and striking each other with their fists. Calls for a five-minute penalty and ejection for the player who instigated the fisticuffs.
Forechecking: Harassing opponents in their own zone to try to gain possession of the puck.
Forwards: Three players—the center and the left and right wingers—comprise a hockey team's forward line. The forwards are primarily attackers whose aim is to score goals.
Frank J. Selke Trophy: Awarded to the player judged the best defensive forward in the NHL.
Goal: A goal is scored when the puck completely crosses the red goal line and enters the net.
Goals-Against-Average (GAG): Average number of goals a goaltender surrenders per game. Determined by multiplying the total number of goals allowed by 60 and dividing that figure by the total number of minutes played.
Goaltender: A heavily padded player who protects his team's goal.
Hart Memorial Trophy: Awarded to the player judged the most valuable to his team during the NHL regular season.
Hat Trick: One player scoring three goals in one game. A player who scores three consecutive goals in one period is said to have scored a 'natural' hat trick.
High sticking: Carrying the stick above the shoulder level. Calls for a faceoff if a player strikes the puck in this fashion. Calls for a two- or five-minute penalty if a player strikes an opponent with his stick.
Holding: Using the hands to impede the progress of an opponent. Two-minute penalty.
Hooking: Using the blade of the stick to impede an opponent. Two-minute penalty.
Icing the puck: Shooting the puck from one side of the center red line so that it crosses the opponent's red goal line. Calls for a play stoppage and a faceoff in the offending team's zone.
Interference: Using the body or stick to impede an opponent who is not in possession of the puck or was the last one to touch it. Two-minute penalty.
James Norris Memorial Trophy: Awarded annually to the player who is judged to be the best defenseman in the NHL.
Kneeing: Using the knee to check an opponent. Two-minute penalty.
Lady Byng Trophy: Awarded to the player who best combines playing excellence with sportsmanship.
Linesmen: Two on-ice officials responsible for calling offside, icing and some infractions, such as too many men on the ice. Linesmen drop the puck for faceoffs excluding those after a goal has been scored.
Neutral zone: The area of the ice surface between the two blue lines and bisected by the center red line.
Neutral-zone trap: Also called the delayed forecheck. A checking system designed to choke off offensive attacks in the neutral zone and enable the defensive team to regain possession of the puck.
Offside: A player who crosses the opposition blue line before the puck does is offside. Play is stopped when this occurs and a faceoff is held outside the blue line. A player also is offside if he accepts a pass that has crossed two lines (e.g. his team's blue line and the center red line). When this occurs, play is stopped and a faceoff is held at the point where the pass was made.
Original Six: In common usage, it refers to the six NHL teams in the pre-1968 expansion era: Toronto Maple Leafs; Montreal Canadiens; Boston Bruins; New York Rangers; Chicago Blackhawks; Detroit Red Wings.
Overtime: During regular-season play, teams play a five-minute, sudden-death overtime period if the score is tied at the end of regulation time. Teams play as many 20-minute sudden-death overtime periods as is necessary to reach a final result during the entire playoff schedule. Sudden-death means the game is over as soon as a goal is scored.
Penalty: A rules infraction which results in a player serving a two- or five-minute penalty in the penalty box, or in expulsion from the game. The penalized player's team must play one man short while he serves a minor or major penalty, but is not so handicapped if the player is assessed a ten-minute misconduct. The player cannot play until his time is up, but the team continues at full on-ice strength. A player assessed a game misconduct penalty cannot play for the rest of the game.
Penalty kill: A four- or three-man unit of players assigned to prevent the opposition from scoring while a teammate serves a two- or five-minute penalty.
Penalty Shot: Called when an attacking player, on a breakaway, is illegally prevented from getting a shot on goal. The puck is placed at center ice and the fouled player skates in alone on the goaltender.
Period: A 20-minute segment, during which time the clock stops at every play stoppage. A hockey game consists of three stop-time periods.
Playing Roster: A team may only dress 18 skaters and two goaltenders for each NHL game.
Plus-Minus: A 'plus' is credited to a player who is on the ice when his team scores an even-strength or shorthanded goal. A 'minus' is given to a player who is on the ice when an opponent scores an even-strength or shorthanded goal. A player's plus-minus total is the aggregate score of pluses and minuses. It is a barometer of a player's value to his team.
Point man: A player, usually a defenseman, who positions himself along the blue line near the boards and orchestrates an attacking team's offensive zone strategy. Often teams try to isolate the point man for a shot on goal.
Pokecheck: A sweeping or poking motion with the stick used to take the puck away from an opponent. Perfected by Frank Nighbor of the Ottawa Senators teams in the 1920s.
Power play: A situation in which one team has one or two more players on the ice than the other team, owing to penalties assessed. It provides the attacking team with an excellent opportunity to create quality scoring chances.
Puck: A vulcanized rubber disk, three inches wide and one inch thick. Game pucks are kept on ice before and during a game, which hardens them even more and helps them slide more quickly.
Rebound: A puck bouncing off the boards, the goaltender or the goalposts. A rebound gives an attacker a second chance for a dangerous shot on goal.
Red line: The red, center line dividing the ice surface in half. In junior and professional hockey, the red line is used to determine icing calls and offside passes. It is not used in U.S. college hockey.
Referee: The chief on-ice official at a hockey game. The referee calls all penalties except too many men on the ice and controls the flow of the game.
Roughing: Excessive pushing and shoving that has not escalated to the level of fisticuffs. Two-minute penalty.
Rink: A surface 200 feet by 85 feet on which a game of hockey is played.
Save: Occurs when a goalie uses his blocker, goalie stick, catching glove or pads to prevent a puck from entering the goal.
Scout: A man or woman who travels to junior, college and high school games, evaluating players who will be available in the Entry Draft. NHL teams also have pro scouts, who evaluate the play of opposing teams.
Shift: The period of time—usually 35-45 seconds—that a player spends on the ice playing the game. Normally a player will play several shifts each period. Some players log as much as 30 minutes in ice time in any given game.
Shot On Goal: Any deliberate attempt by a player to shoot the puck into an opponent's net that, without the intervention of the goaltender, would have scored a goal. Therefore, a shot that hits a goalpost or the crossbar and bounces away, is not a shot on goal.
Shutout: A game result in which the opponent does not score a goal, usually owing to excellent work by the goaltender.
Slap shot: Shooting the puck by swinging the hockey stick through the disk, in a manner similar to a golf swing, except with the hands several inches apart on the stick.
Slashing: Swinging a stick at an opponent. Two-minute penalty.
Slot, The: The area in the offensive zone directly in front of the crease, extending back between the two faceoff circles, about halfway toward the blue line. Teams work hard to create scoring opportunities inside this area.
Spearing: Using a stick as a weapon, jabbing it, like a spear, into an opponent. Five-minute penalty, with expulsion at the discretion of the referee.
Stanley Cup: A silver trophy, originally donated by Lord Stanley, Earl of Preston in 1893 to be emblematic of Canadian hockey supremacy. Since 1926 only NHL teams have competed for the trophy.
Stickhandle: Manipulating the puck back and forth, or any direction, with the blade of the stick in order to deceive an opponent and carry the puck up the ice.
Tip-In: A goal that results when one player shoots on net and a teammate, positioned near the crease, uses his stick to redirect the puck past the goaltender.
Vezina Trophy: Awarded annually to the player judged to be the best goaltender in the NHL.
Wrist shot: Shooting the puck by sweeping the stick along the ice, snapping the wrists on the follow-through.
Zamboni: The box-like, motor-powered vehicle used to resurface the ice in all NHL arenas. The machine collects the snow that builds up during a period of play and lays down a fresh coat of water, providing a smooth ice sheet to begin each period.

INDEX

Caption entries indicated in **bold**